A Tumble in the Night

❧

Cecilia awoke early after a night of strange dreams that had her tossing and turning. She wondered if it had been a full moon, or maybe the Blue Lady had been wandering the corridors, stirred up by newcomers and break-ins.

She rolled over and drew the quilted satin coverlet up around her shoulders. Jack had come into her room in the night and was burrowed under the blankets at her feet. The housemaid had already been in to lay the fire, but the autumn mornings were turning chilly now, and Cecilia was happy to stay in the cozy haven of her bed a little longer, remembering the rally last night.

As the clock struck the hour, the door opened and Jane slipped quietly into the chamber, a tray in her hands. Since she had come to Danby, she had quickly learned all the discreet arts of being a lady's maid—except one. Cecilia should really go down to breakfast, as an unmarried young lady, but Jane always brought her some tea in bed first so they could chatter before Annabel awoke.

"I'm awake already, Jane," Cecilia said. She pushed herself up against the pillows as Jane set the tray on the bedside table and went to open the draperies. It was a gray day outside, clouds lowering over the old medieval tower.

"Good morning, then, my lady," Jane said, gathering up the pink silk dinner gown from last night, along with the more practical blue wool walking dress she had worn to the rally, and putting them in the wicker basket to send to the laundry. It was all like every morning—except that Jane's eyes were red rimmed, her skin pale under her freckles.

Cecilia was immediately concerned. Jane was that rare

creature—a real morning person, eager to chatter even as the sun was low in the sky. Today her quiet demeanor and wan face made Cecilia sit up straighter. Jack peeked out from under the blankets. "Jane, what's wrong? Is someone ill? Are *you* ill?"

Jane glanced up, biting her lip. "Oh, my lady. I hardly know how to say it. It's too terrible."

Now Cecilia was almost panic-stricken. "Is it my grandmother?"

Jane shook her head. "It—it's Mrs. Price, my lady. Amelia Price. We just heard she's dead!"

"Mrs. Price, dead?" Cecilia gasped, a feeling of numbness spreading over her. How could that be? They had seen Amelia just the night before, giving her impassioned speech. "But how? Was her fall worse than had been thought? Was she . . ." A terrible thought occurred to her. "Was she attacked by someone like Lord Elphin?"

"No one knows yet, my lady! The delivery boy from Mrs. Mabry's grocery brought the news from the village just as I was making your tea. It looks like she took another tumble down the stairs at Primrose Cottage, still fully dressed after the rally. Cora Black found her when she got up this morning. She could have been lying there all night!"

"Oh, poor Cora. And poor Anne Price," Cecilia murmured, imaging the horror she would have felt to find her own mother in such a way. She pushed back the bedclothes and swung her feet down to the rug, barely missing Jack, who had crept under the bed to swipe at unsuspecting passersby with his paw. "Help me get dressed right away, Jane. We must go to the village at once."

BERKLEY PRIME CRIME TITLES BY ELIZA CASEY

Lady Takes the Case
Lady Rights a Wrong

Lady Rights a Wrong

~

Eliza Casey

BERKLEY PRIME CRIME

New York

BERKLEY PRIME CRIME
Published by Berkley
An imprint of Penguin Random House LLC
penguinrandomhouse.com

(Penguin logo)

Copyright © 2020 by Penguin Random House LLC
Penguin Random House supports copyright. Copyright fuels creativity,
encourages diverse voices, promotes free speech, and creates a vibrant culture.
Thank you for buying an authorized edition of this book and for complying
with copyright laws by not reproducing, scanning, or distributing any part of it
in any form without permission. You are supporting writers and allowing
Penguin Random House to continue to publish books for every reader.

BERKLEY and the BERKLEY & B colophon are registered trademarks and
BERKLEY PRIME CRIME is a trademark of Penguin Random House LLC.

Library of Congress Cataloging-in-Publication Data

Names: Casey, Eliza, author.
Title: Lady rights a wrong / Eliza Casey.
Description: First Edition. | New York: Berkley Prime Crime, 2020. |
Series: Manor Cat mystery
Identifiers: LCCN 2019055489 | ISBN 9781984803900 (trade paperback) |
ISBN 9781984803917 (ebook)
Subjects: GSAFD: Mystery fiction.
Classification: LCC PS3613.C3226 L329 2020 | DDC 813/.6—dc23
LC record available at https://lccn.loc.gov/2019055489

First Edition: June 2020

Printed in the United States of America
1   3   5   7   9   10   8   6   4   2

Cover art by Alan Ayers
Book design by Elke Sigal

Chapter One

Danby Hall, Yorkshire
Autumn 1912

Just be still for . . . one . . . more . . . second," Lady Cecilia Bates muttered. She bit her lip as her pencil glided across the page of her sketchbook, trying to capture the intricate whorls of a lace-edged cap. Surely, the art lessons she had in London over the summer were going to pay off!

"But, my lady, my nose itches something terrible!" her lady's maid, Jane Hughes, protested.

Cecilia laughed and glanced up again to see that Jane did indeed have a most contorted look on her face. It wouldn't suit the sketch at all. "I am sorry, Jane. By all means, scratch your nose."

Jane rubbed fiercely at the itching appendage and gave a deep sigh. "Oh, that's better."

"Forgive me for keeping you in one place for so long, Jane. I just can never seem to make my pencil match the vision in my head. I fear Monsieur LeClerc's hard work on my lessons was quite in vain."

"I'm sure that's not true," Jane protested. She took off her white cap and smoothed the flyaway strands of her fine, pale blond hair. Her apron and shoes were discarded beside her chair, near the open windows. In Cecilia's own chamber, tucked away in the East Wing and far from the main rooms of the house, their friendship was much easier and more casual than seen by the rest of Danby Hall. "How are your other drawings progressing, then?"

Cecilia flipped through the pages of her sketchbook. Most of her friends and family, as well as the staff belowstairs, had been patient enough to sit for her. Ultimately, she would like to put them all together in a large group portrait, like Queen Victoria's family by Tuxen she had seen at Windsor. But she was a long way from that, she thought with a sigh, as she examined the off-kilter noses and out-of-proportion arms. Her beautiful mother would certainly protest against looking like a hedgehog.

"Not quite where I would like them to be," Cecilia said. "But what else do I have to do except practice? And at least no one can *hear* me drawing, so I don't torment them like when I practice the piano."

After the excitement at Danby last spring, investigating a terrible murder in her own dining room, she had felt so— adrift. Longing for something important, interesting, to do. Choosing gowns, helping with the church fete, and listening to her mother muse about possible suitors had always held limited interest. After being a detective of sorts, it made her want to scream with boredom.

The Season in London had held a few distractions, such as lectures at the Royal Society, visits to museums, art lessons with the (admittedly) rather handsome monsieur, and even a visit to Girton College with her friend Maud Rainsley, who was lucky enough to be a student there. But there had also been endless visits to modistes, the endless parties where other matrons like her mother always asked (subtly) when she would marry, and endless balls where young men with damp palms—even through their gloves—stepped on her toes in waltzes and polkas, and only talked about cricket and shooting.

It was nice to be home again at Danby, but now she was even more at loose ends. She only had her sketches to occupy her, and she was beginning to fear her meager talent would never progress any further. Those cricket-playing boys had so many choices; why did she have none?

"Let me see, my lady," Jane said. Cecilia handed her the sketchbook and sat back in her chair with a sigh. Jack, the large marmalade cat who was a wonderful friend and great distraction to her and Jane—as long as Lady Avebury didn't see him abovestairs—leaped up into Cecilia's lap. She scratched his ears, and he purred loudly and butted his head against her demandingly.

Jane turned the book sideways, studying a drawing of Redvers, Danby's venerable butler. He had bushy, dark brows, very distinctive, but Cecilia had to admit she had made them even too caterpillar-like.

"This isn't so bad," Jane said. "He certainly looks stern enough."

"I had hoped my drawing skills might come in handy if

3

we ever—well, if our detecting assistance is ever called on again," Cecilia admitted. "They would have been useful last spring. But seeing a dastardly murder in one's own house is a once-in-a-lifetime occurrence."

Jane laughed. "You sound disappointed about the lack of blood and gore at Danby, my lady!"

Cecilia laughed, too, and Jack blinked up at her with a flash of his bright green eyes. He had rather enjoyed playing detective, too. "I'm not really disappointed about that, Jane, nor about not having our lives in danger again. That was not terribly fun. I just feel so—so useless now. I don't have anything meaningful to do. Even my mother doesn't need my help so much since she has Annabel. Not that I especially miss passing the sandwiches at the tennis club teas or anything."

Annabel Clarke was an American heiress who was maybe—probably—almost engaged to Cecilia's brother, Patrick. She was meant to save Danby from its financial problems, as well as drag the studious Patrick out of his botany laboratory and into doing his duty as Danby's heir. She was actually Jane's employer, and only loaned her to Cecilia once in a while, since Cecilia hadn't had her own maid for some time. Annabel was tiny, doll-like, pretty, with clouds of golden curls and exquisite, lacy pastel gowns—and she had the organizational skills and determination of Attila the Hun.

"Speaking of useful," Jane said, "I saw this in the village." She took a folded paper from her apron pocket and passed it to Cecilia. "It's an important cause, isn't it?"

Cecilia read over the smudged black ink of the announcement. "It is indeed," she cried in rising excitement. *Mrs. Amelia*

Price will be speaking at Danby Village Guildhall, it said, with a date and a sketch of a tall lady in a fur coat and large, stylish feathered hat behind a lectern, her hand raised imploringly.

"Amelia Price." Cecilia sighed. "In person! I hoped to see her in London, but she had gone to France on a lecture tour for the summer."

"She's famous, isn't she?" Jane said.

"She is indeed. The president of the Women's Suffrage Union. My friend Miss Rainsley is a member. I met her daughter Anne Price briefly at the theater one evening just before we came back to Danby. I think the Prices had just returned from their tour. And now Mrs. Price is coming *here*!"

"Do you really think the women will get the vote one day, my lady?"

"Oh, we must, Jane! We simply must. Or our lives will go on being considered second-rate." She smiled down at the flyer. "We should go to this rally. Her Union might need our help."

"I'm not sure I could get away from Miss Clarke long enough," Jane said doubtfully.

"I'll talk to Annabel. She might like to attend, as well."

Jane gave a little snort. "She says women don't want to vote, we'll all lose our femininity and no man will want to protect us. We're too weak to do without men organizing us. Especially after all those windows got smashed last spring."

"That was only because that horrid Mr. Asquith went back on his promise to support the Conciliation Bill," Cecilia said. "And Annabel sounds like my father." She laughed when she thought of how Annabel "organized" Patrick so adroitly. "But she'll have to let *you* attend."

The little porcelain French clock on the mantel chimed the hour, and she looked up, startled. "Is that the time already? Grandmama is coming to tea! I can't be late." An independent, voting lady Cecilia might want to be, but that didn't make the dowager countess any less fearsome.

"I'll help you, my lady," Jane said, jumping up and opening the carved doors of the armoire to sort through the gowns with her usual efficiency. "The blue tea gown? With the white lace shawl?"

"Perfect." Cecilia tucked the flyer into the back of her sketchbook. Suffrage might have to wait until she did her granddaughterly duty, but she felt a tiny spark of hope for the first time in months.

She sat down at her dressing table, Jack lounging at her feet to bat at his favorite ribbon toy. She moved a small, red-haired china shepherdess, a precious gift from Mr. Talbot's antique shop, to the back of the table so it wouldn't fall and break. Cecilia loved her room, tucked away in the quieter, older East Wing. It was far from her parents' suites and the grander guestchambers, but it had the best views of the rolling lawns, the rose gardens with their fading summer blooms, the woods beyond, and the medieval stones of the ancient tower that was the oldest part of the estate. She had chosen the pale, carved furniture, the sky-blue and pale-yellow draperies, herself. A cozy grouping of satin chairs clustered around the white marble fireplace, surrounded by piles of books and sketchbooks.

It all looked just the same as it always had, pretty and cozy, her own private sanctuary where she could read and think, and now draw. Since Annabel had arrived, all of Danby seemed subtly changed. Annabel and Patrick weren't even officially betrothed yet, and it still felt different, in ways Cecilia couldn't even really explain. She was starting to feel like a guest in her own home.

It also increased the pressure to find her own establishment—to marry and settle in her own life, to not be a responsibility to her family. She had nothing *against* marrying, in itself. It might be rather nice to have a partner in life, if it was the right person. And there lay the rub. The *right* person. Someone who understood and shared her interests, who supported her and who she could support. Who needed her.

Cecilia let down the loose knot of her wavy, reddish-gold hair and reached for her silver-backed brush to run it through the tangled strands as she thought of her suitors, such as they were. There was Mr. Brown, the vicar at Danby Village's St. Swithin's Church. Her mother quite approved of him; he was the nephew of a viscount, and Lady Avebury thought he would be a bishop one day. He *was* rather handsome, with his brown, curling hair and chocolate-brown eyes, from a prominent family, and well-liked by all the neighborhood for his good works and short sermons. Cecilia liked him, too, what she knew of him. But she feared she would make a terrible vicar's wife.

Then there were the young men she met in London, sons of her mother's friends. Lord Battingly-Gore and Mr. Henderson. The dreadfully boring cricket players. Cecilia shuddered.

Against her will, a pair of Viking-blue laughing eyes popped into her mind, an insolent smile, a gentle hand on hers. *Jesse Fellows*. He was one of the newest footmen at Danby, and had only arrived last spring just before the fatal dinner party. Though he was the nephew of Mrs. Mabry at the greengrocer in the village, no one really knew much about him. He had been quick to help at the terrible events of the dinner, coolheaded and kind. And he was much too bold to be a really good footman. Footmen were supposed to be invisible, after all.

Cecilia laughed. A rather motley, and poor, selection of romantic prospects. And she had no desire to marry yet, to tie herself down to one fate. But she did so very much want to be useful.

She thought about the flyer for Mrs. Price's rally. If women had the vote, had their own choices to make—how much her world would open up. The world for all women.

Jane finished laying out the tea dress, along with matching blue silk shoes and the lace shawl. "Will you be having tea on the terrace, my lady? I saw the footmen carrying out chairs earlier."

"I'm not sure. It *is* rather a warm day for autumn. I should probably take a parasol just in case."

Jane found a white, ruffled lace parasol hidden under the bed, perhaps dragged there by Jack, who did tend to purloin anything not tied down. Jane brushed the dust off its ribbon edging before she came to twist Cecilia's hair into a braided upsweep. The daughter of a grocer in New Jersey, Jane had started off as a chambermaid in an American hotel, but had

8

learned all the arts of being a lady's maid very quickly. Not to mention sleuthing, and also being a good friend.

But Cecilia had begun to wonder if Jane had some romantic notions of her own in life. She did seem to spend quite a bit of her free time in the garage with Collins, the handsome chauffeur. Not that she *had* much free time, between Annabel's demands and helping Cecilia.

Cecilia gazed thoughtfully out at the garden as Jane deftly fastened pearl combs into the braids she had just created. It was indeed a warm and sunny day, making Danby look even more beautiful than usual, and marital duties seemed so far away. Yet the thought of them followed her everywhere.

"Have you seen the Blue Lady run across the lawn lately, my lady?" Jane asked.

Cecilia laughed. The Blue Lady was the family ghost, the specter of a Bates who was said to have died in the Civil Wars hundreds of years ago, and who came to visit Danby whenever disaster was near. "Not recently, luckily. She's only supposed to appear when something terrible is about to happen, you know. I think we had enough of that in the spring."

Jane shivered. "We did, at that."

Once Cecilia's hair was tidied to Jane's exacting standards, she helped Cecilia out of her plain skirt and shirtwaist and into the fashionable tea gown. She fastened the tiny pearl buttons up the back and smoothed the intricate pleats and lace inserts.

"Do I look like a proper young lady now, Jane?" she asked, twirling her bell sleeves back and forth until Jack leaped up to beat at them.

"Jack, no!" Jane cried, trying to keep his needle-sharp claws away from the delicate lace ruffles. "I do think even the dowager countess might approve, my lady."

Cecilia sighed. Her grandmama had spent a lifetime learning Society's rules, and she was always the first to apply them—to everyone except herself. The whole family was quite terrified of her. "I do hope so. I don't know what I would do without your help now, Jane." She caught up her shawl and parasol and hurried out of the room, closing the door firmly before Jack could follow. He could help Jane tidy up. Her grandmother, and especially her grandmother's terrier-terror Sebastian, didn't much care for Jack, and the feeling was mutual. No one wanted the tea table overturned.

Danby Hall was actually two houses cobbled together as one, older wings from a pre-Reformation priory connected by the grand Palladian mansion her great-grandfather had built. Cecilia's chamber was in the older wing, and she had to go up and down a few flights of short stairs and along narrow corridors to the old Elizabethan gallery.

She had always loved the gallery, a vast space she and Patrick had played hide-and-seek in when they were children. One of the walls was all windows, curtained in heavy tapestry fabric that half hid the view of the ornamental lake and the medieval tower, while the other wall was dark-paneled wood. Three enormous fireplaces were carved with fruit and leaves and strange, grinning faces that had terrified her when she was a child. Old portraits of Bateses in frilled ruffs and velvet doublets frowned down at her as she passed, interspersed with old battle flags and swords captured by her forebears in battle.

She paused to say hello to Ralph, the ancient suit of armor at the end of the gallery, and patted him on his rusty shoulder before she turned out the door to the main staircase. Local guidebooks to historic houses called it "the best open-well staircase in the neighborhood," a gorgeous creation of thickly carved dark wood, cherubs, flowers, feathers, elaborate Bs, with niches for sculptures. At the landing hung a portrait by Winterhalter of her grandmother, when she was a young lady at the French royal court. Even with dark ringlets and ruffled pink crinolines, she looked intimidating.

At the foot of the stairs, she was in the "new" Danby, built by her great-grandfather in the latest Palladian style of clean, classical lines and pale colors. She heard the echo of voices coming from the Yellow Music Room, the more informal family gathering place. Her grandmother must not have arrived yet, she thought; she always insisted on being received in the grander White Drawing Room.

Cecilia found her parents, Patrick, and Annabel in the music room, gathered around the white marble fireplace despite the warm autumn day outside the windows. Danby was always rather chilly, with its large rooms and carved stone trimmings. Cecilia wondered if Annabel would install some American central heating once she was Viscountess Bellham, future Countess of Avebury.

If she was ever the countess. The engagement did seem long in coming.

"Ah, there you are, Cecilia," her mother said with a sigh, as if Cecilia was hours and hours late instead of five minutes. Emmaline Bates had been a great beauty in her youth, and was still very lovely, tall and slim in her stylish green silk gown that matched her eyes, her dark hair barely touched with silver. Cecilia often wished she had taken after her mother, instead of the Bates reddish hair and tendency to freckle. "What on earth took you so long? Your grandmother will arrive at any moment."

Cecilia crossed the room, pasting a smile on her face. She kissed her mother's cheek and gave her ancient spaniel a pat on the head. He didn't even stir. "I'm sorry, Mama, but I'm here now. Can I help with anything?"

Her mother sniffed. "No, it's all arranged now. Dear Annabel suggested Grandmama might enjoy tea on the terrace, as it will soon be too cold to enjoy the garden."

"We've been chatting about the church bazaar, so exciting," Annabel said. Annabel, too, was a beauty, golden and ivory and roses like a Sevres china shepherdess, dressed in a ruffled white lace gown and the grand pearls her wealthy American father had gifted her. She was always most enthusiastic about Danby doings, or anything English at all. But Cecilia tended to wonder what really went on behind her large blue eyes.

"And I am sure Cecilia will be most happy to judge the annual cake-baking competition, won't you?" Lady Avebury said. "Or run the bring-and-buy tent."

Cecilia, who had been idly flipping through her mother's copy of *The Lady* she had found on one of the little gilt Louis

XV tables, glanced up, startled at the sound of her name. She did rather tend to daydream a bit when talk turned to her mother's local activities. One event seemed to be rather like another, even when the cause was one she supported, as she did the new church roof, and she usually ended up fetching and carrying for whatever her mother needed on the day. Annabel was proving much more adept at upholding the Bates duties in the village. She was like a major general organizing a campaign with every Women's Institute event and charitable assembly.

"I beg your pardon, Mama?" Cecilia said, trying to be all wide-eyed innocence, as if she had really been hanging on every word. "I was just reading about the new winter hats, so riveting." She had actually been reading an account of a women's suffrage meeting in London, where the famous Mrs. Pankhurst had evaded the authorities yet again. But that would never do to tell her mother. She had to plan her strategy most carefully to attend Mrs. Price's rally.

Lady Avebury sighed and ran a bejeweled hand over her sleeping dog's ears. "Really, Cecilia, you do become more distracted every day. I'm beginning to think we shouldn't have bothered to take you to London this summer at all. So many dancing partners for you there, and you barely said a word to them."

"That's because I know nothing of cricket and had not a jot to add to any conversation, Mama. What is a no ball anyway? Nor have I hunted in ages." Cecilia did adore riding, racing along with the wind in her face, as if she could take a hurdle and fly free. But it was just the blood and carnage at the end of the hunt she wasn't interested in at all. And that seemed to be all the London swains cared about.

"It's a penalty against the fielding team," Patrick said, glancing up from his botany book.

"What's a penalty?" Cecilia asked him, puzzled. They were his first words since she'd entered the room. He did tend to live in his own world, one of Latin genus names and such. If he hadn't been an earl's heir, he would have surely worked his days away happily at Kew Gardens.

Alas for Patrick, he was an only son, and the Danby estate and all its problems would one day be his.

"A no ball," he said. "It's a penalty against the fielding team, usually the fault of the bowler. That's about all I know. They tossed me off the village team years ago."

Annabel gave him a sweet, indulgent smile and patted his hand. "You needn't worry about such things, Lord Bellham, darling. Emmaline and I have all the village matters well in hand at the moment, don't we, Emmaline dear?"

Emmaline. Cecilia almost snorted in laughter. American manners. Her mother would never tolerate anyone else calling her by her first name. Not even Cecilia's father did that in public. But everyone knew Danby needed Annabel's American dollars.

She set aside the magazine. "What were you saying about the cakes, Mama?"

"That I am sure you would be happy to help out at the church bazaar by assisting, to judge the baking competition this year," her mother said. "Mrs. Mitchell, the doctor's wife, always wins for her lemon drizzle, of course, but we must put on a good show. And Mr. Brown is also judging, as he always does. So charming."

Ah, so that was the purpose of the cake eating. She was to assist the vicar. The handsome, young, *eligible* vicar. "Surely, everyone would prefer to have Annabel give the prizes. She's the local celebrity."

Annabel smiled and smoothed her shining golden curls, also expertly dressed by Jane. "I *have* made some lovely friends here, it's true. It feels as if I've been here for years, I feel so at home! But I'm already organizing the flower show and the tea tent."

"And she is presenting the prizes for embroidery work," Cecilia's mother added. "Really, Cecilia, you must show some interest."

Cecilia remembered too well what happened the last time she herself ran the tea tent, all the spilled drinks and toppled strawberry bowls. Judging the cakes should be easier, anyway. "I will try, Mama. But I might be busy around that day. I just learned that someone famous, Mrs. Amelia Price, will be having a rally in the village."

She knew it was a mistake the minute she said it. Her mother startled so much her old spaniel snorted awake. "That woman! Here?"

"Yes," Cecilia said carefully. "I thought it was rather exciting. It's usually so quiet."

"It is *appalling*!" Lady Avebury cried. "Don't you remember what happened in London back in March? All those windows smashed. What if they intend to break up our own village? And right at the time of the church bazaar."

"That wasn't Mrs. Price's group, Mama," Cecilia protested. "I'm sure this will be most peaceful, just speeches and such. I, for one, am rather curious about what she has to say."

"Clifford! Can you believe what your daughter has declared?" Lady Avebury turned to her husband with a furious expression. Her delicate, pale, heart-shaped face looked like a thundercloud, and after almost thirty years of marriage, Lord Avebury knew enough to look rather wary. "She wants to rampage through the streets, breaking windows and chaining herself to gates."

"Cecilia wants to do what?" he said carefully.

"I only want to hear a speech, Papa," Cecilia protested. "I am not chaining myself to anything."

"That Mrs. Price is coming to the village," Lady Avebury said.

"Amelia Price? That votes-for-women nonsense?" Lord Avebury said, his tone puzzled. "I don't know what she's on about. You ladies have us to speak for you. Why would you want to do such things, Cecilia?"

"Oh, really now." Cecilia tossed aside *The Lady*, feeling ridiculously like a child again. "You are not me, Papa, as kind and dear as you are. I might have my own opinions on things, you know."

"I don't see why any lady would want to vote," Annabel said. "It's so—unfeminine. What do *you* think, Patrick?"

Patrick blinked up again from his book. It was obvious he had heard not a word of the quarrel. "What are we talking about, then?"

Fortunately, Redvers chose that moment to enter the music room with a discreet little cough and a bow. Cecilia did think she had done rather a good job on his sketch, with his bushy eyebrows, large nose, and forbidding expression. But she knew that underneath he was a soft heart who had always brought her extra sweets at tea when she was a child. "I beg your pardon, my lady, but the dowager countess's car has just turned in through the gates. Should I have Rose and Bridget set the linens on the terrace table now?"

Cecilia's mother took a deep breath and smoothed her face into a serene smile. Long years of being the countess had taught her how to compose herself in any situation. Cecilia wished *she* could learn how to do that. Her cheeks still seemed to burn with anger simmering inside of her at being treated as a child. But she couldn't let her grandmother see that.

"Yes, thank you, Redvers," Lady Avebury said. "We shall be out directly. I think we are quite finished here. Aren't we, Cecilia?"

Cecilia gritted her teeth. "Yes, Mama." Yet she knew they were *not* finished. Not by a mile.

Chapter Two

The terrace of Danby on a sunny autumn afternoon should have been the most idyllic place in the world, Cecilia thought as she followed her mother to the tea table laid out near the marble balustrade. The gardens at Danby were looking especially lovely in the last gasp of summer, autumn golds and ambers touching the leaves, all peaceful and elegant. It didn't look real at all, after the weeks of crowded London streets, but like a world in a Constable painting. The English countryside, eternal and peaceful, smelling of fresh greenery and the apple-crispness of fall.

Yet Cecilia couldn't entirely shake the feeling of restlessness and anger that seemed to creep over her like an itch she couldn't brush away. It had actually been there for months, vaguely humming away in the background as she went about the motions of her everyday life. Changing clothes, sipping tea, looking in shops, dancing, but always as if she was some-place else entirely. *Should* be someplace else.

That hum was like a shriek ever since she'd heard about Mrs. Price's rally. Mrs. Price and her cohorts were women with a purpose in life, an important cause. Women who knew how to use their talents and abilities, where Cecilia wasn't even sure she had real talents.

She glanced back at the tall windows, covered now with heavy red brocade draperies, that led into the grand dining room where Mr. Hayes had been killed last spring in the middle of dinner. It had been a truly awful event, a shocking sight, but Cecilia had surprised herself by dealing with it all. She was needed then.

And now . . .

She just wasn't sure about anything.

She studied her family, her mother and Annabel chatting again about the plans for the bazaar, some complex bit of maneuvering because Mr. Smithfield's flower arrangements from his florist's shop had to be in place before the Misses Moffat from the tea shop brought in the urns for the tea tent, and her father and Patrick studying the lawn before them in the midst of their own thoughts. No doubt her father was envisioning the days of shooting to come, while Patrick wished he was in his laboratory. They all loved her; she knew that. Even her mother cared, despite her constant faultfinding. They wanted the best for Cecilia's life. But maybe their ideas of *best* were not really her own. The wide world was changing fast, but Danby always stayed the same.

The glass doors to the terrace opened, and Redvers announced, "The dowager countess, my lady."

"Oh, Redvers, surely I am quite capable of announcing myself. Or perhaps it is meant as a warning?" Cecilia's grandmother said with a hoarse laugh as she swept onto the terrace, her ebony walking stick click-clacking on the flagstones. She was no longer the dark-haired, crinoline-clad beauty of her Winterhalter portrait, but her eyes were just as bright blue and piercing, just as all-seeing. She stood straight and erect in her gray velvet and lace suit, her hair thick and silvery-white beneath her velvet toque. Her Scottie dog, Sebastian, trailed behind her, not snapping and growling for once.

"Mama," Cecilia's mother said, hurrying to make sure her mother-in-law's chair was carefully placed in the shade. "We are so happy you could come today. We thought we should take advantage of these last fine days and have our tea out here. It's lovely, don't you think?"

"Are you quite sure it's not too breezy, Emmaline?" the dowager said.

Cecilia's mother's smile stayed carefully in place. "If it becomes too chilly, we can simply move into the White Drawing Room. Is that not so, Redvers?"

"Indeed, my lady," the always unflappable butler answered. "Shall we bring out the rest of the tea service, then?"

"Yes, thank you," Lady Avebury said. "I am sure you'll want to hear all about the London Season, Mama, since we haven't seen you since we returned."

"Hmph." Cecilia's grandmother waved her stick in the air,

as if to banish any hint of Town from her presence. "Much the same as it was in my day, I'm sure, when my husband took his seat in the Lords. Overcrowded ballrooms and too many carriages in the park. One does hear the new king is quite dull."

Cecilia's father laughed. "Compared to good old Bertie, how can he help it? King George fell asleep in the royal box at the theater one evening when we were there. Remember, Emmaline? Snoring away while the queen tried to ignore it all."

Cecilia giggled at the memory of that evening, King George nodding away while Queen Mary, sparkling like Aladdin's cave in all her diamonds, stared fixedly at the stage, but her mother gave her a stern frown.

"King George and Queen Mary are most worthy, I am sure," her mother said. "We saw Her Majesty at the British Museum one afternoon, as well, looking at the new Assyrian friezes; she is so cultured. She had the loveliest silver velvet hat. And she did speak so kindly to us at the palace garden party. I am sure she will wish Annabel to be presented next year."

The dowager countess sniffed. "An overdressed partridge compared to dear Queen Alexandra. I hope that poodle fringe of hers won't start some unfortunate fashion in ladies' coiffures now."

Redvers led the footmen, Paul, James, and Jesse, onto the terrace, all of them bearing tiered Limoges china cake plates of Mrs. Frazer's prettiest confections. The raspberry tarts, chocolate éclairs, currant scones with lemon curd, and tiny sandwiches of smoked salmon, egg salad, and cucumber and watercress, were laid out like jewels in a shopwindow, shimmering and enticing. Mrs. Frazer's cooking was renowned all over the neighborhood, and Cecilia's mother lived in terror of losing her to a grander house that entertained more often.

Annabel, though, was sure to make her mark as a grand hostess once she was Lady Avebury. If she was Lady Avebury.

Redvers laid the silver tea service before Cecilia's mother, and she poured out the smoky Lapsang Souchong with an elegant, practiced twist of her wrist. Cecilia caught the eye of Jesse Fellows, who stood just beyond Lady Avebury's chair, and he actually *winked* at her, the saucy lad. She pressed her damask napkin to her lips to hide a laugh.

"That evening when we saw the king at the theater," Annabel said, "wasn't that when those horrid women tried to break the windows of the royal carriage?"

The dowager countess froze as she leaned down to feed a bit of salmon to Sebastian. "Someone tried to attack the king? Dull as the man is, I am sure he doesn't deserve that."

"They were suffragettes, Mama," Lord Avebury said. "It happened as the king and queen were leaving. We didn't see anything, only heard a bit of commotion. The constables took care of it quite smartish."

"Suffragettes?" the dowager cried. "Terrible women. In *my* day, no one would behave like that for something so ridiculous as the vote. It hardly matters *who* is in Parliament anyway; nothing changes. Now, if someone was flirting with someone else's lover at a ball, that might be a different tale. I saw two countesses nearly tear each other's hair out one time at the Duchess of Sefton's rout." She snorted with laughter at the memory.

"The suffragettes were causing such a disruption this

Season," Cecilia's mother said. "Chaining themselves to buildings, blowing up letter boxes."

"And they tore up the orchid houses at Kew," Patrick added, sounding as if that was the worst thing anyone could do. "Those plants were one of a kind, invaluable. Why would someone do such a thing?"

"It was not proved *who* did that," Cecilia protested. "And if they did, it's because no one will listen to them otherwise. They just pat them on the head and give them empty promises of support. And that night at the theater, they were only trying to present a petition to the king."

"You just say that because you want to be one of them, Cecilia," Annabel said with a little smile.

Cecilia gritted her teeth. She was nearly twenty, and yet they treated her as a child, too. It was not the way it should be. "I am not one of them. Not yet. I merely wish to hear what Mrs. Price has to say when she comes to the village."

Her grandmother frowned. "Who is this Mrs. Price?"

"She is the leader of the Women's Suffrage Union, Grandmama," Cecilia answered. She took a long sip of her tea and then a deep breath to calm herself. "She is going to be holding a rally at the Guildhall, and I'm curious about what she has to say."

"Oh, dear heavens," the dowager gasped, and Sebastian growled. He wriggled away from the dowager and ran into the house. "Does that mean we must guard our letter boxes in Danby Village now? And what if you are arrested there, Cecilia? What a scandal. It will be like Lady Constance Lytton."

"I'm quite sure no one will burn anything down *or* be arrested, Grandmama," Cecilia said. "Surely, Colonel Havelock will see to that. And Mrs. Price is not a militant, anyway." The colonel was the local magistrate, a sensible, no-nonsense military man, a veteran of the Boer War, and very involved in local matters. He had been of great help when Mr. Hayes was killed.

"She won't be arrested because she won't be going," Lady Avebury said. She nodded to Redvers, who discreetly led the footmen away.

"Mama . . ." Cecilia protested.

"*I* certainly would not attend such a thing." Annabel sniffed. "Making a public spectacle. So unladylike. I have everything a lady could want right now." She delicately dabbed at her lips with her napkin, and Cecilia remembered her true history. Eloping from her millionaire father's San Francisco home, then returning in time to come to Danby, at least according to her cousin. It wasn't all that "ladylike." But then, Annabel was so mysterious sometimes.

"I did say we shall not discuss this any further today," Lady Avebury said firmly, offering a plate of pink-iced petits fours. "It is too lovely an afternoon to spoil with such unpleasantness. Now, Mama, did we tell you what a success darling Annabel was this Season? So many invitations!"

Cecilia half listened as her mother, grandmother, and Annabel chatted about all the London parties they had attended, the latest styles in narrow skirts and lacy sleeves, and studiously avoided any mention of suffrage and rallies. She tried to eat her sandwich, but it tasted like sawdust in her mouth.

"Oh, all the lemon tarts have gone," her grandmother said with a tap of her stick. "They are Sebastian's favorites. Where is the little scamp?"

A sudden howl from inside the house, followed by a series of furious barks, said that Sebastian had found his nemesis Jack once again. Surely, Jack needed a puzzle to help solve soon, or he would be forever getting into such scrapes.

"I'll go call for more cakes—and bring back Sebastian," Cecilia quickly offered, glad for the chance to escape, even if only for a few moments. Before her mother could protest, she jumped up and hurried through the half-open glass doors. The footmen waited just inside, in case they were needed, and they looked quite surprised to see Cecilia suddenly appear there. They ignored the dog and cat noises, too accustomed to such contretemps by now.

"Just going to see if Mrs. Frazer has any more lemon tarts," she said cheerfully.

Jesse fell into step beside her. "Let me help you, my lady," he said, as she made her way through the foyer. The foyer was the one space in Danby most meant to awe visitors, pale, carved stone walls soaring up to a blue-inlaid dome, the Bates coat of arms gilded and shining over the double front doors, tall blue-and-white vases brought from China by her grandfather guarding the entrance. In the corner was a hidden door to the kitchens, her goal.

"Oh, there's no need . . ." she said.

"I think there is, my lady," he said with a grin. "Not if I don't want a dressing-down from Mr. Redvers for failing in my duties."

Cecilia laughed. "Yes, of course. We can bring more hot water while we're at it. Grandmama does like her Lapsang, and scolding me is always thirsty work."

At the door that separated the main part of the house from the narrow stone staircase that led down to the kitchens, they paused. When Cecilia was a child, she had dashed down there without a thought, begging for biscuits from Mrs. Frazer to satisfy her sweet tooth or watching Redvers in careful silence as he decanted the wine, which was almost a religious ritual for him. Now she hesitated to intrude on that busy, bustling world.

"Lady Cecilia," Jesse said quietly.

She glanced up at him, surprised to see him look so solemn. "What is it?" she said, just as quietly. She had a sudden flash of memory, of when he had saved her from a drunken man's assault just steps from there in the foyer, and she knew she could trust him.

"I couldn't help but overhear a bit about that suffrage rally in the village," he said. "If you want to go, my lady— well, you should go. It's important to have options in life, for everyone."

Cecilia remembered that once he had confided he might one day like to be a butler himself, or even own his own restaurant or hotel. Options in life, ones that a footman might not have had even ten years ago. "Are *you* a supporter of women's suffrage, Jesse?"

He gave a wry smile. "I grew up with just my mum and my aunt, my lady." Cecilia knew his aunt was Mrs. Mabry, who owned the greengrocer in the village, but she had never met his mother. She wondered who she was, where he really came from. "Heaven help anyone who ever tried to tell them what they can or can't do. They have brains and opinions, just like everyone else. Just as you do."

He thought she was smart? Cecilia felt her face turn warm, and she tried not to smile. "Why, thank you, Jesse."

The door suddenly swung open, revealing the green baize on the other side, and Mrs. Caffey, Danby's house-keeper, stood there. A sturdy, capable woman in black silk, she had been at Danby for decades, since she was a kitchen maid, and now she ruled the household with a benevolent but firm hand. Her eyes widened at the sight of Cecilia, so far from her own tea party and conversing with a footman. Cecilia felt awful, fearing Jesse would get a dressing-down after all. Not that he didn't seem like a young man who could handle anything at all.

"Is everything quite all right, Lady Cecilia?" Mrs. Caffey asked.

"Perfectly so, thank you, Mrs. Caffey," Cecilia answered. "My grandmother has requested more lemon tarts, and perhaps more hot water for tea. Fellows here was being most helpful."

Mrs. Caffey gave Jesse a doubtful glance. "I'm glad to hear it, my lady. I'll send up more tea trays at once."

"Thank you." Cecilia whirled around and departed, walking as slowly as she dared. At the turn of the corridor, she looked back to see Jesse watching her. He gave her an encouraging smile, and she couldn't help but smile back.

She found Sebastian sitting beside the terrace doors, apparently no worse for wear. And Jack, the naughty fellow, was nowhere to be seen.

Chapter Three

"Did you hear?" Bridget, one of the housemaids, whispered to the kitchen maid Pearl. "Mrs. Amelia Price is going to be in the village! You know her. She just got back from a speaking tour in France, telling women they have the right to make up their own minds in life. My own aunt is part of her Union, I think. Now she'll be *here*!"

Pearl peeked nervously at Mrs. Frazer, who was carefully stirring her consommé. The tea trays had just been cleared away and dinner preparations were in full action. Even though it was just the family that night, the kitchen was a hive of activity, meats being roasted, trifle being constructed. Pearl herself was meant to be chopping a small mountain of vegetables, but she was caught by Bridget's words.

"You mean the lady who says we should be able to vote, however we choose?" Pearl whispered back. "She's going to be right here?"

"At the Guildhall in the village. I saw a flyer about it when I went to my uncle's bakery this afternoon. It says everyone is welcome. We should go! We might see my aunt there."

"Oh, I don't know." Pearl would *like* to go, to be sure. It sounded nice to have a choice in life besides chopping carrots forever. But she needed her job. Mrs. Frazer, for all her stern impatience, was a fair woman who said Pearl might even make a cook herself one day, if she worked hard enough. But Pearl was quite sure Mrs. Frazer wouldn't approve of political agitation on the part of her maids. It could reflect badly on the house, and no one wanted to work in a house that was the subject of gossip.

Yet it was very tempting.

"When is it, this meeting?" she asked.

"In just three days."

Pearl sighed in disappointment. "That's not my half day."

"Well, it's mine. Maybe that new kitchen maid would change with you."

"I'll see about it. I don't know."

"What are you two whispering about?" Mrs. Frazer cried. "Here I am, slaving to get this soup finished, and you have time for a gossip! Pearl, those vegetables won't chop themselves, and there's the potatoes to roast and the jam for the trifle to finish. And I'm sure Mrs. Caffey is looking for you, Bridget."

"Yes, Mrs. Frazer," they muttered together, and Bridget ran up the stairs to find the housekeeper. Pearl redoubled her efforts at the carrots.

The kitchens at Danby were, even with the estate's recent financial troubles, large and airy. The flagstone floors were scrubbed to a shine even though some of them were cracked, and the walls were painted a bright white. Unlike most kitchens in grand houses, broad, high windows let in plenty of light, so they could see as day turned to lavender-silvery twilight outside the high windows, even now that summer was slipping away and days were getting shorter. Autumn meant more work, since the family was back from London and shooting parties would visit. There might even be engagement celebrations soon. No one was sure what would happen now, but dinner would always have to be on the table at the same time every evening. It was the way Danby was run, and always would be. Properly.

In the adjoining servants' hall, Mrs. Sumter, Lady Avebury's maid, brought in her ladyship's apple-green satin dinner gown to press, and Rose, the housemaid who sometimes helped Lady Cecilia when Jane was busy with Miss Clarke, carried in a pair of silk evening gloves to mend. Redvers soon appeared with the evening newspapers, which Lord Avebury liked to peruse before dining and which had to be ironed to keep the print from smudging off. He scowled in irritation to see that Mrs. Sumter already claimed the iron. It was their nightly battle.

Redvers harrumphed but sat down to glance over the headlines as Mrs. Sumter arranged and smoothed the chiffon ruffled sleeves of the gown. Beyond the door was the crash and clang of the final food preparations for dinner, Mrs. Frazer's shouts, the clatter of a tray falling to the floor. The aromas of lamb with rosemary and roasted potatoes with the last of the summer peas floated through the warm air.

Mrs. Caffey and Mrs. Frazer came in, the cook with a harried expression on her reddened face and her hair frizzing from under her crooked cap. "The consommé has gone off, just as I feared. They'll have to have pommes de Parmentier for soup instead."

Redvers frowned. "Pommes de Parmentier?"

"Will that mess with your wine choice, Mr. Redvers?" Mrs. Caffey asked.

"No, I think the Riesling will still do well enough," he grudgingly admitted. "But they are having potatoes with the lamb. And one does not like to have plans changed about once they are set."

"Indeed not," said Mrs. Caffey. "But one soup instead of another is nothing to the chaos of what happened last spring, I should think. The dining room has been perfectly peaceful since then."

"Hmph." Redvers rustled the papers. He did not like to be reminded of the most disruptive thing that had ever happened on his long watch over Danby. "Speaking of chaos—I see that Mrs. Price woman will be here in the village, holding a rally of some sort."

"Here?" Mrs. Caffey gasped. "Oh dear. I do hope no windows will be broken at Danby."

"Perhaps his lordship can set some extra guards at the gate," Redvers said.

"Well, I think *someone* needs to stand up for us women," Mrs. Frazer muttered. "We do all the hard work and get none of the credit, and precious little of the money." She spun around and marched back into her kitchen.

"I'd be so frightened to go to such a thing," Rose said with a shiver. Her head was still bent over the tear she was mending in Lady Cecilia's glove, which had no doubt been torn by a cat's needlelike claws. "All that shouting and pushing, so many people everywhere." Rose was shy by nature, gentle, wanting only to marry her footman-beau Paul soon and set up her own home.

"They're not all an argy-bargy like that, Rose," Mrs. Sumter said, casting a careful eye over the pressed ruffles. "Most of them are only speeches and questions. You might do well to educate yourself, dear. You will have to help teach your children one day."

Redvers frowned at her. "I hope *you* have not been to such a thing, Mrs. Sumter."

Mrs. Sumter pursed her lips. As her ladyship's personal maid, she was not actually under the butler's jurisdiction, and they both knew it. "We must all have our little secrets, Mr. Redvers. I am quite finished here. You should use the iron while it's still warm."

Chapter Four

"And how is your cousin's shop faring, Collins?" Cecilia asked the chauffeur as the Bateses' car jounced along the rutted road into Danby Village. The neighborhood lanes were not quite ready for automobiles, but her father had been one of the first to enthusiastically adopt the technology, including importing a chauffeur from London.

Collins hadn't been with the family very long, but Cecilia liked him. He was kind and funny, polite without being obsequious, and a very good driver. He had been of great help in solving the Hayes unpleasantness, plus his cousin owned the loveliest little antiques shop, full of tempting things.

Cecilia also suspected Jane might be the tiniest bit sweet on Collins, judging from the way her freckled cheeks blushed and she grew uncharacteristically tongue-tied when they took a drive. She glanced at Jane now and saw that she was distinctly pink.

Cecilia bit her lip to keep from smiling. She did like romance, when it was not her own!

"Business has been quite brisk, my lady," Collins answered, glancing back at them in the mirror. Did his own gaze linger just a wee bit long on Jane? Cecilia contemplated if she should actually try her hand at a spot of matchmaking.

She wondered what Collins thought of women's suffrage.

"I'm glad to hear it," she said. "I do so love that seventeenth-century toilette set he found for me."

"He said to tell you he has a new snuffbox, Russian enamel, that the earl might like for his collection," Collins said.

"I'll stop by after we go to the milliner," Cecilia said. "It *is* almost my father's birthday. And I do quite look forward to seeing Mr. Talbot again."

They swung around a corner, swerving to avoid an especially large rut on the road, and Cecilia's brown velvet hat tumbled over her eyes. When she straightened it and pinned it tighter to her coil of hair, they had come into the village itself.

Danby Village, with its green at the center, was as familiar to Cecilia as Danby Hall. In the middle of the green stood an obelisk to memorialize the village's war dead surrounded by benches and pathways where everyone gathered on fine days. Shops ringed the green with gray Yorkshire stone, dark slate roofs, and shining display windows. Cecilia spotted the Mabrys' grocery, the milliner, Mr. Smithfield's florist, the Misses Moffat's tea shop, the branch of Coutts bank, Mr. Jermyn the attorney, and Dr. Mitchell's surgery. Just beyond was the whitewashed Crown and Shield pub with its wooden tables lined up in a small courtyard, and the sturdy, Norman-era St. Swithin's Church with its large yard and pretty brick vicarage. On the corner was her very favorite place, Mr. Hatcher's bookshop.

The other side of the village housed a row of pretty cottages, and the largest dwelling of all, her grandmother's dower home.

"Why don't you wait for us at Mr. Talbot's shop, Collins?" Cecilia said, gathering up her scarf and handbag. "We'll come find you there when we finish up our errands."

"Very good, my lady."

Jane followed Cecilia along the high street, past Mrs. Mabry's grocery, Dr. Mitchell's surgery, and Mr. Smithfield's florist shop with large arrangements of dark-red roses in the windows. Cecilia was meant to pick up a hat for her mother at the milliner, but she thought she could grab a cup of tea and some strawberry cakes at the Misses Moffat's tea shop. She was in no hurry to get back to Danby.

"I hope Annabel doesn't need you back anytime soon, Jane?" she said.

"I think she and Lady Avebury were meeting Lady Byswater about the church bazaar," Jane answered. "Miss Clarke is very curious about the new renovations the Byswaters are doing on their house, so I doubt they'll return until after teatime."

Cecilia laughed. The Byswaters were quite wealthy, thanks to Lord Byswater's clever investments and Lady Byswater's inheritance from some factory or something, and they always had a new, lovely bit of house being added, or large stables built and Italian fountains installed in their gardens. They sometimes made overtures about buying some Danby land, but with Annabel that would no longer be necessary. "Wonderful! A whole day of freedom."

They stepped into the milliner's shop at the end of the lane and, after a pleasant hour of examining ribbons and feathers, left with Lady Avebury's new chapeau along with a darling little beret for Cecilia. Large, feathered and bowed, swagged hats were still all the vogue, but Cecilia grew tired of the weight and not being able to see at all to either side of her. Leaving off such styles was one of the advantages of being in the country again. Though she did notice there seemed to be more people than usual strolling the streets and on the green.

"Lady Cecilia!" she heard someone call, and turned to see Mrs. Mabry at the greengrocer arranging a display of brussels sprouts outside her door, along with pyramids of orange and purple carrots and the last of the summer peas laid out enticingly in baskets. "How fortunate to see you. I was just going to send a message to Mrs. Frazer to see if she'd like some of these sprouts, the first of the season. Just arrived."

"I'm sure she would, thank you, Mrs. Mabry," Cecilia said. "Her roasted sprouts with béarnaise sauce is one of my brother's favorites."

Mrs. Mabry's smile turned a bit sly, and she wiped her hands on her gingham apron. "And how *is* Lord Bellham? Any interesting news to be expected soon?"

Cecilia knew very well what she meant. Patrick's maybe-engagement to Annabel had been the talk of the village all summer, everyone hoping for a grand wedding soon in St. Swithin's and American dollars to pour into the shops. "He is in excellent health, thank you, Mrs. Mabry, as are we all. And your nephew Mr. Fellows is doing very fine work at Danby."

"I'm glad to hear it." Mrs. Mabry glanced down at her display with a sigh. "Though I could certainly use his help here right now. So many people are coming into the village for that Mrs. Price business, I don't know how we'll feed them all!"

"Large crowds are expected, are they?" Cecilia asked. That would explain why the village seemed more populated than usual.

"All the rooms at the Crown and Shield are full, and every cottage to be spared is let. I just hope all my vegetables come in time!"

"Of course. I'll stop on the way back to Danby and pick up the sprouts, and maybe some tinned pineapple if you have it to spare?"

"Right you are, my lady."

Cecilia took Jane's arm as they walked away, whispering excitedly, "Did you hear that, Jane? It sounds as if Mrs. Price really will have a great success here!"

"Only if it's the right sort crowding into the village, my lady," Jane answered doubtfully.

Cecilia watched as a quartet of ladies in stylish suits strolled past them toward the tea shop. "What do you mean?"

Jane gestured toward a group gathered in the small front garden of the Crown and Shield pub. It was usually quiet there at that time of day, with only a few elderly farmers sitting at the long wooden tables with their pints, talking about the good days of the "old queen." Today, though, quite a crowd was gathered, their voices rough and loud even at that distance.

To her dismay, Cecilia recognized Lord Elphin at the center of the group, obviously the ringleader of whatever was going on, pounding his hammy fist on the planks of the table.

The Byswaters were Danby's nearest neighbors, and even though they made no secret of the fact that they would like to acquire some Danby land to expand their own estate, they were friendly and easy to get along with, hosting a grand hunt ball every year that kept the neighborhood on their good side. Lord Elphin owned the estate on the other side of the Byswaters and was a different kettle of fish. Though his family was a very old one, there was little money, and his house was crumbling. He seemed to enjoy drinking and feuding with everyone else in the neighborhood more than trying to restore his fortunes, though he ran his farm as he always did. And his wife, who might have served as some sort of good influence, had died many years ago. The Bateses mostly avoided him whenever possible.

As they came closer to the Crown, Cecilia saw that most of the men gathered around Lord Elphin were his own tenants and farmworkers, a rough lot who seemed as shiftless as their employer. No one enjoyed seeing them in the village, and luckily, they seldom appeared, especially in groups.

Until today.

". . . won't stand for it!" Lord Elphin growled, pounding again at the table. His face, beneath the sparse ring of his graying hair and his whiskers, was alarmingly red. "People like that invading *our* neighborhood. Sluts who destroy private property! When they should be home taking care of their families. Next thing you know, women will be drinking in the pubs while we're left to mind the kiddies. You better watch your own houses, boys."

"Tain't right," one of Lord Elphin's men cried.

"He must be talking about Mrs. Price," Cecilia said indignantly. She started to march toward the Crown, to give that horrid old Lord Elphin a piece of her mind, but Jane held her back.

"My lady, we should just let them be for now," she whispered. "I know they're very wrong, but there are only two of us, and they've been drinking."

Cecilia reluctantly nodded. Jane was quite right, of course. Two women against a group of drunken men might not end well at all. Cecilia knew she was often too impulsive, too quick to jump in, when cool, careful consideration, not to mention patience, would be more likely to win the day.

But her blood still boiled to see Lord Elphin and his cavemen cronies. The village did not belong to *them*, nor did their wives, who were no doubt locked up at home cooking or cleaning, or both.

"You are quite right, Jane," she said. "But we must get a message to Mrs. Price before her rally to watch for those bullyboys. They seem just the sort to try and break things up with violence." She remembered tales of suffrage meetings in London, windows and bottles smashed all around, women beaten, banners torn down.

"Maybe Colonel Havelock should know, as well," Jane suggested.

"Of course. We can stop at Mattingly Farm on the way back to Danby."

"Shall we go to the bookshop, then?" Jane said, in that coaxing tone Nanny had once used to employ when cajoling Cecilia into a better humor. It was rather irritating, but Cecilia had to admit it was also rather effective. Jane was coming to know her too well. Stepping into Mr. Hatcher's bookshop, inhaling that delicious scent of glue, dust, and old leather, always made her feel calmer.

By the time they emerged with a package of the latest French poetry, Lord Elphin and his crowd were luckily gone. But someone equally surprising was on the green, just beyond the war memorial. A tall, burly man in a blue policeman's uniform held another man by the collar of his shabby coat, giving him a good shake.

Cecilia peered more closely at the bobby. There was something rather familiar about that face beneath the helmet, the pockmarked cheeks and crooked nose. "Is that— Sergeant Dunn?"

Sergeant Dunn had come with his inspector to Danby all the way from Leeds to look into the Hayes matter this past spring. Cecilia hadn't seen him since then.

Jane gasped in surprise. "I think it is, my lady. Surely no one else looks quite like that. What could he be doing here?"

"Let's go find out." Before Jane could stop her, she marched across the lane and along the gravel pathway that wound around the green. "Sergeant Dunn! Is that really you?"

The sergeant looked up, and a grin broke out across his fearsome face, completely transforming him. Cecilia remembered how he had been kind and methodical while his horrid inspector tried to arrest her brother. Was his smile just a bit brighter when he looked at Jane now? "Lady Cecilia, Miss Hughes! Fancy seeing you here." His grip never loosened on the kicking, protesting man.

"Well, we do live here, Sergeant," Cecilia said. "But whatever are you doing in Danby?"

"Seconded from Leeds for a few days, to keep an eye on that Mrs. Price," he said. "There was a bit of trouble when she was in Leeds a few weeks ago, and no one wants that here."

"Indeed they don't," Cecilia agreed. She gestured to the struggling man. "Is he part of this expected trouble, then?"

Sergeant Dunn looked down at him in surprise, as if he forgot he held on to anyone at all. "This? No, he's just a bit of a lucky find. Georgie Guff, a well-known thief."

"That ain't true!" Mr. Guff yelled. "That's a foul lie. I'm a law-abiding citizen now. I done my time in Wormwood Scrubs."

"That's not what I heard, Georgie, not when that jewelry shop was turned over last month," Sergeant Dunn said, giving him another shake. "I saw him lurking around Mr. Talbot's antiques shop over there. Eyeing the silver service in the window. A gift for your mam, then, Georgie?"

"No law against looking in windows," Georgie muttered.

Sergeant Dunn pushed him away, and Mr. Guff straightened his threadbare coat and smoothed his thin, pale hair. "Just stay away from me and out of trouble while I'm here, then, Georgie. We've got enough to worry about what with them suffragettes."

Georgie seemed to agree and ran off without another word, disappearing into the alleys behind the shops.

"Why would a notorious thief from Leeds come to someplace like Danby Village?" Cecilia asked, watching as the man tripped and dodged away. "Unless there is a new profitable line in books and scones."

"Maybe he's waiting for Mrs. Price and her group?" Jane suggested. "The ladies we saw walking around today were dressed nicely."

Sergeant Dunn scoffed. "Lot of coin in smashing lampposts, now?"

Cecilia frowned and decided she didn't have time to enlighten another ignorant man that Mrs. Price's Union was much more about intelligent speeches concerning justice than smashing anything. And Danby didn't have many lampposts, anyway.

"I've heard that Mrs. Price's husband was something high up in the law; he even worked for Queen Alexandra," Cecilia said. "I am sure Mrs. Price is comfortable without pawning lampposts."

Jane tapped at her chin in thought. "Didn't one of her daughters study the law, as well?"

"Yes, Anne Price. At the University of Manchester. She can't practice, though, even though she took high marks. I think I read she was third in her class." Cecilia tried to remember what she knew about Anne Price, but all she could recall was that Anne was second-in-command to her mother, along with Mrs. Price's secretary, Cora Black, and her vice president, Harriet Palmer. She had seemed a quiet, sensible sort when they briefly met at the theater in London. "I think there's another daughter, as well, who is also married to a solicitor. I don't think she's in the Union, though."

"Very wise of her," Sergeant Dunn said. "You ladies be careful while rabble like that is around."

"Oh, we will, Sergeant. And you keep an eye on Mr. Guff. I wouldn't want my mother's jewelry to go missing." Cecilia gestured to where the thief had reappeared, eyeing the marble facade of the branch of Coutts bank. With a curse, Sergeant Dunn took off after him.

Laughing, Cecilia and Jane turned toward the tea shop. "I don't think Mrs. Price should count the sergeant as an ally," Jane said.

"But he does seem rather sweet, in his old-fashioned sort of way," Cecilia said. She glanced at the pub where Lord Elphin and his crowd had been whipping themselves into anger. "Some men, though, are clearly nothing but trouble . . ."

Chapter Five

"Oh, Mother, why *did* you bring that thing? We have cars to take you wherever you need to go," Anne Price said, scowling as she watched her mother wheeling a bicycle into the flagstone foyer of Primrose Cottage.

Amelia Price patted the handlebars with a fond smile and adjusted the basket. "A car won't give me exercise in the fresh air I need. A good pedal around the lanes is required if I'm going to keep up with the Union's schedule. I'm not getting any younger."

As Amelia took off her stylish straw and satin hat, she revealed a luxuriant pile of dark hair barely touched by gray. Only the faintest of lines surrounded her large gray eyes, though her skin was a touch unfashionably golden from those long pedals, and her stylishly narrow-cut cream cashmere suit made her look even younger.

Anne felt rumpled and worn next to her mother, tall and

gawky and dressed all wrong as she always had. She worked so very hard for the cause, studying law, sitting up all night plotting rallies and extracting ladies from jail, and still it was only her mother everyone saw. Her mother who floated through life, as easy as a drifting silk scarf and as bright as a diamond.

Anne sighed. It was always thus, her racing to catch up with her mother and her pretty older sister, Mary. At least Mary had no use for the cause. Quite the opposite.

"Why can you not just go for a walk when you need fresh air, Mother?" Anne asked.

"And what if I need to run an errand while I'm out? I need my basket."

Anne frowned. "You mean, if you need to fetch more bottles of wine from the pub?"

Amelia just laughed and drifted into the cottage's sitting room. She tossed her hat and gloves onto a large, round, heavy oak table and sat back on a burgundy velvet settee. The whole cottage was like something from decades ago, all dark wood, small windows, swagged velvet draperies, and waxed flowers under glass. But it was cheap, and large enough to house some of their committee members and hold meetings. And for storing bicycles.

"Oh, Annie, don't be such a wet blanket," Amelia said lightly. "Wine is an *art*. If only you had paid attention when we were in France."

"I was too busy studying when we were in France, remember?" Anne said. She glanced out the old mullioned window and saw that the van had arrived, with four men removing their trunks and cases. Amelia preached freedom for women, a lightening of expectations that held their lives tethered, a new simplicity of dress and demeanor. Yet she herself never traveled light.

Anne turned to see that memories of France had indeed affected her mother again, and Amelia was pouring a glass of Bordeaux from her ivory-inlaid carrying case.

"Well, you're not studying now, my dear," Amelia said. "Do try some of this; it's lovely. A '98."

"Mother, it's not even teatime yet. We should go over the plans for the rally. Maybe visit the Guildhall to make sure the stage is set up properly."

Amelia waved an airy hand, the ruby on her finger flashing fire. Even though she had been separated from Anne's father for many months, she always wore his rings. "Cora is seeing to all that; there is nothing to worry about."

"Of course she is," Anne muttered. Ever since Cora Black had become her mother's secretary, she had carefully taken over almost every aspect of the Union. The financial books, the logistics of getting members to far-flung rallies like this one, even the ordering of sashes. Between her and the Union's vice president, Harriet Palmer, there was little for Anne to do anymore. Nor for Amelia, though she did not see and would not admit the way she was being slowly pushed aside and made a mere figurehead, no true work to do at all. "I thought she had been ill for a while?"

"Just a slight fever, I think. It barely slowed her down. I

don't know what we would do without Cora," Amelia said, closing her eyes blissfully as she drank down half the glass of wine. "She has even agreed to conduct a séance while we're here. I think this table would be perfect for it, don't you?"

"What!" Anne cried. Typing and filing and bookkeeping were all very well, but now *séances*, too? She knew Cora enjoyed reading about Theosophy, chatting about the Eternal Veil and such, yet she had never seemed to do more than that.

"Yes. She met Madame Breda in Brighton last month; it seems that Madame sensed a great gift in Cora. She must develop it."

"Here?"

Amelia shrugged. "I don't see why not. I wouldn't mind hearing what your grandmother might have to say." Amelia's mother had been dead for decades, and Anne knew little about her.

"And give the press even more fuel to declare us figures of fun? Hysterical women who will believe in any nonsense and cannot be trusted to vote rationally?"

"It's merely a spot of fun, Annie," Amelia said, pouring more wine. "You worry far too much. It can't be good for you."

Yes, Anne thought, she *did* worry. Someone had to. Their work could change millions of lives, not only their own but those of women who were trapped in existences not of their own making. Unable to use their talents and intelligence, their desire to live as full humans. It was work to change the whole world. Anne knew her mother believed in that, and her beauty and charisma drew followers to her by the hundreds.

But Amelia had no care for the hard work behind the drama and applause. Anne took care of that.

Or she had, until Cora Black arrived.

Anne sighed and peered again out the window. She didn't see the pretty garden, with the last of the climbing roses over the arbor, the vines twining along the fence, the graveled lane beyond, the gorgeous spreading plane trees that cast their shadows over the cottage. She saw all that had happened lately in the Union, all that *was* happening. Cora had come to them as everyone did, an acolyte of Amelia's cause, eager to help in any way, recommended by Harriet. Now she did all the tasks. Even illness didn't slow her down.

And she was a medium now, too, it seemed. Cozying up to the spirits of the dead as well as to Anne's mother. The living were quite complicated enough.

As Anne watched, a little Topeka Touring car swooped into the drive, so fast it was practically on two wheels, and came to a halt. Cora stepped out, unwinding the gauzy veils of her motoring hat, unbuttoning her creamy canvas duster. She reached onto the seat and pulled out a large, flat box. No doubt the apparatus for calling the dead.

Cora saw Anne watching out the window and waved merrily. Her eyes glowed brightly, and her cheeks were very pink. "Isn't it the most rustic place you've ever seen? Like something in a Hardy novel!" she called.

Anne gave a little wave back. Danby Village was indeed quintessential country England, all half-timbered shops and hedgerows. She just hoped that, like Hardy's Wessex, it did not conceal wickedness behind every herd of sheep.

ॐ

"Oh, Monty! Why must *we* go to Yorkshire? It's sure to be gloomy and gray and dull. And you hate spending time with my mother." Mary Price Winter flopped back onto her chaise, the box of chocolates perched beside her on the satin cushions sliding off and spilling across the rose-embroidered carpet. Her dark hair slipped out of its loose knot and over the shoulders of her ruffled dressing gown.

"That is exactly the point," Montgomery Winter gritted out between his teeth. He studied himself carefully in his wife's dressing table mirror, straightened his tie, and smoothed his silk pocket handkerchief. Just because a man was in a bit of a pickle, that didn't mean he should let the side down.

Especially when he was in a pickle. Appearances counted for everything. And this was all that woman's fault.

"I don't understand what you mean," Mary said.

"I mean—your mother owes you. She had too many distractions here in London to listen to any reason from us, and she hasn't answered your letter. It will be different in the country. She will *have* to listen. You must make it up with your mother and sister."

"Why must I?" Mary cried. "Mother always makes me feel so stupid, and Anne is just a dusty old stick. My headaches have been plaguing me so much of late. We should go to Bath instead."

Monty slammed his hand down hard, rattling glass bottles and silver picture frames, making Mary sob even harder. "Bath won't help us now. We need your blasted mother, whether we like it or not. Now, stop being a ninny and get dressed. Something somber and respectable, none of your ruffles and bows. Don't make me angry again, Mary. I am warning you. Women like your mother and her unnatural harpies might not do as they're told, as they're meant to, but it's a very different matter in my own home. I know you agree with me."

Mary sniffled and reached for her chocolates. It didn't matter if her dressing gowns were getting too tight; she needed their creamy comfort now. Sometimes it felt as if no one was on her side. Not her husband, not the mother who ignored her letters, not her stern father who refused to help Monty any longer. No one. "Of course, Monty darling. Always."

Chapter Six

W hat do you think, Jack? Do I look quite suitable for a suffrage rally?" Cecilia spun around in front of her looking glass. She had decided on one of her favorite country suits, a light caramel-colored tweed, with a cream silk blouse and sensible, brown lace-up boots. She wanted to look smart and respectable, but not too frivolous.

She straightened her hat, a narrow-brimmed brown felt trimmed with caramel silk roses, and then she remembered seeing photos of Mrs. Amelia Price, dressed in the height of Parisian fashion, with large hats, flounced sleeves, and narrow skirts. She frowned. "Maybe I *should* dress up a bit more."

Jack yawned and stretched from his perch on her bed. He didn't look especially interested, and Cecilia wished Jane was there to offer her opinion. But Jane was occupied in looking after Annabel that evening, as Annabel had a headache, and had forbidden Jane to attend the rally anyway. Cecilia herself had pleaded for an early night after dinner so she could slip out, and she knew she had to leave soon or she would be late. She fastened a small pearl brooch to her brown velvet lapel and reached for her gloves and handbag.

"Wish me luck, Jack darling," she said. "And don't tell anyone where I've gone!"

Jack blinked his green eyes and sat up on his haunches.

"Very well, you can tell Jane, but no one else," Cecilia said. "I won't be late."

"Mrow," Jack agreed.

Cecilia carefully opened her door and tiptoed down the gallery to the head of the staircase. She couldn't hear much; her mother had also gone to bed early, and Patrick was surely back in his laboratory for a few hours. She saw a faint glow flickering from beyond the half-closed door of the music room and heard her father chuckle. He was obviously taking the opportunity to have some more brandy and laugh over the sporting papers without her mother's disapproving glances. Which meant Redvers would also still be around somewhere.

Cecilia rushed down the stairs, glad of the thick old carpet that muffled her bootheels, and turned toward the dining room. She decided she would slip out the doors to the terrace and then out around the lawn to the road. She was less likely to be seen there than on the front drive.

She hadn't counted on the dining room still being occupied, though. She ducked around the door only to come face-to-face with Jesse Fellows. Still wearing his livery from dinner, but with a basket in his hands for collecting the silver-ware, he looked as startled as she was.

Then he grinned.

"Why, Lady Cecilia," he said. "Eloping in the middle of the night?"

Cecilia straightened her shoulders and tried to look stern. "Nonsense. I was just—feeling a bit peckish. I thought I might see if there was any of Mrs. Frazer's apple charlotte left."

"So you came down for a snack in your hat and walking suit?"

Cecilia bit her lip. She remembered how many times Jesse had helped her in the past; surely, she could trust him now? Or a bit of bribery, if need be? "Can you keep a secret?"

He smiled and leaned closer. "You know I can, my lady."

"I'm going to Mrs. Price's rally in the village. I just don't want anyone to see me. It's easier not to argue about it tonight."

"Oh, I see," he said with a nod. "And how are you going to get there?"

"I thought I would walk."

"At night?"

"I do know the way. Papa might usually insist Collins drive us there, but it's not very far, you know."

"You still shouldn't walk in the dark alone. It'll be late when you come back. I should go with you."

"Redvers would never let you," Cecilia protested. "You would get into such trouble, and I would feel awful about it."

He looked doubtful. He set down the basket of silver. "At least let me hitch up the governess cart for you. You do know how to drive it?"

"Of course. But don't you have to finish your work in here?"

"It's just the silver from the sideboard. Mr. Redvers thinks it needs a good polishing. It'll only take a few minutes to get you set up in the cart."

Cecilia nodded, glad of his help. They hurried out the terrace doors to the garden, crossing the manicured lawn and the wall of the kitchen garden to the stables. The old medieval tower behind seemed to loom over everything in the shadows, and she could see the light from Patrick's laboratory. She stumbled on a cobblestone, and Jesse caught her hand. Through their gloves, his fingers were warm and strong, holding her steady. She was rather sorry when he let her go.

In the stables, Cecilia lit a lamp and Jesse brought out the little wicker cart from its stall, along with the placid gray mare who always drew it. The stalls were warm, rich with the familiar old scents of horses and hay, the sounds of snuffles and snorts. It held all kinds of memories.

"You're very good at that," she said, watching Jesse's efficient, calm movements as he hitched up the cart in no time. She remembered how cool-headed and brisk he had been when Mr. Hayes was killed, too, keeping her steady, and she wondered how many other occupational skills he had, who he had been before he came to Danby.

He smiled as he stroked the gray's soft nose. "My father was assistant to the master of the hounds at the Pryde Hunt near Melton Mowbray, before he died. I spent part of my childhood with such creatures around all the time."

"And you didn't follow in his footsteps?"

Jesse frowned. "He died when I was just a lad, and my mum and I moved to London. It's nice to get outdoors again sometimes, though." He turned to her with a smile, and that tiny glimpse of his past was gone. "Come on, then, my lady, or you'll be late."

Cecilia suddenly remembered the rally, how important it was to be there, and she took his hand to step up on the cart. She suddenly felt a tug at her hem, holding her back.

"What's this, then?" Jesse exclaimed. "A stowaway?"

Cecilia glanced down to see Jack at her heels, one paw caught in her hem. "You scamp!" she cried. "He must have followed me from the house."

Jesse tried to pick up the cat, but Jack clung closer to Cecilia with an affronted "mrow!"

"Oh, he might as well come along," Cecilia said with a laugh. "He does seem determined to demand votes for women."

Jesse laughed, too, and it made him look younger, carefree. He helped her up onto the narrow seat and settled Jack on a carriage blanket beside her. "I'm glad you'll have someone with you, my lady."

Cecilia nodded and flicked at the reins to set out from the stables. She found she was rather glad of that, too.

❧

The village Guildhall, one of the oldest structures in the neighborhood, dignified, stolid, and square in its darkened medieval stones and cloudy stained glass windows, surely hadn't seen such excitement in years, Cecilia thought as she left the cart at the livery stable and hurried toward the entry with Jack tucked under her arm. Lights glowed from the opened doors and through the red and blue glass, and she could hear the echo of music and laughter. She glimpsed Mrs. Mabry, Jesse's aunt, going in, with the Misses Moffat from the tea shop behind her.

A woman was handing out green, purple, and gold sashes at the door. She looked friendly and full of vivid energy, with her pale red curls escaping from their pins. Up close, though, her cheeks were a hectic red in an otherwise pale face, her eyes feverishly bright, as if she wasn't as healthy as her energy suggested.

"Hello!" she said to Cecilia, offering a sash. "Is this your first time at a meeting? I don't think we've met."

"It is my first time, yes," Cecilia said, feeling rather shy as she took the sash.

Jack let out a loud "meow," making the woman laugh. "And I see you've brought a friend."

"He wouldn't be left behind, I'm afraid. He won't cause a fuss."

"He certainly wouldn't be the first if he did. I wish I had a little sash for him; he does look so wonderfully fierce." She shook Jack's little paw and offered her hand to Cecilia. "I'm Cora Black, Mrs. Price's secretary."

Cecilia shook her hand and shifted Jack so she could fasten on the sash. "I'm Lady Cecilia Bates."

Miss Black's eyes widened. "Lady Cecilia *Bates*? From Danby Hall?"

"Yes, that's me," Cecilia answered warily.

Miss Black clapped her hands in delight. "We're certainly glad you're interested in the cause, Lady Cecilia! Mrs. Price has never been so far north before. She'll be very happy to hear it's so receptive to her message. Please, come with me, we'll find you a seat."

Cecilia felt her cheeks turn warm. "Oh no, I don't want to make a fuss. You must be so terribly busy."

"No trouble at all. Do follow me, Lady Cecilia—and what is young Sir Feline's name?"

"This is Jack."

"What a good lad you are, Sir Jack." Cora scratched him behind his ragged ear and made him purr, which made Cecilia quite like her, too. Jack was a good judge of character.

Cora led Cecilia down the side aisle of the hall. It was a large room, with a vast, hammer beam medieval ceiling and rows of cushioned benches along three aisles, and a dais overlooking it all from the front. Cecilia recognized a few local ladies, like the Moffats, but most of the women were unfamiliar, dressed in white suits and frocks with the sashes. They came to a short row of folding chairs near the front and to the side, with a good view of the dais. It was lined with flowers, no doubt from Mr. Smithfield's florist shop, large brass buckets of purple, gold, and white blossoms. Behind it were more rows of chairs and a lectern, with a banner hung overhead that read, "How Long Must Women Wait for Justice?" Many of the ladies around the room held placards as well, some of which read, "Women Bring All Voters into the World, Let Women Vote" and "What Will *You* Do for Women's Suffrage?"

"Have you worked for Mrs. Price very long, Miss Black?" Cecilia asked as the secretary drew out a chair for her and looked for a cushion for Jack.

"Oh, do call me Cora, please. I've only been her secretary for a few months, but I've worked for the Union much longer, ever since I left secretarial school." She gestured to the ladies who sat at the front of the dais, one a plump, middle-aged matron in a navy blue and green dress, and one a tall, slim brunette in a white suit and the Union sash. "That is Miss Anne Price, Mrs. Price's daughter, and Mrs. Harriet Palmer, the vice president of the Union. We all work together to coordinate the actions of our members across the country."

"How fascinating," Cecilia said. And how lovely, she thought, to have such an important cause to dedicate oneself to.

"Will you be comfortable here, Lady Cecilia? Have you a good view?"

"Oh yes, it's wonderful, thank you."

"Do come and look for me after. I'll lend you some of the literature about our work." She pressed Cecilia's hand, and her fingers were burning-warm.

"Of course I will," Cecilia said, and watched Cora hurry away. She did so envy the woman's sense of energetic purpose, her air of sharp, alert intelligence.

More people were filing into the hall, and Cecilia recognized a few of the women she had seen walking on the green earlier. It reminded her of Lord Elphin and his men, and she hoped they would stay away that night.

She settled Jack on his cushion at her feet and told him, "Now, you stay just there, Sir Jack, and don't go wandering and interrupting the speakers. You are quite a different sort of fellow from the likes of Lord Elphin, you know."

He made a huffy "mrow" and started grooming his paw. After a few more minutes, the chatter of the crowd faded away as Anne Price stepped to the podium. "Good evening, everyone. I am Miss Anne Price, Mrs. Amelia Price's daughter," she said, her voice deep and resonant. She was more reserved and watchful than her famous mother, but Cecilia could tell she was an accomplished speaker and passionate advocate of the cause. "I cannot tell you how happy we are to visit Danby Village and bring the message of the Women's Suffrage Union to the north. And now, I am very pleased to introduce my mother, Amelia Price."

Another woman swept onto the dais, and Cecilia felt a lightning bolt of excitement shoot through her. She slid to the edge of her seat as if she might miss something, even though Mrs. Price had not said a word yet. She had a distinct presence that made Cecilia see clearly why she had become famous. She was tall and lithe, like her daughter, with thick, dark hair swept up and held with pearl combs that shimmered like her white satin gown. She raised her arm, and lace ruffles fell back from her wrists like ocean waves.

"I am so pleased to see such support for our sacred cause," she said, her voice soft and musical, yet carrying through the ancient hall. "Women's rights *are* human rights, and we must spread that message far and wide. Our daughters and granddaughters shall not suffer as our mothers and grandmothers, unable to use their full intellects and talents to achieve their dreams in life. They shall not live at the mercy of men, denied careers and education, simply because they were born female."

"Hear, hear!" the woman next to Cecilia cried, brandishing a placard high, and a cheer went around the hall. Cecilia nodded, thinking of her fierce grandmother, her restless mother, of her friend Maud Rainsley at Girton, of her own useless Season just past. What *would* she do, if she were free to choose? To follow her own dreams? She scarcely even knew, had never dared to think of it at all, because it was impossible.

But now, as she listened to Mrs. Price and watched the mesmerizing gestures of her hands, the flash of a ruby ring on her finger, a tiny hope dared to bloom deep inside Cecilia's secret self. Maybe things *could* be different. Maybe she could have choices. As she listened to Mrs. Price's speech go on, that hope expanded.

". . . each individual deserves dignity, responsibility, personal attainment," Mrs. Price finally concluded. "We must stand tall together, and change *will* come!"

Thunderous applause swept through the hall, and the audience jumped to their feet. Cecilia picked up Jack so he wouldn't be crushed and tucked him under her arm as she stood. She felt that bright, sunlit hope expand and grow as the crowd around her sang "Shoulder to Shoulder," and Mrs. Price bowed.

As the women on the dais filed out and the crowd began to thin, Cecilia sat down to wait for things to quiet a bit more before she found Miss Black and then went to fetch the cart. "That was quite stirring, wasn't it, Jack?" she said.

He squeezed his eyes, as if in agreement. Or perhaps he just thought they should stop by Mrs. Mabry's grocery on the way home to ask for scraps.

"Maybe Mrs. Price should take on feline rights next," she

said with a laugh, remembering Jack's story, how he was rescued by Jane from the sinking ship carrying them both from America. "We can't just sit around waiting for someone to save us, I suppose."

Jack just licked his paw.

"Lady Cecilia," someone called, and Cecilia glanced up to see Cora Black hurrying toward her. Her hair was even more tangled now, the tie at the neck of her shirtwaist askew, as if she had been rushing around the whole time. "I'm so glad you're still here. Would you have a moment to meet Mrs. Price?"

Meet Mrs. Price? *Her?* Cecilia felt her stomach lurch, and she patted at her hat. "Oh, I should like that very much indeed, Miss Black. But I must get home before I'm missed."

"Of course. Mrs. Price would not take up much of your time; she's often very tired after a speech. We just so much appreciate your visit, and Mrs. Price was eager to say so herself."

Cecilia knew that it was not herself that warranted a private word but the earl's daughter. Yet she still couldn't help but feel excited and eager. "Then I would be honored."

She followed Cora to one of the smaller chambers just behind the dais, where once guild members had negotiated the price of wool. Tonight there were just a few ladies there, gathered around an urn of tea, chatting quietly. Cecilia recognized Harriet Palmer, the vice president, and Anne Price. Behind them sat Amelia Price, a cashmere shawl wrapped around her shoulders, a glass in her hand.

"Mrs. Price, this is Lady Cecilia Bates, who I met before the speeches," Cora said, tidying up a small table nearby as if she couldn't quite keep still.

"Lady Cecilia, how very charming." Mrs. Price gave a radiant, though slightly tired, smile and held out her hand. That ruby ring and a wedding band shimmered. "Such a delight to meet you. I was very glad when Cora told me you attended tonight."

Cecilia shifted Jack under her arm and shook Mrs. Price's hand. Her fingers were soft and slight. "Thank you, Mrs. Price. It was such a stirring speech."

"I was quite hoping to meet someone from Danby Hall while we're here. I knew your father once."

"Really?" Cecilia couldn't quite hide her surprise at the thought of her conventional, conservative father who was against suffrage being friends with Mrs. Price. He had said nothing of that.

Mrs. Price laughed. "Oh, it was ages ago, before I even met Mr. Price. I was Miss Merriman then. Clifford was such a handsome devil! All of us debutantes were in agonies of love for him." She gestured to the ladies close to her. "You have met Cora, of course, and this is my daughter Anne."

"How do you do, Lady Cecilia," Anne Price said. Up close, she looked even more like her mother, tall and slim with dark hair, but her eyes were darker, more solemn, and she seemed slightly wary. "I remember you from the theater in London. How nice to see you again."

"And this is the vice president of our Union, my oldest friend, Mrs. Harriet Palmer," said Mrs. Price.

"Lovely to meet you," the plump, partridge-like, but sharp-eyed Mrs. Palmer said before turning back to her tea.

"I am sure you must get home before it grows too late, and

I don't want to keep you, but I hope you will visit us before we leave. Perhaps tomorrow?" Mrs. Price asked with another smile. "We are staying at Primrose Cottage."

"Thank you, I would enjoy that," Cecilia answered, determined to pay that call, even if she had to sneak out again.

"And do bring Sir Jack!" Cora added. "And any friends."

The Guildhall was quiet when Cecilia made her way out, but the night was not yet completely deserted. When she opened the door, she found herself facing a cluster of angry, red-faced men—led by Lord Elphin.

"Go home to your babies!" one of them shouted. "What are you going to do, go to the pub and leave your husbands to change nappies?"

Cecilia thought that sounded like a splendid idea, despite the cold touch of nervousness she felt deep inside as they pressed closer to her. Who wouldn't prefer cider to baby nappies? Jack seemed to agree, as he hissed in her arms.

"Women are irrational, emotional creatures who can't make logical decisions at a ballot box," Lord Elphin shouted. "Britain would be in chaos!"

And Cecilia thought *that* was rich, coming from men waving torches and mucking around in the dark to whine about women going to the pub. She stepped forward to say how ridiculous they were, when she felt a gentle touch on her arm. She looked back to see Mrs. Price herself standing behind her, pale and perfect as a statue in the torchlight, a slight smile on her lips.

"You cannot stop us—we are your equals whether you like it or not," she said, in her musical, carrying voice. She smelled of roses and wine. "I pay my taxes, so I demand my say." She waved her beringed hand at them. "Now begone to your beds. Maybe some beauty sleep would make you less cranky." She glimpsed Lord Elphin, and her eyes widened for an instant, as if she recognized him. Maybe he had harassed the Union before.

The men shouted incoherently and waved their torches, but Mrs. Price just ignored them and turned her smile to Cecilia. "Is that by any chance your friend over there, Lady Cecilia?"

Cecilia was confused by the whole strange scene. She couldn't be talking about anyone in the crowd of angry men. "My friend, Mrs. Price?"

Mrs. Price gestured to the other side of the lane, along the edge of the village green. Cecilia saw that Jesse Fellows had just driven the cart around the corner, and he looked quite anxious.

"Oh yes, that's Jesse," Cecilia said, in surprise and relief. Maybe a tiny bit of rescue from being a stowaway wasn't so terrible.

"Come along, then. You should not keep such a handsome lad waiting, my dear." Mrs. Price took Cecilia's arm and walked with her down the stone steps.

"Mother!" Anne called from the doorway. "Where are you going?" Mrs. Price just waved her back, and even the angry men seemed to fall away a step as she marched serenely past them, as if they weren't even there. Jack hissed at them.

"Does this happen everywhere you go, Mrs. Price?" Cecilia whispered.

Mrs. Price laughed. "There are certainly misguided people everywhere. Nothing to worry about. They will come to see the light of truth. And do call me Amelia."

One of the men suddenly lunged forward to push Amelia, who stumbled against Cecilia. Jack howled and puffed out his orange-striped tail.

"Hey!" Jesse shouted, and jumped down from the cart.

Amelia glared at the man, who surprisingly retreated into the crowd of his mates. Lord Elphin himself had vanished. "You go on with your friend now, Lady Cecilia. And don't forget to call on us at Primrose Cottage tomorrow! I do want to hear how your father is doing these days."

Still feeling a bit shaken, Cecilia just nodded and let Jesse lead her and Jack to the cart. She glanced back to see Amelia marching back into the Guildhall, the crowd dispersing into the night now that the excitement was over.

"Are you all right, my lady?" Jesse asked tightly. He helped her up onto the narrow seat and carefully tucked the carriage blanket around her and Jack. "Some people have no manners."

"You are quite right about that, Jesse. But it was a fascinating evening. I quite enjoyed it before all that ruckus. And thank you for showing up like that," she answered. "You didn't need to come."

He smiled and jumped up beside her to gather the reins. "I wouldn't have been able to sleep, thinking about you and Jack all alone in the night. But you and Mrs. Price seemed to have everything well in hand. That Elphin is a boor who should be put in his place more often."

"I certainly won't disagree with that. Even my mother is hard-pressed to be polite to him when they meet, and she's the perfect social actress. But Mrs. Price *is* rather extraordinary. I'm sure nothing much goads her."

"Joining up with the cause, then, my lady?"

"I'm not sure about that. I doubt I have much to offer them. But Mrs. Price did invite me to call on her tomorrow, and I'm looking forward to talking to her more." She hugged Jack close as they drove on through the night, still dizzy with all the sudden possibilities out there.

Chapter Seven

I'm so excited you could come with me today, Jane! You'll like Mrs. Price; she is so charming," Cecilia said as the two of them hurried down the lane toward the village. Collins had taken her father out in the car for the day, and Jesse was too busy with his duties to secretly hitch up the governess cart again, so walking it was. Cecilia thought that for the best, anyway, as the fewer people who knew about the suffrage meetings, the better. She had to gather her strategy before anyone could stop her from attending any further meetings.

"Miss Clarke is working with your mother on that church bazaar again today," Jane said, taking a small leap over a rut in the road. "It's nice to be out for a while. Jack was rather put out about being kept back, though."

Cecilia laughed. "Poor Jack! He did seem quite interested in all the excitement last night, but he never likes walking on the lead."

"Was there really a commotion outside the Guildhall with that Lord Elphin and his stooges?"

Cecilia frowned as she remembered their shouting and the shove someone gave Amelia. "It wasn't much, really. Just a few men behaving badly, yelling about women and the pub. I'm sure Mrs. Price has faced much worse. She seemed very calm about it all."

"Weren't you frightened, my lady?"

"I was, a bit," Cecilia admitted. She thought about life at Danby, how every day was just as expected and manners were everything. Maybe she had to get used to a different world if she wanted to be free. "We cannot let men like Lord Elphin stand in our way, not if we want to fulfill our potential in life."

Jane gave her a cheeky grin. "So you're a full-fledged suf-fragette now?"

Cecilia remembered the sash she had carefully tucked away in her dressing table drawer. "Of course not. I'm not sure how I could manage that, or be of help to them." Yet.

They turned at the end of the lane and hurried toward the village. A wagon clattered past, kicking up a small cloud of dust, but it was a warm, sunny, blue-sky day on the high street and the green. "How did you know there was a com-motion?"

"Mrs. Mabry's delivery boy brought some crates for Mrs. Frazer this morning, and he told us about it. It sounds like nothing so exciting has happened in the village in ages!"

"It hasn't. Not since we won a Prettiest Village Green prize from the Yorkshire Garden Society a few years ago."

Jane gave her a strange, almost searching glance. "I also heard that Jesse Fellows helped you with the governess cart, my lady. And disappeared from the servants' hall later."

Cecilia felt her cheeks turn warm at being found out. "He was being kind. He didn't think I should be out alone at night. It was thoughtful."

"Thoughtful, yes. He's handsome, too. I think Bridget and Pearl are half in love with him."

"Is he—is he in love with one of them, too?" Cecilia gasped.

"Not a bit of it. He's just polite to them, like he is to everyone. Bridget thinks he must have a sweetheart back wherever it was he lived before."

"Does she indeed?" Cecilia murmured.

"It's just gossip. Jesse is too closemouthed about everything personal to let something like that slip by. No one really knows much about him." Jane frowned thoughtfully. "I have the feeling he *is* sweet on someone, though. Maybe a certain pretty lady with red-gold hair . . ."

"You should write novels, Jane. You do seem so secretly romantic," Cecilia said, wishing she was not "secretly romantic" herself. Jesse Fellows was handsome and considerate, yes, but he was also a footman. It would make their lives very difficult indeed. "Oh, here we are!"

She was relieved to see Primrose Cottage just ahead. She did not like even *thinking* about her love life, and the fact that she had just had her second Season and would have to settle down somewhere suitable soon, let alone talking about such things. She took Jane's arm and tugged her along to the garden gate.

Primrose Cottage had once belonged to the widow of the last vicar, until she went to live in Brighton with her sister, and it was a charmingly old-fashioned, rambling house of old red brick with a wide veranda looking out to the garden that in summer would be a riot of color. Wavy, ancient glass windows peeked out from under the thatched roof. But a modern bicycle leaned against the garden wall, all shiny novelty. Cecilia pushed open the rickety garden gate and went to knock at the door, which was quickly opened by Cora Black.

Like last night, Cora seemed a whirlwind of flying reddish curls and wide, bright eyes, a dark smudge on her shirtwaist sleeve, and account books balanced in her hands.

"Lady Cecilia! I'm so glad you could come today. And you've brought a friend!"

"This is Miss Jane Hughes," Cecilia said as Cora ushered them into the dim, cool, flagstone-floored foyer. Coats, umbrellas, and hats were piled there haphazardly. "Jane, this is Cora Black, Mrs. Price's secretary."

"It's such a pleasure to meet you," Jane said.

"How do you do, Miss Hughes!" Cora said. "We've met so many fascinating people here in Danby. Mrs. Price has decided to stay on for a few days and hold another rally."

"What wonderful news," Cecilia answered.

"I'm sure Amelia will want to tell you all about it herself," Cora said. "Do come in; everyone is in the sitting room. I am afraid we had a bit of a puzzling experience this morning."

"A puzzling experience?" Cecilia asked as she and Jane followed Cora along a narrow, cool corridor, with a flagstone floor and lined with old paintings of pastoral scenes. They stepped around a set of rickety, steep old stairs that no doubt led up to the bedchambers.

"It seems as if there was a robbery in the early hours," Cora said with a shiver. "Or rather an *attempted* robbery. It doesn't look as if anything was taken."

"A robbery!" Cecilia cried. She exchanged glances with Jane, remembering the thief Guff, who had been collared on the green by Sergeant Duff. Had he been scoping out the village after all?

"A window in the kitchen is broken and the latch messed about with is all," Cora said. "These old houses are quite sturdier than they look. He got no farther."

"And no one heard anything?" Jane asked.

"Not at all. Anne and I were in our rooms upstairs, and Mrs. Price took a small chamber just beyond the sitting room for her own parlor. She says she doesn't like managing those rickety old stairs until bedtime."

"No one else stays in the house? Like Mrs. Palmer, maybe?" Cecilia asked.

"No. Mrs. Palmer and the rest of the executive committee are at the Crown, and Nellie, Mrs. Price's lady's maid, doesn't arrive until this afternoon." Cora opened a door and ushered them into the sitting room.

It was a round-shaped room, with a large, smoke-blackened fireplace at one end displayed with a portrait of the old queen on the mantel. Old-fashioned, heavy, darkly carved furniture was scattered on a faded red-and-blue carpet, and red velvet upholstered the seats. Embroidered cushions were scattered about. One desk, a modern, pale oak table, held folders and documents and books for serious work, along with unopened post and a letter ripped in half. Anne, Harriet, and Amelia examined the papers there, whispering among themselves.

Another table, shoved into a corner, was quite different. Draped with a white cloth, it was scattered with a crystal ball and various tarot cards. Burned-down candles spilled wax onto the linen. Had the ladies been trying a bit of séance along with the business?

Anne whispered something to her mother, and for an instant Amelia's ivory-like face puckered in an angry frown. But that frown vanished as she looked to greet the newcomers with her usual serene smile. Yet Cecilia noticed that Anne Price still looked irritated as she gathered up the papers in short, rough gestures, and Harriet Palmer stared fixedly out the window.

Those windows looked out onto the front garden, beyond to the lane and all the passersby of the village.

"Lady Cecilia, so marvelous to see you again." Amelia glided forward to take Cecilia's hand in a cloud of heavenly rose and wine scent. She wore a morning gown of lavender cashmere and chiffon, the sleeves and high neck embroidered with tiny crystal leaves that matched her earrings. She still wore her ruby ring. An impressive double row of perfectly matched pearls nestled creamily against the chiffon panel of her bodice.

"Amelia, this is Lady Cecilia's friend, Miss Jane Hughes," Cora said.

"So lovely! We've met so many wonderful people here in Danby. I was just telling Anne that we must establish a northern branch of the Union."

"But we don't have anyone suitable to run it at the moment, Mother," Anne protested. She sounded weary, as if this was an argument she'd had many times before. "We are all needed in London."

Amelia waved this away with a sweep of her lacy, bell-shaped sleeve. "I'm sure the right person will be found in no time. When a need appears, so does the solution."

Mrs. Palmer and Cora exchanged a long glance, as if they doubted it was quite as easy as all that. Amelia was the queen, and they were the worker bees.

"Do join us for tea, Lady Cecilia, Miss Hughes," Amelia said, ushering them toward the cozy grouping of chairs and settees by the fire. Anne seemed to shake away her irritation and gave them a polite smile as she arranged the tea service where the papers had been. Harriet Palmer tucked them away into locked drawers, and Cecilia longed to know what they said. Harriet, though, was still quiet and warily watchful.

"Or perhaps you would care for something else?" Amelia continued. She sat down on a throne-like velvet and gilt armchair, arranging the froth of her long skirts around her. "I do have a lovely pinot gris from Alsace."

Cecilia glanced at the clock on the mantel, a Black Forest confection of tiny couples in lederhosen and dirndls. It was almost noon now, and there was that whiff of wine under the rose scent Mrs. Price wore. It felt quite daring. "That sounds scrumptious. Thank you, Mrs. Price."

"Oh, Amelia, remember! And you must call us all Cora and Anne, too, and even Harriet. Just ignore her sour frowns. I am sure we will all be great friends."

As Amelia uncorked and poured glasses of the shimmering, golden wine, Anne went on with the teacups, her lips pursed.

"I must say I did enjoy the rally so much," Cecilia said. "It has made me think of, hope for, things I dared never even say before."

"That is the point—to open women's eyes to their true potential. We've done tours to America, you know, Lady Cecilia, as well as France and Germany. Poor Cora here was quite ill in France, but their spas are the best in the world, and luckily they did wonders for her!" Amelia said. "We were well-received everywhere. Now I see I must reach every corner of our own country, as well. England is much bigger than it looks."

"I heard you had a break-in last night," Cecilia said, taking a salmon sandwich from the flowered china plate Anne offered. She recognized the sandwich as the Misses Moffat's creation. Anne gave a tight smile. She did look much like her mother, with her cameo features and dark hair, but she was all edges and anger where her mother was soft persuasion. Cecilia rather felt for her; she did know what it was like to live in a mother's perfect shadow.

Amelia looked confused for a moment, before she waved away the break-in with her wineglass. "An attempt, perhaps, but no one got in and we heard nothing, thankfully." She put a protective hand over the impressive pearls at her throat.

"We have guards in London, ladies of the Union who have been taught a self-defense course," Anne said. "But Mother thought them unnecessary in the country. Though she *will* travel with her jewel case rather than leave it at the bank."

"A lady must be properly attired, my dear," Amelia said. "A ballot box, and pearls and a stylish hat, can go together. I do wish you would think of that sometimes, darling."

Cecilia glanced at Anne, at her austere expression and plain dark suit. Anne held her head high and did not answer.

"Is someone here a spirit medium?" Jane asked, thankfully breaking the awkward moment. She nodded toward the dark, solidly Victorian round table in the corner. "I see you have a crystal ball and tarot cards."

Cecilia was surprised. She didn't know Jane was a connoisseur of the spirit world.

"That would be me," Cora said solemnly, quietly.

"Madame Breda said she has great gifts," Amelia said. "And Madame Breda is a leading member of the Psychical Society in London."

"I'm just an amateur, though I've had unusual gifts and feelings ever since I was a small child," Cora answered. "I was sure a house of this age must contain many entities, and I thought it could be fun to contact them, hear their stories."

"How fascinating," Jane said. "Have you been successful?"

Cora gave a rueful smile. "Not yet, I'm afraid."

"You live at Danby Hall, do you not, Lady Cecilia?" Harriet asked, speaking for the first time. She sounded hoarse, rather rough and low. Her small, dark eyes glittered with curiosity—or maybe malice.

"Yes," Cecilia answered, shaking off Harriet's strange gaze uneasily. "I'm sure we have our share of ghosts, though I'm disappointed to say I've never actually seen one. Though my brother used to try to frighten me with the speaking tube in the nursery."

"When I met your father, so many years ago I hate to think of it," Amelia said, "he liked to scare all of us silly debs with tales of the Blue Lady."

Cecilia wondered again how close her father and Amelia had once been for him to have told her about the spirit of her ancestor—and did he remember her now? Her father seldom mentioned the Blue Lady to anyone. "She's an ancestress from the time of the Civil War. They say she appears when disaster is about to befall a Bates."

"Then it sounds as if you're lucky she hasn't appeared to you," Harriet said.

"Indeed," Cecilia agreed. "I would probably scream my head off if she did, or run and hide in the linen cupboard. I'm quite a coward at heart."

"I'm sure that's not true, Lady Cecilia," Amelia said. "You seem quite interested in new ideas. You came to our rally, after all, and faced down that dreadful Lord—oh, what's his name?"

"Lord Elphin, Mother," Anne said, slicing the Victoria sponge from the tea shop. It looked like the Prices were settling well in the village, finding the best shops and making acquaintances.

"Lady Cecilia is not a coward at all," Jane declared loyally. "She even caught a murderer in her own home last spring!"

"*We* caught him, Jane," Cecilia murmured.

Amelia grinned. "Oh, how fascinating! I do love a detective novel. Tell us more."

After Cecilia and Jane told the tale of the murder of Mr. Hayes, everyone looked at them like they were marvels.

"Oh, Lady Cecilia, I am quite sure you and Miss Hughes are exactly the sort of people we need here in Yorkshire," Amelia said. "Don't you think so, Anne?"

"I certainly do, Mother," Anne answered, with a rare smile.

"I—well it's certainly something I would like to think about," Cecilia said slowly. "And tell me, Miss Price, is that your bicycle I saw in the garden?"

Anne looked surprised at the change in subject. "No, it's Mother's."

"It is the finest exercise to be had, Lady Cecilia," Amelia said, pouring herself another glass of wine. "Are you a cyclist yourself?"

"No, but I would like to learn," Cecilia answered. "I often have errands in the neighborhood, and a bicycle would make it so much easier."

"A bicycle can greatly aid in a lady's freedom," Amelia said emphatically. "We can't always rely on handsome young men and their carts. I can teach you to ride, if you like."

"I would love that. Thank you, Amelia," Cecilia cried happily.

A knock suddenly sounded at the door, loud and rapid, making them jump.

"Oh, who on earth can that be?" Amelia asked, a touch of irritation to her tone. "We don't have any committee meetings until this afternoon."

"Aren't you expecting Nellie today?" Cora asked.

Anne glanced out the window. "I don't think it can be Nellie. Unless she's bought herself a Mercedes HP."

There was another knock, even louder and more impatient. "I'll go see," Cora said, hurrying out of the room.

". . . about time!" a man's voice echoed through the foyer. ". . . kept standing on the doorstep like a tradesman. But one can't expect a proper household *here*, can we?"

"Oh no," Anne whispered. Cecilia looked at her, startled to see that the usually unflappable, stoic Anne had gone pale.

Amelia rose to her feet just as two people burst into the sitting room, Cora hurrying behind them. The man was tall, well-fed, and full cheeked, with bushy, graying brown sideburns and a goatee below a gray bowler hat. His brown eyes were narrow and close together, giving him the look of an unfortunate badger.

The woman who hovered behind him was shorter, slighter, very pretty, with an impressive bosom, in a tan lace and muslin dress under her half-unfastened canvas motoring coat. Dark curls escaped like a cloud from the veil of her hat, and her hands fluttered as if she didn't quite know what to do with them.

"Whatever are you doing here?" Amelia cried.

The lady gave a tired little smile. "Hello, Mother. Monty and I just wanted to see how you were faring. Who would have imagined you *here*, in Goldilocks's cottage?" She giggled. "One never knows what might happen next . . ."

Chapter Eight

The next day was Sunday, and Cecilia knew she wouldn't be able to escape her family duties to go back to Primrose Cottage. There was the church service, where she had to (badly) play the organ, and luncheon at the dower house with her grandmother. Yet she couldn't stop thinking about the people she had met at the rally, and then at the cottage: Mrs. Price, her daughter Anne, her secretary Cora, and the strangely quiet Mrs. Palmer. And then the Winters couple.

"How Amelia Price could raise such a conventional daughter as Mary Winter, one would never know," Cecilia said as Jane put the finishing touches to her hair. Jack lolled in a patch of sun near the window, lazily batting at his ribbon. "Though I suppose we all have relatives we wish would stay far away." She grimaced to remember her father's cousin Timothy and his damp, lecherous hands.

Jane laughed. "My uncle, my mother's brother, was always off in Atlantic City dreaming some get-rich-quick schemes. Mines in Ecuador; desalination stations in the middle of the ocean; selling cut-rate petticoats door-to-door. He spends a lot more on those cockamamie ideas than he ever gets out of them. He went off to South America a few years ago, and we haven't heard from him since."

"My grandmother's sister did something like that. She went to explore Lebanon. But she was a marchioness, so no one really cared. She was just thought to be eccentric, not crazy."

"Sure. If you're poor, you're insane. If you're rich, you're an individual," Jane said, biting her lip as she placed a comb carefully at the back of Cecilia's hair.

"Too true, Jane. Which would people call the Prices, I wonder?"

"From what I've read in the papers, my lady, a lot of people would call them sensible. And a lot would call them crazy."

"Or maybe eccentric? Those pearls Mrs. Price wore weren't cheap, and someone went to the trouble to try and break into their cottage. After her jewel case, maybe? Or those papers Mrs. Palmer locked away?"

"Traveling abroad can't be cheap, and didn't they say Miss Black went to a health spa? I think I did read that Mr. Price is a solicitor, one who did some work for Queen Alexandra herself, but the couple no longer lives together. Maybe that was why he was left off the last Honors List."

"Interesting. I wonder if it's because they just don't get

along, or because Mr. Price knows his wife's work is important so he lets her lead her own life."

"Then he'd be a very unusual gentleman." Jane put the last touches to Cecilia's hair and reached for the navy blue and lavender dress that hung on the wardrobe door, freshly pressed.

Cecilia stepped into it and stood still as Jane fastened the lavender pearl buttons. "What did you make of the Winters? There didn't seem to be a great deal of love lost between them and Amelia and Anne. I wonder why they came all this way. Perhaps we shouldn't have departed right after their arrival. A little nosiness can go a long way."

Jane smoothed the lavender feathers on Cecilia's navy blue hat, fluffing at the net veiling. "I doubt even a family like the Prices would air their dirty laundry in front of everyone, my lady, especially not an earl's daughter they're wooing to their cause. But you're right—them showing up like that seemed strange. Most people want to stay far away from family members they feud with, don't they?"

Jane sorted through the glove box and held up a pair of fine lavender kid gloves embroidered with small blue flowers.

"Those look perfect," Cecilia said. "And the hat, too. Fashionable enough for my mother, but not so heavy I'll have a headache throughout Mr. Brown's homily."

Jane gave a teasing smile as she pinned the hat in place. "And how *is* the handsome vicar, my lady?"

Cecilia bit her lip, remembering the conversation she had overheard between her parents last spring, speculating on a match between her and Mr. Brown, considering he was going to be Archbishop of Canterbury one day—maybe. "Oh, don't you tease, too, Jane! I'm sure Mr. Brown has no interest in me at all."

Jane smoothed the hat's veil. "I wouldn't say that, my lady. He comes to call on Lady Avebury about the bazaar all the time, and he always asks after you. Rose said he was very disappointed yesterday to hear you had gone to the village."

Cecilia shook her head. "I'm sure Mr. Brown knows I would make a terrible vicar's wife. I am far too unorganized and scatty."

"I don't know, my lady." Jane held out a navy blue shawl. "A vicar's wife should be caring and concerned about people, and you have that in spades."

"Do you really think so, Jane?" Cecilia asked hopefully.

"Of course. You're always the first to offer help, to organize a fundraiser or take donations to people's homes, to rescue a kitten and run a charity bazaar, even when you don't want to. You even want to help women get their rightful votes."

"But could a vicar's wife really attend suffrage meetings?"

"Are you going back to see the Prices, then?"

"Yes. Apart from anything else, Mrs. Price promised to show me how to ride a bicycle."

Jane handed Cecilia her handbag and parasol with a grin. "A bicycle would be an excellent way for a vicar's wife to visit parishioners, my lady."

Cecilia laughed. "Oh, Jane! Then *you* should marry Mr. Brown's new curate, and we could make a parishioner-visiting, mystery-solving team."

"Except you would never get me on a bicycle, my lady."

A knock sounded on the door. "The car is waiting downstairs, my lady," Redvers called.

"Thank you, Redvers, we will be there directly," Cecilia answered. "And as for you, Jane—no more teasing! I have no intention of getting married just yet. I have a few things to do first."

If only she knew what those things could really be . . .

❧

St. Swithin's Church in Danby Village was not the most elegant church in the county, perhaps—it was too square, too plain, too solid, an old Norman church that had once formed the chapel of a larger monastery that had long ago been swallowed by the village. Yet Cecilia had always loved it, loved its quiet solidity, its hushed coolness within the thick ancient walls, the scent of candle smoke, flowers, and old dust from the prayer books. One of the stained glass windows, the largest over the altar, was in memory of her great-grandfather, who had restored the old bell tower and bought a new organ, and generations of Bateses lay in the vault beneath the stone floors and in the churchyard. When she was a little girl, she had imagined they would gather close and listen to the hymns with her.

Today, as she filed in behind her mother to the Bateses' pew just below the spiral staircase to the carved lectern, her thoughts were on more worldly concerns. On the future, and her place in it. She glanced across the aisle to see Amelia and Anne Price, along with Cora Black, all dressed in stylish

London fashions for the service, though Amelia's hat was by far the largest of anyone's except Lady Byswater's. Cecilia didn't see the Winters anywhere.

She waved at Amelia, who smiled and waved back with her lace-gloved hand, but there was no time for any other pleasantries as the organ signaled the opening hymn. Lady Byswater usually played the opening songs, while Cecilia played the interlude. She opened her prayer book and rose to her feet with everyone else as Mr. Brown and his new curate (who *was* handsome, and would look quite nicely next to Jane) processed down the aisle.

Mr. Brown, too, was good-looking, Cecilia had to admit. Tall and classically handsome, with glossy brown hair and a kind smile, the sort of vicar who might appear in a romantic novel. Not a Mr. Collins in the Austen vein at all. He also seemed kind and cheerful, energetic in his duties, and certainly hardworking. Their last vicar had been at St. Swithin's for decades and had long since lost the energy to even deliver a coherent sermon, let alone perform the charitable work of the neighborhood. Mr. Brown had come like a fresh breeze through Danby, energizing not only the church but the school, the WI, and all the charitable committees.

And he was the nephew of a viscount, and everyone seemed sure he would make a bishop one day. Not a ducal match, maybe, but very suitable, and Jane was right—it would give Cecilia a job to do. An important one, if she made it so. And if she could love Philip Brown.

Thinking about it all gave her a headache. Cecilia shook it away and glanced over at the Prices again. *They* chose not to be married, or at least Cora and Anne went their own ways. Anne was a lawyer, or had studied to be one, and Cora was Union secretary. And Mrs. Price hadn't lived with Mr. Price for some time, though Cecilia wondered why.

The doors at the end of the aisle opened, letting in a swirl of leaves on the breeze along with a low murmur of disapproval. No one ever came late to St. Swithin's. Cecilia peeked over her shoulder to see the Winters slipping into the back pew. Mr. Winter wore a black overcoat with a glossy fur collar, his bowler hat in hand, his hair patent-leather smooth with fashionable pomade. Mary wore a purple-and-white-striped suit, an ermine stole over her shoulders, a purple feathered hat balanced on her head. She held her husband's arm but didn't look up at him.

Anne Price frowned, but Amelia went on serenely smiling at the altar.

Cecilia's mother nudged her, and Cecilia snapped her attention back to Mr. Brown. Luckily, the rest of the service proceeded as usual, and Cecilia was able to find Amelia in the churchyard afterward, chatting with the curate. Cecilia's parents, along with Patrick, Annabel, and Jane, waited at the lych-gate for her, but she dared take a few minutes to speak to the Prices. The Winters had vanished again.

"Lady Cecilia, how nice to see you again," Amelia said with one of her charming smiles, as if her errant daughter and son-in-law hadn't even cast their small shadow on the day. "I do hope you'll come to tea this afternoon. I can show you my bicycle."

"I would certainly enjoy that, Mrs. Price," Cecilia answered. "I must have luncheon at my grandmother's house, but I can stop by Primrose Cottage after."

"We shall look forward to it, then."

"Cecilia, darling, won't you introduce me to your new friends?" she heard her mother say, in her most frighteningly cheerful "social" voice.

Cecilia turned to see Lady Avebury and Annabel standing nearby. They looked elegant and perfect in the shade of the old oak trees, their pastel gowns and furs shimmering, their faces framed in lacy hats. "Of course, Mama. This is Mrs. Amelia Price, and her daughter Miss Anne Price, as well as their secretary Miss Cora Black. This is my mother Lady Avebury and Miss Annabel Clarke." Cecilia glanced around, but her father had vanished. Perhaps he did not want to run into a figure from his youthful past.

The ladies all exchanged pleasantries about the warmth of the day, the prettiness of the village. As Lady Avebury smoothed her gloves, a signal to move along, Cecilia decided to be truthful. "Mrs. Price is going to teach me how to ride a bicycle, Mama. I promised to call at Primrose Cottage after luncheon with Grandmama."

Lady Avebury's lips tightened. "A bicycle, Cecilia? Are you quite sure that is wise?"

Cecilia thought quickly and remembered what Jane had said. "I can do so many errands for the parish, Mama, if I can ride a bicycle. Papa needs Collins and the car most of the time, after all."

Her mother still looked doubtful, but she nodded. "I suppose it could be useful at times."

"Bicycles *are* becoming quite fashionable in America," Annabel said. "The magazines say it's a good way to keep one's girlish figure, and the outfits are ever so cunning. Perhaps I should learn as well!"

Cecilia knew her mother would never speak against Annabel *and* increased parish duties, but she still didn't look terribly happy. "Will you be staying in the village long, Mrs. Price?"

"A few more days at least, Lady Avebury. This is certainly one of the most charming places I have ever visited. Don't you agree, Anne?"

Anne seemed doubtful.

"Then you must call on us at Danby Hall," Lady Avebury said graciously. "Cecilia, we should speak to Mr. Brown about the bazaar before we go to the dower house. He will be so pleased to hear of your new zeal for parish duties."

They bade goodbye to the Prices, and Cecilia's mother held her arm tightly as they made their way toward Mr. Brown, who was in the shadow of the church porch, chatting with Colonel and Mrs. Havelock. Lady Avebury's kid-gloved fingers were curled tightly around Cecilia's sleeve, as if she feared her daughter might suddenly run off to set fire to a letter box.

"Cecilia, I thought we made our views on suffrage clear," she whispered fiercely. "You must think of your position. Your future!"

"That's just what I *am* thinking of, Mama," Cecilia whispered back. What *was* her future? Marriage—to who? Social duties, children? Maybe college, like Maud Rainsley? A job, like Cora? Travel? "I was just talking to the Prices, anyway. It's 1912, not 1512."

"They certainly seem more respectable than I would have imagined, even if they *are* misguided," Annabel said. "Did you see Mrs. Price's pearls? And that hat. So elegant. I'm sure it must come from Paris. I had imagined these suffrage women would barely even bathe! Yet Mrs. Price wore La Rose d'Orsay scent, very chic. Cecilia, if you do learn how to ride a bicycle, you must show me. It will be such fun!"

Cecilia knew that her mother wouldn't argue with Annabel, and she was glad of the unexpected ally.

Mr. Brown's smile widened when he saw them. "Lady Avebury! Lady Cecilia, Miss Clarke. How lovely you are all looking today. And your organ playing was as elegant as ever, Lady Cecilia."

"Mr. Brown, your homily was excellent as always," Lady Avebury said with her most charming smile. "You must come to dinner this week at Danby. Cecilia has so many new ideas for the St. Swithin's bazaar, and I know you will want to hear them all . . ."

❧

It was quite late in the afternoon when Cecilia could escape from the dower house to make her way to Primrose Cottage. All the lunch talk had been of the bazaar, Patrick's botany work, or the newest styles in hats, and her grandmother's constant certainty that everything was so much more elegant and clear-cut in *her* day, all while Sebastian growled and snapped under the luncheon table. Cecilia was glad to escape it, and she took Jack with her, just to be sure he wouldn't make trouble with Sebastian.

To her surprise, the cottage door was ajar, and she heard raised voices from inside. She clutched Jack's basket a little closer. "Hello?" she called uncertainly.

Cora appeared in the doorway. Her hair fell down her back in an untidy plait, and she wore a loose canvas jacket over her white dress. "Oh, hello, Lady Cecilia."

"I came for a bicycling lesson with Mrs. Price, but if it's a bad time . . ."

"Not at all, it's just—well, it seems Mrs. Price has taken a fall."

"A fall?" Cecilia exclaimed in concern. "Is she badly hurt? Should I fetch Dr. Mitchell?"

"Not at all," Mrs. Price shouted from the sitting room. "Everyone just insists on fussing! Do show Lady Cecilia in, Cora."

Cora gave Cecilia a helpless shrug and closed the front door behind them. The sitting room was crowded, with Anne Price, Harriet Palmer, and a slight, pretty blond woman she did not recognize. Judging from the black dress with white collar and cuffs, Cecilia guessed she must be Nellie the maid. Cecilia knelt next to Mrs. Price, who had her foot up on a stool; her fashionable coiffure was all undone. Mary Winter stood in the corner, fidgeting with her ermine stole, but "Monty" was nowhere about.

"What happened?" Cecilia cried.

Mrs. Price gave a hoarse laugh, but her usual gesture of waving things away seemed listless. "A tiny tumble down the stairs, that's all. I just missed a step."

"If you would wear more rational skirts, Mother . . ."

Anne said. She knelt down on her mother's other side and pressed an ice pack to her mother's ankle. Jack made an indignant "mrow" from his basket, so Anne let him out, and he sniffed at Amelia's skirts curiously.

"I doubt it's the skirts, Anne," Mary muttered. She shot a long look at the bottle on a side table. "Wine and old, rickety stairs don't mix, Mother. You need to moderate your habit."

"Don't be such a ninny, Mary," Amelia said with a snort.

Cecilia thought the ankle did look terribly swollen under the ripped silk stocking. "Won't you let us call the doctor?"

"If you can't stand at the lectern tomorrow night . . ." Cora said.

Anne suddenly shot a glance at Cora, full of daggers. "Oh, you would like that, wouldn't you? A chance to heroically stand up for the fallen leader and dazzle with your own speech."

Cora's mouth fell open. "I—I don't know what you mean, Anne."

"Girls, really," Amelia said sternly. "I have hardly *fallen*; it was just a tiny misstep. I don't need a doctor. I'll just keep my foot up with ice, and I will be quite well tomorrow."

"Please, I can call Dr. Mitchell," Cecilia offered. She sensed that whatever quarrel was going on there was an old one, a rivalry for control of Mrs. Price and the Union, and she wanted to dissipate it. "He's been our family's physician for ages. He's very good and so kind."

"You are considerate, Lady Cecilia," Amelia said. "If the swelling is worse in, say, an hour, I will call for him. In the meantime, I know you have come for your bicycle lesson. Do let us go outside. I could use the fresh air."

"Mother, you shouldn't move about," Anne protested.

"Oh, pooh, I am just going a few steps to the front garden. Nellie, dear, bring the footstool. Cora, if you will give me your arm? And Mary, do stop standing there like a hooked fish! Come along with us. Master Jack can come, too, I think."

They made a strange little procession to the garden, Nellie carrying the stool as if it were the crown-bearing cushion, Mary scurrying behind them, Anne looking uncertain, and Jack prancing with his tail high like a king. Cecilia trailed after them, unsure what she should do, but once Amelia was settled with an armchair and her stool under the shade of an ancient plane tree, with Mary and Cora beside her, she gave Cecilia a gentle smile.

"Come, Lady Cecilia, I'll show you how to start with the bicycle, even though I can't ride myself today," she said. "Anne, dear, can you fetch it?"

Cecilia followed Anne to the cycle propped up by the garden gate, and they wheeled it into the lane. "Are you a cyclist as well, Miss Price?"

"Oh, call me Anne, please. After you've witnessed all my family's scenes, it seems silly to stand on ceremony." She held up the bicycle, pointing out the pedals and brakes, the way to keep skirts out of the wheels. "I'm not the enthusiast my mother is, but I know how to ride well enough. All a part of being a new woman, you know."

Cecilia glanced back at Mary, who was fidgeting in her

fashionable striped gown and furs. "And your sister? Is she at all a—new woman, too?"

Anne laughed wryly. "Mary? Not half. She married Montgomery Winter when she was eighteen, and that was that. No hope for her, poor thing."

"Mr. Winter does seem very, er, decisive." She remembered the impression he gave when he arrived, swaggering into Primrose Cottage as if he owned it.

"That's one way of putting it. He's practically kept Mary in a prison since then. We rarely see them."

"But they came to find you here in Danby?"

Anne frowned. "It's all very odd. We haven't heard from Mary in months, except for one letter, and then she and Monty show up on the doorstep. I'm not at all sure why. It's hard to imagine Monty would take time away from his work just to harangue us. He usually does that from a distance."

"What is his work?"

Anne studied the wheel of the cycle. "He's a solicitor. With a very prestigious firm in London, Bird and Wither. My father helped him find the position when he married my sister. My father was a lawyer, too, you know."

And Anne had studied law—but could not practice it, as she was a woman. Cecilia wondered how that made her feel now. It couldn't be pleasant.

Anne suddenly looked up and smiled. "Here, Lady Cecilia, let me show you how to get on this beast and start the pedals. You should tie your skirt up a bit. I promise it's simpler than it looks, and you could even put a basket here for Jack. He does seem the curious sort . . ."

Chapter Nine

"I'm so glad you could come with me tonight, Jane!" Cecilia said as they clambered over a stile and turned toward the village. It was almost sunset, the sky pale lavender and peach at the edges, the air with the cool nip of early autumn. "You'll enjoy Mrs. Price's speech, I'm sure. Her message is so very important for all women to hear."

"I'm not sure how having the vote will help me when Miss Clarke is ticking me off for pressing her tea gown wrong," Jane grumbled, but she looked excited, too. She'd had so many questions about the last rally, and about Cecilia's visits to Primrose Cottage. "But I am glad Miss Clarke went off to dinner at the Byswaters' with Lord and Lady Avebury and Lord Bellham. She won't miss me for hours."

"As long as we're back before they are." Cecilia thought of her own excuse for not attending the Byswater dinner, a sick headache that absolutely required Jane's ministrations at home.

She could hear the noise from the Guildhall before they saw it, a hum of voices laughing and shouting, the strains of "Shoulder to Shoulder." As they turned the corner on the high street, she saw the building was lit from roof to basement, the stained glass windows glowing.

She looked around warily for Lord Elphin and his men, but there were just a few of them, sullenly drinking their pints outside the Crown and Shield and watching the proceedings. She wondered how they felt with some of the Union members actually lodging there at the Crown, right above their heads.

A movement at the edge of the green caught her attention, and she turned her head to see Georgie Guff, the thief Sergeant Dunn had caught. He lurked there in the shadows, shuffling his feet on the grass, peering out from beneath his ragged felt hat. She was surprised he was still dangling about; surely, a good shaking by the sergeant was enough to put fear into any miscreant.

"Jane, isn't that Georgie Guff?" she said.

"The thief?" Jane answered, briefly distracted from her wide-eyed fascination with the color and noise of the Guildhall. "Where?"

"Over there." Cecilia pointed, but the man had vanished.

"Lady Cecilia!" Anne Price called, and Cecilia hurried over to find Mrs. Price's daughter handing out sashes and leaflets at the door along with three other ladies. Anne looked much more cheerful since her mother's fall, as if things were looking up with her work. "I see you brought your friend."

"Yes, Miss Hughes," Cecilia said.

"So pleased you could come, Miss Hughes," Anne said, handing Jane a sash. "The response here in Danby has been so gratifying."

"No trouble yet tonight?" Cecilia said, and gestured toward the staring men at the pub.

Anne gave them a scornful glance. "They'll stay away tonight, if they know what's good for them."

Cecilia was not so sure, not at the rate they were putting away their pints. But for now they kept their distance. "And your mother? Has she recovered from her fall?"

"She says she feels quite well. I'm afraid that wasn't the first time such a mishap has happened with her. I think she's more upset about Mary and her horrid husband appearing like that than she'd like to tell. Mix that with wine . . ."

"You did say you hadn't seen the Winters in some time."

"Monty thoroughly disapproves of us, as I'm sure you noticed, and Mary does what he says. Thank goodness I never married! I truly have no idea why they're here now. I would have thought they'd leave as soon as they could, but I heard they rented a cottage near the florist shop."

"How strange." Cecilia longed to ask more—family drama was always so odd and complicated, like something in a novel. But more ladies came up behind them, and Cecilia and Jane hurried into the hall.

"Be sure and look for Cora!" Anne called. "She'll be saving seats for you."

Cecilia did find Cora, who was arranging chairs at the front of the hall just beside the dais. She smiled at Cecilia, but Cecilia thought she looked a bit pale that evening, with deep-purple shadows ringing her eyes. Perhaps she had been up all night tending to Amelia—or using her medium skills to commune with the spirits.

"Oh, Lady Cecilia, hello," she said softly, pushing back the hair falling from its pins.

Cecilia introduced her to Jane, but her worry increased when Cora swayed on her feet. "Miss Black, are you quite all right? You do look tired."

"Here, miss, sit down," Jane said quickly, holding out one of the chairs Cora had just arranged.

Cora gave a faint smile. "I *am* a bit tired, that's all. A lecture tour can get a bit taxing at times, though of course anything is worth it to spread the message of suffrage."

Cecilia saw some ladies dispensing tea from a table on the other side of the room. "Do let me fetch you something to drink."

"You are kind, but I must make sure everything is ready for Mrs. Price! Tea and sandwiches after the speeches. Do sit here at the front, Lady Cecilia, Miss Hughes. It should be quite an exciting evening."

She gave one more pale smile and hurried away. Cecilia sat down, but she felt rather worried about Cora. It seemed like looking after Mrs. Price, as important a job as that was, could be quite tiring.

"Exciting," Jane murmured. "I'm not sure about the sound of that. Will someone take another tumble?"

"I'm sure you'll enjoy the speeches," Cecilia said, but she did know what Jane meant. There was always Lord Elphin and his crowd to worry about. They might break some windows this time, beat down the door, accost the ladies of the Union as so many barbarians had in London. And someone had already tried to break into Primrose Cottage, quite aside from Amelia's fall down the stairs.

A row of women in white dresses and suits, fashionable hats, and the ever-present sashes of purple, gold, and green filed into their places on the dais with their placards, below the Union banner.

"And who are the others on the stage?" Jane asked.

"You met Cora Black; she's the secretary. She also says she is a spirit medium, which must be fascinating. And Harriet Palmer."

"And Mrs. Price has that other daughter? The overdressed one?"

"Mrs. Mary Winter. She's against women's suffrage, and her husband is as pompous looking a stuffed shirt as you can imagine. I admit I'm rather curious about why they're here. Anne Price says they seldom hear from them."

"And the elder Mr. Price?"

Cecilia shook her head. "I don't know anything about him at all, except that he's a solicitor. Rather an important one, too, I believe. It seems husband and wife don't share a roof, or at least don't often see each other."

Jane laughed. "Some would call that an ideal marriage, then."

"Indeed," Cecilia murmured, thinking of some Society friends of her parents who only seemed to meet at dinner parties.

The lights dimmed a bit, and Anne Price made her introduction to a burst of wild applause. When Amelia appeared, she leaned on a walking stick but otherwise appeared no worse for her tumble. She smiled and waved, and Cecilia couldn't help but notice something odd—she didn't wear her ruby ring.

❧

Cecilia awoke early the next morning, after a night of strange dreams that had her tossing and turning. She wondered if it had been a full moon, or maybe the Blue Lady had been wandering the corridors, stirred up by newcomers and break-ins.

She rolled over and drew the quilted satin coverlet up onto her shoulders. Jack had come into her room in the night and was burrowed under the blankets at her feet. The housemaid had already been in to lay the fire, but the autumn mornings were turning chilly now, and Cecilia was happy to stay in the cozy haven of her bed a little longer, remembering the rally last night.

As the clock struck the hour, the door opened and Jane slipped quietly into the chamber, a tray in her hands. Since she had come to Danby, she had quickly learned all the discreet arts of being a lady's maid—except one. Cecilia should really go down to breakfast, as an unmarried young lady, but Jane always brought her some tea in bed first so they could chatter before Annabel awoke.

"I'm awake already, Jane," Cecilia said. She pushed herself up against the pillows as Jane set the tray on the bedside table and went to open the draperies. It was a gray day outside, clouds lowering over the old medieval tower.

"Good morning, then, my lady," Jane said, gathering up

the pink silk dinner gown from last night, along with the more practical blue wool walking dress she had worn to the rally, and putting them in the wicker basket to send to the laundry. It was all like every morning—except that Jane's eyes were red rimmed, her skin pale under her freckles.

Cecilia was immediately concerned. Jane was that rare creature—a real morning person, eager to chatter even as the sun was low in the sky. Today her quiet demeanor and wan face made Cecilia sit up straighter. Jack peeked out from under the blankets. "Jane, what's wrong? Is someone ill? Are *you* ill?"

Jane glanced up, biting her lip. "Oh, my lady. I hardly know how to say it. It's too terrible."

Now Cecilia was almost panic-stricken. "Is it my grandmother?"

Jane shook her head. "It—it's Mrs. Price, my lady. Amelia Price. We just heard she's dead!"

"Mrs. Price, dead?" Cecilia gasped, a feeling of numbness spreading over her. How could that be? They had seen Amelia just the night before, giving her impassioned speech. "But how? Was her fall worse than had been thought? Was she . . ." A terrible thought occurred to her. "Was she attacked by someone like Lord Elphin?"

"No one knows yet, my lady! The delivery boy from Mrs. Mabry's grocery brought the news from the village just as I was making your tea. It looks like she took another tumble down the stairs at Primrose Cottage, still fully dressed after the rally. Cora Black found her when she got up this morning. She could have been lying there all night!"

"Oh, poor Cora. And poor Anne Price," Cecilia murmured, imaging the horror she would have felt to find her own mother in such a way. She pushed back the bedclothes and swung her feet down to the rug, barely missing Jack, who had crept under the bed to swipe at unsuspecting passersby with his paw. "Help me get dressed right away, Jane. We must go to the village at once."

Chapter Ten

The village seemed strangely deserted as Cecilia and Jane made their way along the high street, really quite eerie for the hour when business should be bustling in the shops. Cecilia held tightly to Jack's basket as they proceeded down the street. Only a few people hurried down the walkway, nodding at Cecilia as they passed but not stopping to chat. A dog barked somewhere in the distance, perhaps Sebastian in her grandmother's garden; nothing would faze the terrier. Yet even he quickly fell silent, and Jack didn't respond to the provocation, as he usually would.

As they walked, Cecilia exchanged a quick glance with Jane and saw her own shock and disbelief in the maid's eyes. They had just seen Mrs. Price atop the dais at the Guildhall, so alive, so full of passion for her cause! So beautiful. How could that suddenly be cut short? It hardly seemed real.

Cecilia could see a few signs of life. Pink gingham curtains swaying at the tea shop window, a light above Mr. Hatcher's bookstore, an early funeral wreath of dark purple delphiniums already laid out in the florist's window. She knew that behind the scenes gossip would be flying like birds on the wing. Nobody's business stayed secret in the country, especially not when that business was the sudden death of a scandalous celebrity.

She noticed Mr. Talbot, Collins's cousin, opening the door of his antiques shop. His shop was near Primrose Cottage. "Good morning, Lady Cecilia, Miss Hughes," he called. "Though it's hardly a *good* morning, of course. Such a shocking thing."

"Indeed it is, Mr. Talbot," Cecilia agreed. She hoisted Jack's basket higher so he could "mrow" a greeting to the shop owner. "Did you see or hear anything at all strange last night?"

He shook his head sadly, touching a finger to Jack's velvety nose through the bars of the basket. "Not a peep, after everyone settled down after the Guildhall rally. It was an evening like any other. I had my cocoa and got ready to retire. Most of the lights in everyone's windows were out by then." His eyebrow suddenly went up. "Though I did notice something before I closed my curtains."

"Something strange?"

"Just a man walking down the street. He had a sack over his shoulder, heavy I would say, since he was moving slowly, a bit unsteady on his feet. I thought he might just be a late straggler from the Crown. With that Lord Elphin and his men hanging about lately, I'm sure the pub is doing a brisk trade."

"Do you think it *was* Lord Elphin?" Jane asked.

Mr. Talbot frowned in thought. "I wouldn't think so. Lord Elphin is a portly man, isn't he, and this man was thinner. Taller, I think. But I couldn't see his face."

"Was he coming away from Primrose Cottage?" Cecilia said, wondering if the attempted thief had come back.

"Perhaps, but anyone from that direction would be. Primrose Cottage is set a fair ways back from the other houses along here." He shook his head. "Are any of us safe in our beds these days, I wonder? Danby is usually such a quiet place."

"Yes, usually," Cecilia murmured. But now this was two murders in only a few months! Surely, a record since the wild days of Civil Wars over two hundred years ago. "Do come up to Danby Hall if you feel at all unsafe, Mr. Talbot. Collins does have his own flat over the garage."

"That's kind of you, Lady Cecilia, but I daren't leave my shop. I will certainly put my best wares in the safe at night now. I hear that Colonel Havelock has sent for Inspector Hennesy from Leeds again, as a precaution after that break-in with the Prices. I'm sure this will all be over in no time."

Cecilia sighed inwardly. Not Inspector Hennesy again! She hadn't cared for him very much during the business with Mr. Hayes. Though she supposed she couldn't be surprised, not with Sergeant Dunn already in the village and Mrs. Price being famous. She and Jane bade goodbye to Mr. Talbot and continued on to Primrose Cottage.

If the village was strangely quiet, the cottage was the opposite. The door and windows were flung open, and loud, angry voices, cries, and sobs floated out on the morning breeze.

Sergeant Dunn's bicycle leaned against the gate with Mrs. Price's, but there was as yet no sign of the inspector.

Cora sat alone on a bench under the oak tree, her face buried in her hands, her shoulders shaking. She wore a blue silk kimono over her nightdress, and her hair fell in an untidy plait down her back.

"Oh, Miss Black! Cora," Cecilia cried, feeling a deep wave of pity wash over her. She and Jane hurried to her side. "I am so very sorry."

Cora looked up, her eyes red, her cheeks flushed and puffy from crying. Jane dug a handkerchief from her coat pocket and pressed it into Cora's hand with a gentle smile. Cecilia opened Jack's basket, and he jumped into Cora's lap for a comforting meow and a pat.

"Lady Cecilia, Miss Hughes," Cora said, hugging Jack. "Thank you for coming. Everything is in such confusion! Poor Nellie has even locked herself in her room, refusing to come out. And they say some police inspector is on his way, that there must be an inquest. It's too awful for words! Mrs. Price—gone like that. What will happen to us all?"

"Did you find her?" Cecilia asked softly. She remembered from the terrible Hayes business that it could be important to remember things when they were fresh, not clouded with time and fear and hope.

Cora blew her nose in Jane's handkerchief and nodded. "When I woke up and came downstairs. I'm usually the first one about. Mrs. Price likes to sleep late, especially after a speech. And—and there she was. Just lying at the foot of the stairs, her head all twisted! I'll never forget it, ever."

"And you heard nothing at all during the night?" Cecilia said.

Cora shook her head, watching as Jack jumped down to sniff at the doorstep. "I haven't been feeling quite well of late, you see, and I took a dose of laudanum last night. If only I hadn't! I should have stayed up with her. She wanted a brandy before bed, but I was just too tired."

"A brandy?" Cecilia said, thinking of the tumble Amelia had already taken once on the stairs, her enjoyment of French wines.

Cora seemed to sense what she was thinking and shook her head vehemently. "It wasn't like that at all! She only had a glass once in a while. Mrs. Price was entirely respectable in her habits."

"Was anyone else in the house?" Jane asked.

"Anne, of course, and Nellie. Harriet had taken a room at the Crown—she said it was too crowded here, but she stayed for a while after we returned from the Guildhall." She blew her nose again, then seemed to remember something. "Oh, and Mr. and Mrs. Winter!"

Cecilia was surprised. There certainly seemed no love lost between Amelia and her elder daughter and son-in-law. "Really? At such an hour? What did they want?"

Cora shook her head. "I don't know. Mrs. Price wanted to be alone with them when I said I was tired, so I went ahead to bed. There didn't seem to be an argument, though, no raised voices. Anne might know, I suppose."

Cecilia glanced at the open front door, where Jack still sniffed about, and glimpsed Colonel Havelock just inside.

"Jane, can you and Jack stay with Cora for a moment? I'm just going to speak to the colonel."

"Of course, my lady." Jane murmured soothingly to Cora, putting her arm around the woman's heaving shoulders. Jane was always so good in a crisis; Cecilia feared her own Bates reserve reared up when she was faced with tears, no matter how strong her own emotion, but she hoped she was improving thanks to Jane's friendship and example.

She hurried through the foyer and past the sitting room door of the cottage, where she could hear Sergeant Dunn and Anne Price speaking, to the scene of the crime—if of course it was indeed a crime. Amelia Price lay sprawled on her back on the carpet at the foot of the narrow old stairs, her legs pointed up on the steps, her torso and head on the floor, as if she had fallen straight backward. Unlike Cora, who was in her bedclothes, Amelia was still wearing her white lace and chiffon evening gown from the night before, her purple, gold, and green sash over her shoulder. But the sash was ripped, half of it jaggedly separated from the rest and missing. One of her elegant, Louis-heeled kid shoes was gone, and the sight of that bare, silk-stockinged foot made Cecilia choke back a sob. She couldn't help but think of the old tale of Amy Robsart, neck broken on the stairs in Cumnor Place in the time of Queen Elizabeth. *That* death had never been solved.

She took a deep breath and forced herself to study the rest of the scene. The cause of death did seem obvious; a pool of half-dried, darkened blood was under Amelia's head, her hair disarranged though not loosened from its pearl pins. One arm was flung out at an awkward angle, as if broken in the fall, or maybe grabbed and twisted. Aside from the carpet along the stairs being a bit askew, nothing else seemed out of place. She wore her wedding band but no ruby ring.

"Good morning, Lady Cecilia," she heard Colonel Havelock say, and she turned to give him a sad smile. He was a kind man, an intelligent and observant one, whose equally smart wife often served on charity organizations with Cecilia and her mother. She wondered what he made of the whole business.

"Hello, Colonel Havelock," she said. "This is certainly a terrible thing."

"Terrible indeed. We fear the press may descend at any moment, so we are about to seal the area. Are you friends with the deceased?"

Cecilia glanced at Amelia and was struck again by the utter *absence* of a soul that had been so very vital. "Of a sort, yes. I called here a couple of times and attended two of Mrs. Price's rallies at the Guildhall. She was a remarkable lady."

Colonel Havelock frowned. "Remarkable, yes, so my wife tells me. And, shall we say, controversial."

"I heard that Inspector Hennesy has been summoned. Does that mean foul play is suggested?"

"Sergeant Dunn was in the village on another case and suggested it might be wise, in the case of such a well-known personality as Mrs. Price, to cover all possibilities. I have taken a preliminary look and see nothing to suggest anything other than a tragic accident. It seems the lady was, shall we say, fond of a nightcap."

"Miss Black said she didn't drink all that much," Cecilia said. "And she did also have enemies."

"Of course, as anyone in public life would."

"And one of them came here last night and killed her!" Anne Price cried.

Cecilia turned to see Anne standing in the sitting room doorway. Unlike Cora in her nightdress and kimono, Anne was neatly dressed in a navy blue wool skirt and crisp white shirtwaist, a purple tie knotted at her starched collar. A black band circled her arm. Her hair was up in a braided knot, but like Cora she looked as if she had been crying. Her eyes were puffy and red rimmed, but dry.

"Miss Price," Cecilia said, going to her side. "I am so very sorry. Are you quite sure this was not just some terrible accident?"

Anne glanced over her shoulder, and Cecilia could see that she was looking at the round séance table in the corner. It held wine bottles and a glass stained with the remains of a dark brandy, a hint of lip rouge on the rim. There was only the one glass, though Cora had said Mr. and Mrs. Winter had also been there last night. Scraps of paper were scattered around them. Sergeant Dunn stood next to the table, notebook in hand, and Cecilia wondered if he had also questioned the amount of wine.

For an instant, something like doubt flickered across Anne's face, but then her expression hardened. She fiercely shook her head.

"My sister and her husband were here for a time, and Mother sent me to bed, saying she would look at her speech before she retired. I heard Monty's car not long after that, so they must have left," Anne said. "I didn't hear Mother come upstairs, but she often stayed up late. It's true she enjoyed a glass of wine at times, but not when she was going to work. She *must* have been pushed. Her sash was torn away, don't you see?" Her voice cracked.

Cecilia gently took her hand. She had the definite sense that Anne was not a woman who let many people close, but she did allow Cecilia to lead her back into the sitting room, away from the stairs. The sergeant nodded and discreetly departed. Anne went to the fire as if to stir it up, but faltered on a sob.

Cecilia helped Anne to sit down on an overstuffed velvet settee near the fireplace, before she knelt down to try to stir up the embers. Cecilia didn't often make a fire, but she was sure she could do it. It was turning into a warmish day, but Anne rubbed at her muslin-covered arms as if in cold shock.

"Should we not—move her?" Anne said quietly, gesturing to the doorway.

Cecilia remembered what it had been like when Mr. Hayes collapsed in the Danby dining room. "I'm afraid not, Miss Price. An inspector has been called, and he'll want to gather all the clues he can to present at the inquest. I am so sorry. But our village undertaker is quite good and I'm sure will come as soon as possible to help you make the arrangements." She prodded at the ashes and noticed what seemed to be scraps of paper.

Anne nodded. "You're quite right, Lady Cecilia," she said softly.

"I think this may be one time we might indulge in a spot of wine ourselves, even if it's still morning," Cecilia suggested,

and Anne nodded. As Cecilia left the fire and poured out two
glasses of a port she found on the sideboard, she noticed a pile
of torn papers near Cora's séance paraphernalia. Curious, she
peered closer, smelled a faint perfume of sweet lilacs, and saw
a few words in smeared black ink: . . . *forced to take action . . .
hope it does not come to this . . .* And there was a bit more,
harder to make out.

"Is everything all right, Lady Cecilia?" Anne said.

Cecilia nodded and pushed the papers half under the box
of tarot cards in case a closer look would have to be taken
later. She handed Anne the glass.

"To Mother," Anne said, and Cecilia nodded with a sad
smile.

"To Mrs. Price."

They sipped at their wine in silence for a moment, listening to the comings and goings outside the door, the sounds of
sobs from Nellie in her room upstairs, and slowly, Anne seemed
to steady herself. She sat up straighter and shook her head.

"Thank you, Lady Cecilia," she said. "You are kind.
Mother did say you were a good sort of lady."

"That was very nice of her," Cecilia said, and sat down
next to Anne on the settee. "So you heard nothing at all last
night, Miss Price? After your brother-in-law's car left."

Anne shook her head. "I read for a while, then went to
sleep. I'm a fairly heavy sleeper. I thought I heard Nellie moving about in Mother's room, but that was all."

Cecilia thought of the man Mr. Talbot had seen walking
away with the sack. "Perhaps there was another attempted
theft, and Mrs. Price surprised the thief this time?"

Anne shrugged helplessly. "Possibly. Mother would insist on taking her jewels everywhere she went, and she could be a bit—well, careless with them at times. I noticed she was not wearing her ruby ring last night, and she wore it all the time, despite her estrangement from my father. But she did have many enemies. Any of them could have gotten in late at night."

"Enemies?"

Anne took another sip of her wine. "Those who possess all the power, Lady Cecilia, will never give it up easily, simply because it is the right thing to do. They will fight us with everything they have to keep us as slaves, cleaning their houses and raising their children. Those of us who fight back, who stand up for ourselves, are hated simply because we insist on our own humanity. So yes, my mother did have enemies. Starting with my father and sister, I'm afraid."

Before Cecilia could ask her more about those shocking words, Colonel Havelock and Sergeant Dunn appeared in the doorway, followed by two local constables. They looked most solemn. Jane and Cora were behind them, Cora leaning heavily on Jane's shoulder. Jane held Jack in her other arm, but he looked very much as if he wanted to leap down and explore.

"My apologies, ladies, but if everyone could remain here for the time being, I would be most grateful," the colonel said. "I am sure we will have more questions after a longer look around the cottage."

"May I take Miss Black upstairs to change her clothes, Colonel Havelock?" Jane asked. "She also has not been well and tells me she needs to take her medication."

"Yes, of course, if you tread carefully, Miss Hughes. And perhaps you can ask Mrs. Price's maid if she will kindly leave her room soon," the colonel said. "Sergeant, will you escort Lady Cecilia and Miss Price outside to the garden for a moment?"

"Certainly, Colonel," the sergeant said, flashing Jane a shy smile as she led Cora past him. "Ladies, if you will follow me?"

"Perhaps I might just fetch the decanter, Sergeant? As it seems we will be here for a while." Anne sighed and drained her glass before setting it carefully on a small table. "Maybe we should ask Cora to use her spirit medium skills to ask Mother what happened."

"And what do you think Mrs. Price would say?" Cecilia asked.

"I think I know what *Cora* would claim Mother said."

"What do you mean?"

"Cora and Mrs. Palmer have been thick as thieves lately. And they have their own ideas of how the Union should be run."

"And those ideas were not your Mother's?" Cecilia asked. Could Union politics really have something to do with Mrs. Price's death? She didn't know much about Harriet Palmer, but Cora seemed to worship Amelia.

Anne opened her mouth, but then she seemed to think better of whatever she had been about to say. She shook her head and took up the decanter and her glass before heading toward the door. "We all have our own ideas about how life should be run, do we not?"

A scream suddenly erupted through the cottage, shrill and full of terror. "Mama! No! How can this be?" a woman shouted.

Anne groaned. "I see Mary has arrived."

"Mary?" Sergeant Dunn asked in a bewildered tone.

"My sister," Anne said.

Cecilia ran to the sitting room door to see that Mary Winter had indeed "arrived." Her hair was loosely pinned atop her head, and she wore a lace jacket hastily thrown over a pink muslin morning gown, as if she had started her morning toilette and been a bit interrupted. There was no sign of her husband.

One of the constables held her back from the staircase. She fell to the floor, her shoulders heaving. Cecilia was strangely reminded of a performance by Mrs. Patrick Campbell in *Bella Donna* she had seen at the Lyceum that summer.

Anne seemed to agree as she peered down at her sister with an exasperated frown. "Oh, Mary, do stop that caterwauling and come outside with us. You are not being helpful in any way."

Mary stared up at her sister with an equally exasperated expression. "How can you be so heartless at a time like this, Anne? You always were so cold! Not human at all. Our mother is *dead*."

"Our mother who you have refused to speak to for months," Anne said. "You only appeared here because you and Monty want something, though who could ever say what."

Mary's face contorted, and she jumped to her feet to stalk toward Anne. She didn't even seem to see the constable or

Cecilia. "You know what she did to us, to Monty and me! How could I talk to her after that? But I never wanted to see her dead! I'm not ruthless like you and your unnatural friends."

Jane and Cora reappeared, Cora dressed hastily in a white skirt and shirtwaist, her hair twisted back. Jack hissed a bit at the commotion but was quickly shushed by Jane. Cora stepped between the warring sisters, her hands held up. "Please, not now!" she cried.

"Colonel," Cecilia said, fearing things were about to become even more dramatic. "Perhaps Jane and I could take the ladies to the tea shop while you finish here? I'm sure they will be ready to answer any questions you might have afterward."

Colonel Havelock looked quite relieved. "I'm sure that is acceptable, Lady Cecilia, thank you."

"Miss Price, Mrs. Winter," Cecilia said, taking them each firmly by the arms and leading them out of the cottage, keeping them facing away from the terrible sight at the stairs. Jane and Cora followed close behind, Jack stuffed back into his basket and mrowing irritably at it.

The breeze outside was fresh after the close, coppery tang of the cottage, and Cecilia took a deep breath as she kept a firm hold on the warring Price sisters. But her relief was short-lived when she glimpsed a man at the gate, a short gentleman in a cheap tweed coat and bowler hat, with the telltale notebook and pencil of a reporter. His face lit up when he saw them.

"Miss Price! What's happened to your mother?" he called. "Is it true she was found bludgeoned in a pool of blood? Do you suspect anti-suffragists?"

Cecilia gave him a freezing look, learned from her mother when some social parvenu tried to get too close, and marched their small party past him, slamming the garden gate behind them. He fell back, but she feared he was just the vanguard. She thought Danby Village was going to get much less sleepy very soon.

Chapter Eleven

O̲h, you poor dears," one of the Misses Moffat clucked as
she led their strange and forlorn little party up to a private parlor above the public tea shop. "What a terrible morning you have had! What an inspiration Mrs. Price was. You
just sit down here; no one will bother you in *my* shop. There's
a Victoria sponge with raspberry sauce, fresh from our
kitchen. I am sure it will fortify you."

As she left, one of the pink-aproned maids placed the tea
service on the table, gawking at them wide-eyed. But she was
obviously under strict instructions from her employers and
quickly left them alone despite her curiosity.

It seemed Mary and Anne had already burned out their
ire with each other, at least for the moment. The silence of
the parlor, muffled by heavy pink and white satin draperies
at the bow window, was almost deafening after all the drama
and clamor outside, as thick as the Misses Moffat's famous

clotted cream for scones. Anne and Mary did not look at each other at all.

Cecilia and Jane exchanged a quick grimace. Cecilia wasn't really sure *what* to say or do now. Ever since childhood, she had been taught the proper behavior for every possible social situation, every awkward moment or sudden challenge. A burned menu item at a dinner party, the sudden appearance of royalty, an unwanted marriage proposal. Taking tea with two newly bereaved but warring sisters had never been taught by her governess.

Miss Moffat brought the cake herself, and Cecilia played mother, filling the teacups and passing them around the table. Anne and Mary smiled briefly at her but still did not look at each other.

"You live in London, I believe, Mrs. Winter?" Cecilia said, trying desperately to find something to talk about that wouldn't make Mrs. Winter cry again.

Mary nodded. "In Ebury Street. With my husband, Mr. Montgomery Winter. He is a solicitor."

"And yet you managed to come to Danby Village so quickly," Anne said dryly. "Just before Mother's passing."

Mary scowled. "That was a hideous coincidence, and you know it! Monty and I wanted to make amends with Mama, and I fancied a bit of country air. I never expected to find it like this. I wrote to her before we came!"

"I never saw any letter from you," Anne said.

Mary pursed her lips. "I suppose you do read all her post. I wouldn't be surprised if you kept my letter from her on purpose."

"Cora takes care of Mother's correspondence now, don't you, Cora?" Anne said. Cora stared at her in silence, and she went on, "I am sure Mother would have mentioned hearing from you after all this time. Why would you be writing to her now, anyway? Making amends, ha. You and Father would never do such a thing." She pushed away her plate of cake without taking a bite.

Mary looked furious. "I am not the one who needed to make amends! You know what happened because of Mother. Because of you both, and your horrid ideas. You behave like such barbarians, parading around in public, neglecting your proper duties. Poor Father! How he has suffered, just as Monty and I have, because of you."

"Father, suffering?" Anne said with a bitter little laugh. "He tossed Mother out."

"He was the head of our household, and she would not listen to him! It was his right. We could all have been so happy, so socially secure, if only you and Mother had *tried*. Instead it's all just . . ." Mary's eyes filled with tears, and she stuffed a large bite of the cake into her mouth.

Anne gave a tired sigh. "Is that why you've come, then, Mary? To tell Mother again what a misery she had made of you and your precious, prosperous Monty, all because she insisted on being herself, her own person? You could have saved the effort."

"We only wanted to see if common ground could be found somehow," Mary said around her cake.

"Where is Monty today, then?" Anne said. "I don't suppose he lets you wander around by yourself now."

"Of course not! I am a proper lady, something you would know nothing about. He is at the cottage we rented behind the church. He was still asleep when I heard about poor Mother. He has not been sleeping well lately, and it's no wonder. I had wanted to come see Mother this morning anyway, before I heard she had—died. I hoped this early she would be—well . . ."

"Sober?" Anne said shortly, and Mary let out a sob.

"That is not fair," Cora cried. "You know Mrs. Price was not like that. She would never have had so much to drink that she . . ."

Anne sighed, and Mary started crying again. Jack hissed in his basket.

Cecilia handed Mary a napkin and patted her hand. "It must have been a terrible shock to hear what happened, Mrs. Winter."

Mary nodded and took another bite of cake. "A woman cleaning in the churchyard told me as I was walking past. I hadn't been able to awaken as early as I had hoped. I slept so heavily after Monty sent me home. That poor woman in the churchyard, she didn't even know who I was when she told me, but she was just so—so gossipy. We are always such a scene of tittle-tattle wherever we go now! It is quite unbearable."

"I suppose not so unbearable for Mother now," Anne said shortly. "She can't hear it. And now you and Monty and Father won't have to put up with it any longer."

Mary sniffled even harder, and Anne sipped at her tea. Cora looked mortified, and Jane sadly shook her head. Cecilia thought she could tell what Jane was thinking—the Prices were an odd clan indeed.

She thought of her own parents, how they sometimes drove her quite mad with their old-fashioned ideas, her mother's matchmaking attempts. Her grandmother's bossy, seemingly all-knowing ways. And Patrick—she sometimes wondered how they came from the same parents, he was so intellectual, so distracted. She had grown up knowing the world of Danby Hall worked in a certain way, and she had her place in it, no matter how she fought against it. Yet she had also known they loved her, they wanted her happiness as they saw it, and she loved them in return. They had their quarrels, their misunderstandings, but never anything like this icy indifference and animosity between the Price sisters.

What had happened between Amelia Price and her husband? What drove Mary and her husband so far away from her mother and sister? Was it really only Mrs. Price's suffrage work? And what was Mary doing in Yorkshire now?

There was a knock at the door, and Sergeant Dunn peeked into the parlor. Cecilia was suddenly rather glad to see his battered, crooked-nosed face. The anger and grief that tightened around them in that small parlor was starting to cut off her breath.

"Inspector Hennesy is on his way," the sergeant said. "He wires that he will set up an office of sorts at the Crown, if you would care to speak with him there later today, Miss Price, Mrs. Winter. I know he will want to talk to you, as well, Lady Cecilia."

Anne nodded and pushed back her chair to march out the

door, past the sergeant. "Cora, perhaps you would come with me? We can start looking through Mother's papers." Cora nodded and followed her out.

Mary blew her nose in the pink napkin. "I must go to my husband," she said.

"Let me walk you there, Mrs. Winter," Cecilia said. "You said your cottage is near the church, and I need to stop there anyway. Sergeant, perhaps Miss Hughes and I could speak with the inspector at Danby at his convenience? I must be getting home soon; my mother will be wondering where I am. And Jack will want his meal soon."

At the mention of Danby Hall and the countess, the sergeant hastily nodded. "Of course, my lady. And Colonel Havelock said he will send word as soon as the inquest is arranged."

"Thank you, Sergeant." Cecilia took Mary's trembling arm and led her gently back to the street. Luckily, there was no press waiting there; they were probably all gathering at the cottage. She remmebered that Mrs. Winter had said she was on her way to see Mrs. Price that morning when she heard the news. "I am terribly sorry you weren't able to see your mother this morning, Mrs. Winter."

Mary sniffled. "It is like a curse, isn't it? Feelings must go on forever unspoken, love lost and buried by hate." She pressed the back of her hand to her mouth and shuddered.

Cecilia was rather fond of a penny dreadful novel herself, all curses and tragedy, but she wondered if perhaps Mary wasn't laying it on a bit too thickly. She thought again of Mrs. Patrick Campbell.

"I'm sure your mother knew you cared about her, just as

she must have cared about you, no matter what passed before," Jane said.

Mary gave her a startled look. "Cared? My mother never cared about *me*. She never cared about anything except herself."

"Mary! Mary, my darling, I just heard," a man called out, and Cecilia saw Monty Winter running along the pathway that led around the churchyard. She was reminded again that if she had ever imagined what a solicitor married to a lady like Mary Price would be, this was him. Solid, respectable, his hair pomaded to a shine, his suit perfectly tailored. Even as he rushed toward them to take Mary into his arms, all tender, marital solicitude, Cecilia thought it was all a perfect picture. Mary stiffened a bit, but then gave him a watery smile, turning her cheek to his kiss.

"It is true, then? Your mother is—deceased?" he said. "How is that possible?"

"She—she had a fall," Mary answered. "And there is some inspector who wants to speak to us later, so horrid."

"Speak to us?" Monty said, his concerned-husband mask slipping a bit as if he contemplated a scandal. "Surely, he must know we can be of no help! We only just arrived here."

"Then I'm sure he will let us return to London soon. After I make sure proper arrangements are in hand. Anne can't be trusted with such things." Mary smiled again and half turned to Cecilia. "Darling, this is Lady Cecilia Bates, from Danby Hall. We saw her ever so briefly at Primrose Cottage. She so kindly offered to escort me home after this morning's awfulness."

His expression immediately changed to a charming smile. "Lady Cecilia. How very thoughtful of you to see to my wife. I am sure none of this can be of interest to you."

"I actually did meet Mrs. Price a few times since she arrived in the neighborhood, Mr. Winter," Cecilia said. "I am so sorry for what has happened."

"How very kind you are," Mr. Winter said. "I must see my wife home now, but perhaps we might call on you later at Danby Hall? If it is not too much trouble."

"Of course," Cecilia answered, puzzled as to why he wanted to talk to them at Danby. "We are happy to help in whatever way we can."

She watched as Monty and Mary hurried down the pathway. Though they were arm in arm, she could have sworn they were arguing.

"Well, Jane? What do you think of the Price sisters?" Cecilia asked as they clambered over a stile to cut across the fields as a shortcut to Danby. They had already missed luncheon, and her mother was sure to be furious. Maybe Cecilia could fudge a bit and tell her they had seen Mr. Brown at the churchyard? Which they had, for an instant, waving at him as he fastened a notice to the lych-gate. "They don't strike me as exactly Jane and Elizabeth Bennet."

"Not at all," Jane answered, hoisting Jack's basket under her arm. "My brothers go at one another like cats and dogs all the time, and my dad's not above giving them a walloping for it from time to time. But we always have one another's backs.

I don't understand having such—well, such contempt for a sibling, my lady."

"Is it just the fact that Mrs. Winter is anti-suffrage? Or maybe there's some old childhood rivalry? Vying for their mother's affection?"

"They do seem like very different sorts of people. But I would have said Mrs. Price was closer to Miss Black than to her daughters."

"So it could definitely be old family wounds, as well as new politics. But Mrs. Winter said she was here to mend fences."

"Why now? Right before Mrs. Price dies like that."

"That I could not say." They climbed to the summit of a hill, and to one direction she could see the chimneys of Danby. To the other, there was the crumbling, ill-kempt stone wall of Lord Elphin's estate, past the gleaming new chimneys of the Byswaters' grand house. "Tell me, Jane, do you really think it was just a fall? There are plenty of people who would have liked to see the last of Mrs. Price. Men like Lord Elphin, for instance. As Anne said, people who think they are due power won't give it up easily."

Jane frowned thoughtfully. She, too, liked a good, thrilling detective novel and had been a keen observer of what happened when Mr. Hayes was killed. "You do hear of ladies at suffrage meetings being knocked about savagely, my lady, and Lord Elphin seems just the type to do that. And what about Mrs. Price's husband, or that Mr. Winter? He does seem to know all the proper behavior, but there's just something about him . . ."

"I quite agree with you there, Jane. Perhaps Mary Winter

married a man like her father? She did seem to think her mother and sister had done something to wrong her and her husband. But what sort of wrong? And what sort of grudge do they hold about it?"

They climbed over another low wall and onto Danby land, following a pathway through the park. "And another thing," Cecilia said. "What will happen to the Union without Mrs. Price? Who do you think is slated to become the leader now? Anne hinted that there were some disagreements with its direction between her mother and Mrs. Palmer, and even with Cora Black."

"Surely, Miss Price is the logical candidate, my lady? And it looked to me as if she and Miss Black did all the work while her mother took her bows onstage."

"Yes, indeed. But such a system did seem to work well for them. Mrs. Price knew how to draw in a crowd, almost better than Sarah Bernhardt. She created the enticement, but then who managed the funds? The logistics? Budgets would surely have seemed dull to Amelia Price, yet proper management would have been vital to it all. We should find out who does what, and who *wants* to do what. Who has access to the funds. Maybe someone did want to push Mrs. Price out and do things their own way."

"Miss Price? Or maybe Cora? I must say, my lady, she doesn't seem all that robust right now; she had a lot of medicine bottles in her bedroom. And what about the vice president, Mrs. Palmer?"

"Anne does seem like a decisive sort of lady, but I don't know Mrs. Palmer well at all. I shall have to ask around about her. And what about the man Mr. Talbot saw walking away from the cottage?"

"Maybe it was that thief the sergeant was after?"

"Georgie Guff. It could very well be. Anne said her mother's ring was missing, and I didn't see her wearing it at the rally last night." Cecilia sighed. "Mrs. Price did have lots of enemies, yet surely, she had plenty of people who liked her, too. Loved her, even. And we saw where love got poor Mr. Hayes. Do you think Mrs. Price could even have had a lover? I'm sure her husband the respectable solicitor wouldn't have liked that. But who?"

Jane laughed. "And where would she have found the time for an illicit affair? She was always traveling, giving her speeches. Cora said they just got back from France."

"Oooh, maybe a handsome Frenchman? It's true she was busy, and her progress was always followed in the papers. But she was very beautiful. We'll just have to keep our ears open for any gossip."

They opened the gate between the park and the formal gardens and turned toward the house. "There's another thing, my lady," Jane said. "The way the body was lying. As if she had been standing on the landing just above, outside the bedrooms, and fell straight down. And the torn sash. Maybe someone grabbed it, ripping it, and she fell? If she was pushed on purpose, then she clearly didn't just trip and fall down the stairs."

"Oh, very good, Jane!" Cecilia cried. She pictured the scene in her mind, and it was just as Jane said. Except for the crooked arm, Amelia hadn't looked as if she flailed about as she tumbled down. "And no one heard anything, either. Maybe someone surprised her there?"

"Cora was on those medicines, my lady, and didn't Miss Price say she's a heavy sleeper? What about the maid, Nellie?"

"Could you speak to her? She wouldn't even come out of her room when we were there."

Jane sighed. "I can try, but Miss Clarke has me running off my feet every ten minutes lately. Constantly changing her mind about her outfits! She's not usually like this. I wonder . . ."

"Wonder what, Jane?"

"I wonder why she's second-guessing herself all the time. Miss Clarke usually knows her own mind very well, you know, my lady."

Cecilia did know. Annabel was very confident. A lot like Mrs. Price, in fact, though Annabel used her talents for quite other purposes. "Maybe it's my brother? We all thought he would surely propose by now, and it would all be settled. I'll speak to him, if you like. Or maybe it's not Patrick at all. Maybe she's seen life at Danby now and wants nothing to do with it. I couldn't really blame her."

"Oh, I doubt that, my lady. She keeps a copy of *Debrett's Peerage* beside her bed, so she can check on people's titles whenever she likes. No, once she's set on something, I don't think she'll let it go. Like your grandmother's terrier."

Cecilia had to laugh at the image of Annabel as Sebastian. Who, then, would be Jack? "Well, it's up to her, of course, but I do hope she will decide to stay. I never want to lose you, and really I think she would be good for my brother. She's very strong." She remembered stories of Annabel's life before she came to Danby, rumors of elopements from her California millionaire father's home and such. New, strong blood would be good for Danby, just as it was for women in general.

"She is that, my lady. We all have to be strong, don't we?" Jane smiled down at Jack in his basket. "Just like Jack here, a survivor."

Cecilia thought of the pickle they were all in now. "If there is a murder, especially by some anti-suffrage man, I'm afraid the inspector and his men will just brush it under the rug. We must make sure that doesn't happen."

"No, my lady, we can't let that happen at all."

As they turned toward the lawn and the terrace, Cecilia saw Patrick and Annabel strolling together on the croquet green, laughing under her lacy parasol. Maybe Jane's doubts in that direction were wrong? Cecilia quite hoped so. But her hopeful spirit was dashed when she saw that the couple was not alone at all. Lady Avebury sat at a tea table on the terrace, along with the dowager countess, Sebastian, and Mr. Brown. She groaned, fearing her excuse of calling in the village to find out more about the church bazaar was quite found out, and there would be trouble.

"Cecilia!" her mother cried. To Cecilia's surprise, she was not scolded at all, but her mother leaped up from the table and ran to hug her close. Remembering the Prices and their quarrels, she hugged her mother close in return, and inhaled deeply of her comforting lemony perfume. "Your grandmother and Mr. Brown just arrived from the village and said that there was a terrible death, and I was so worried when you were nowhere to be found! Are you quite well?"

How did Mr. Brown get there before them so quickly? She wouldn't have an excuse now. "I'm sorry, Mama. Jane and I just walked into the village, and then I couldn't just leave Miss Price and Mrs. Winter when they had heard about their mother. I would never want to worry you."

"Such kind charity, Lady Cecilia," Mr. Brown said with a smile. "You are always so thoughtful of others."

"Isn't she just?" the dowager countess murmured wryly. "I knew there would be trouble as soon as I heard that sort of woman was coming to Danby. And see! I was right, as usual. I do hope you have learned your lesson about suffrage, Cecilia."

"Come and have some tea, darling," her mother said, leading her to the table and seating her next to Mr. Brown. Jane disappeared around the side of the house toward the servants' hall, no doubt before Annabel could see her and send her on some errand. "Have one of Mrs. Frazer's raspberry cakes; they're your favorite. You must forget all about such unpleasantness and hear Mr. Brown's new ideas for the bazaar. He agrees with me that you would be superb in charge of the bring-and-buy stall!"

Cecilia smiled and took a cake, but she knew her mother was quite wrong—she would never forget.

Chapter Twelve

I beg your pardon, my lady," Mrs. Caffey said, "but Inspector Hennesy is downstairs asking to see you and Miss Hughes. If this is not a good moment . . ."

Cecilia sighed and exchanged a glance with Jane. They had been sitting in her chamber, Jane doing some mending as Cecilia read aloud from the newest penny dreadful thriller, trying to distract themselves from the real terrible events happening just beyond their doorstep. It wasn't really working, though. "No, Mrs. Caffey, now is fine. Better to get it over with, I think."

"Lady Avebury and Miss Clarke have gone into Ripon to do some shopping, and Lord Avebury has gone out with the estate agent," Mrs. Caffey said. "I've put the inspector in the library."

"Thank you." Cecilia put away her book and stood as Jane

tucked the lacy petticoat into her workbox. Jack was nowhere to be seen; no doubt he was hiding from the inspector, the lucky scamp.

Mrs. Caffey led them downstairs. "Should I or Mr. Redvers stay with you, my lady?"

"Oh no, I don't want you to worry yourselves, Mrs. Caffey," Cecilia said, wary of what the inspector might ask. Gossip spread so fast around the house, despite Mrs. Caffey and Mr. Redvers's legendary discretion. "I would hate to add to your tasks for the day. I'm sure the inspector won't stay long. There isn't much we can tell him."

Mrs. Caffey looked doubtful. "Danby has always been such a peaceful place, my lady. And now for such terrible things to happen here . . ." She paused with them outside the library door. Bridget the housemaid was dusting the ancient Chinese vases in the foyer, and Mrs. Caffey shooed her away. "By the way, my lady, Bridget has asked if she might have the afternoon off to visit her aunt?"

"Her aunt?"

"Yes. It seems her aunt has something to do with the suffragettes. A Mrs. Palmer, I believe."

"Indeed?" Cecilia was shocked to find a connection between Danby and the suffragettes so close to home. She remembered the stern-looking Harriet Palmer and the rumors of some rift within the Union. "I had no idea Bridget was a connection of Mrs. Palmer."

"Nor did I, my lady, until today. As you know, Bridget's uncle owns the butcher's shop in the village. Mrs. Palmer was once married to his brother, until the man died and she married again. I'm not sure they were close, but—well, family is family, my lady, especially in difficult times."

"Of course it is. She must go see Mrs. Palmer, by all means." Cecilia wondered what Bridget might be able, or willing, to tell them about the Union. "Tell her she may have the rest of the afternoon off. I'm sure Mama won't mind."

As Mrs. Caffey left, Cecilia whispered to Jane, "Did you know about Bridget and Mrs. Palmer?"

Jane shook her head. "Not at all. She didn't mention it when we were all talking belowstairs about the Prices coming to Danby."

"The world is a small place indeed. Perhaps she can tell us more later." Cecilia eyed the library door as if it were guarded by Cerberus. "Well, come along, Jane. We must get this over with, yes?"

Inspector Hennesy and Sergeant Dunn waited at the far end of the library. The library was quite the most fantastical room in the house, redone by her grandparents in a medieval Gothic style once so beloved by Queen Victoria. The soaring, carved, beamed ceiling, stained dark to look ancient, blended with the wine-red velvet draperies, the stained glass in some of the windows, the red velvet and tufted leather chairs and settees she had lounged on for so many hours with beloved books. At one end of the vast room was a minstrels' gallery, reached by a spiral staircase and concealed by a false rood screen. It was an excellent place to hide and eavesdrop. Or, on quieter days, to curl up and read by the fireplace, massive enough to roast a boar, if such was needed in those modern days.

She had hidden up in that gallery the last time there was trouble at Danby, when the inspector used the library to investigate a crime.

"Inspector Hennesy, Sergeant Dunn, so nice to see you again," Cecilia said with a polite smile. She noticed that the sergeant blushed in a rather adorable way when he looked at Jane. "Please, do sit down. We're quite eager to be of assistance in this awful matter. How can we help?"

They sat down in a grouping of tapestry-covered chairs by the tall windows that overlooked the garden. Inspector Hennesy took out a notepad and gave her a stern look as he opened it. "I understand you knew the deceased, Lady Cecilia?"

"I met her a few times. I attended her rallies at the Guildhall and called at Primrose Cottage," Cecilia answered. "Miss Hughes went with me.."

"And did Mrs. Price strike you as a—clumsy person?" the inspector asked.

Cecilia remembered Mrs. Price's slim figure, the graceful gestures of her hands as she spoke, drawing everyone in. "Not really. She was quite elegant."

"Yet she had fallen before?"

"You would have to ask her daughters or Miss Black about that," Cecilia said. "She had hurt her ankle when I called once before."

"Oh, believe me, we will ask them the particulars. It seems Miss Black is ill at the moment, and Mrs. Winter quite overwrought." Inspector Hennesy gave an impatient sigh. "I'm sure this will all turn out to be an old lady overimbibing and falling down some rickety stairs, a great waste of time. If she hadn't made herself notorious, we wouldn't be here at all."

"I'm not so sure about that, Inspector," Cecilia said.

He scowled at her. "And why would you think that, Lady Cecilia?"

"Some rather odd things have been happening around Primrose Cottage lately," she answered. "There was an attempted break-in, for one thing, and Anne Price said her mother travels with valuable jewels. I myself noticed that her ruby ring was missing when her body was found, as was a torn piece of her suffrage sash. And Sergeant Dunn has been keeping an eye on a notorious criminal in the village."

"That's true, sir," Sergeant Dunn said. "Georgie Guff, you know. He was last collared near here for the Downing theft."

The inspector turned his fearsome scowl onto his sergeant. "Why didn't you say that before?"

The sergeant flushed. "I'd forgotten about the broken window at the cottage. Sorry, sir. Mrs. Price said nothing was taken then. And I didn't know about the ring."

"Mr. Talbot, who owns the antiques shop just down the lane from Primrose Cottage, thinks he saw a man walking away from there late at night with a sack," Cecilia said. "But it was too dark for him to see who it was."

Inspector Hennesy turned his glare back to her. "Put Mr. Talbot on the list to question, then, Sergeant. Is there anything else we should know, Lady Cecilia? Any known enemies of Mrs. Price? Any masked villains lurking in the shrubbery around Primrose Cottage?"

"I wouldn't know about the shrubbery, Inspector, but of course Mrs. Price had enemies. She was a suffragette, after all. Lord Elphin, for one—his crowd was being a nuisance at the rally."

"Lord Elphin?" Inspector Hennesy asked, jotting down the name in his notebook.

"Local landowner, sir," Sergeant Dunn said.

"He owns the estate just beyond that of the Byswaters," Cecilia added. "He's a bit of a curmudgeon, usually keeps to himself. But it seems women's rights have quite aroused his ire."

The inspector looked as if he very much agreed with Lord Elphin. "Have they now?"

"He, or maybe it was one of his men, shoved Mrs. Price outside the Guildhall after one of her rallies, and she nearly fell. He leads quite a group of ruffians."

"Add Lord Elphin to the list, then, Sergeant," Inspector Hennesy said.

"But do be careful," Jane said with a smile to the sergeant. "They say Lord Elphin likes to shoot at trespassers."

"What else have you seen, then, Lady Cecilia?" the inspector asked.

Cecilia tried to think of everything she had noticed in the last few days. "There seems to be some quarrel between Mrs. Price and her elder daughter Mrs. Winter, as well as with Mr. Winter. I'm sure you noticed that when you tried to speak to Mrs. Winter."

"What sort of quarrel, my lady?" Sergeant Dunn asked.

"I'm not sure. Family differences," Cecilia said. "Politics, maybe. I don't think they had seen each other in quite some time until the Winters came to Danby Village."

Inspector Hennesy scribbled some notes. "And is there anything else you can tell us?"

Cecilia remembered her last encounter with the inspector, when he had been so sure Patrick was guilty of killing Mr. Hayes and almost missed the real culprit, and she wasn't sure how much she should tell him now. "Not really, Inspector. I had really only just met Mrs. Price, though I did admire her a great deal."

He snapped the notebook shut and rose to his feet, the sergeant hurrying to follow him. "Then if that's all, I will take my leave. You and Miss Hughes know you must attend the inquest at the Crown in two days?"

"Yes, of course. Thank you, Inspector Hennesy." Once they had left, Cecilia and Jane fell back onto their chairs with sighs.

"What do you think, my lady?" Jane said. "Will he just declare it all an accident and go away as fast as he can?"

Cecilia frowned. "I don't know, Jane. Maybe it *was* a fall."

"Do you really think that?"

It was certainly possible. Primrose Cottage was an old, dimly lit place. But where was Mrs. Price's ring, and the piece of her sash? What about the voices that were heard? "My instinct says—probably not, Jane."

Jane nodded. "So does mine."

"But I do think the inspector will try to hurry things along and be done with it, just as he did with Mr. Hayes. Why don't you talk to Bridget when she gets back, and maybe ask Collins about what Mr. Talbot saw? I can ask around more about any gossip pertaining to the Prices and their family relations."

"Very good, my lady." Jane hurried away toward the garage.

Through the window, Cecilia saw her father appear from around the West Wing of the house clad in dusty walking tweeds. She waved to him and pushed open the glass to call out to him.

"Cecilia, dear, what a surprise to see you downstairs at this hour," he said. "Did I just hear a car drive away?"

"It was Inspector Hennesy, Papa. Perhaps you remember him from the Mr. Hayes business?" Cecilia said. "He's here looking into Mrs. Price's death and had a few questions."

Her father frowned. "Cec, dear, you should have let me or Mr. Jermyn call on him before you talked to him."

"Oh, Papa, I'm hardly a suspect. It was only a few questions. No need to bother Mr. Jermyn."

"Nevertheless, my dear, I don't want you mixed up in this business any more than is strictly necessary," her father said. "There is bound to be gossip."

"I'll be careful, Papa. I promise." Cecilia leaned out of the window. "I understand you once knew Mrs. Price, yourself," she said slowly, hesitant to bring up such a personal topic with her father. And he certainly didn't seem to approve of Mrs. Price's work now.

"Me? Know a suffragette?" he scoffed.

"When she was Miss Amelia Merriman, a long time ago. She said all the young ladies were in love with you back then. Perhaps it was even before you met Mama." Cecilia well remembered the tale of her parents' young romance, her mother the daughter of a respectable but not well-off family of colonial administrators serving in India and South Africa, but so beautiful and charming she won the then-wealthy earl.

Her father's mouth gaped for an instant. "Miss Merriman? How extraordinary. Who would have thought she would become a suffragette, of all things? Though she *was* opinionated, even back then . . ."

"So you did know her?"

"Everyone knew her. She was the 'Diamond of the Season' according to the gossip papers back then, until she ran off with some attorney. So she turned out to be a suffragette? So odd."

"She eloped with Mr. Price?"

"I don't know the details. Gossip was always such a bore. I think her parents didn't quite approve of him. I suppose no one knew Henry Price would end up attached to the household of Queen Alexandra back then." He tapped his walking stick thoughtfully on the grass. "Maybe your grandmama would remember more. She was working so hard in those days to get me married off, she knew everyone." He laughed ruefully. "Mothers don't change, do they, my dear?"

Cecilia thought of her own mother and nodded in agreement. Had it been thus with Mrs. Price's mother, or even with Mrs. Price herself when it came to her daughters? It was something that seemed worth looking into.

❧

Jane found Bridget in the walled kitchen garden, gathering a basket of mint for Mrs. Frazer's dinner. She looked like a painting of "country contentment" as she bent over the plants along the brick wall, but Jane thought she also seemed deep in thought. Jack trailed behind her, as if hoping for a tidbit.

"Is this part of a housemaid's job, then, Bridget?" Jane asked, striding along the narrow pathway between the neat beds of vegetables and herbs.

Bridget looked down at her basket with a laugh. "Not really, no. I just like getting outside once in a while, so I told Pearl I would fetch it. A housemaid could go weeks just seeing the inside of walls, you know."

Jane nodded. She herself was a city girl born and bred, used to being indoors or out on noisy streets, but she had to admit she was getting used to the lovely, green quiet. "Did you grow up in the country?"

"In Danby Village, with my uncle at his bakeshop, after my parents died. I had to work in the shop, but otherwise I could wander a bit in the woods and on the lane." She glanced back at the house, gleaming in the sunlight beyond the walled garden. "Not much wandering here, but the pay is good and the people nice. I've heard of worse situations."

"So have I," Jane answered. She remembered the hotel in New York, the men waiting to pinch unsuspecting maids. No one behaved like that at Danby, at least not in recent days. "And Mrs. Harriet Palmer is your aunt-in-law? The woman from the Women's Suffrage Union?"

Bridget nodded. She bent down to give Jack a bite of vegetable. "My uncle's sister-in-law."

"Do you know her very well? And her work?" Jane picked a clump of mint to add to the basket.

"Not well. She lived in London when I was little, still does, I suppose. She was widowed a long time ago. She visited sometimes and always had such interesting things to say about her work. So different from *my* life."

"Is it still interesting? Mrs. Palmer's life? You've seen her since she came to the village?"

"Just for tea at my uncle's house. She's been even busier lately! She was even in jail for a while, for trying to give a petition to some MP. Just imagine! I could never be so brave."

"She must be upset about what happened to Mrs. Price."

Bridget frowned. "It's hard to tell with Aunt Harriet. She just says the Union needs some fresh ideas."

"What sort of fresh ideas?" Jane asked, wondering if such a thing could drive a woman like Mrs. Palmer to murder. It seemed unlikely, but then look what had happened to Mr. Hayes last spring.

Bridget frowned, obviously uncomfortable with having such a conversation with her employer's maid. Jane gave her a reassuring smile, and Jack helped by touching Bridget's foot with his soft paw. "I'm not sure," Bridget said slowly. "Some of what she says is confusing. But maybe less talk, more action. It's confusing to me."

"And she is going to lead this march forward into more boldness? I'm sure the Union needs a new leader now."

"Maybe. She does get passionate when she talks about it all. She says Mrs. Price could be too slow, too considering. Women need the vote right now. Even I can see that." Bridget suddenly sighed deeply and rubbed Jack's velvety ear. "It must be nice, don't you think, Jane? Doing something so many people think is important. Something that could change the whole world."

"Have you never thought of going to London to live with your aunt, Bridget? To see what her work is all about first-hand?"

Bridget laughed. "Me, go live in London? I wouldn't know what to do. I would just bumble around getting in Aunt Harriet's way. Besides, my uncle needs my wages."

"Bridget!" Mrs. Frazer called from the doorway. "Where are you with that mint? My lamb's sauce won't make itself while you dillydally about."

"Coming right away, Mrs. Frazer!" Bridget called back. She gave Jane a quick smile and hurried out of the garden with her basket.

Jane thought of what she had learned, that Mrs. Palmer was indeed not happy about the pace of the Union under Mrs. Price's leadership. Would a woman like that take drastic steps to get what she wanted, when it came to a cause she was so passionate about?

She was needed to help Miss Clarke dress for dinner, but for just a moment Jane wandered to the gateway that led from the garden across the gravel drive to the garage, carrying Jack with her. Collins was outside washing the car, in his shirt-sleeves. It was rather a pleasant sight. He saw her there and waved with a smile.

Jane thought Bridget was quite right not to leave such a place. Danby had everything it needed right within its walls.

Chapter Thirteen

Cecilia knocked at the door of Primrose Cottage and waited for a moment, but a cloud of silence still seemed to linger around the old house, heavy and sad. Mrs. Price had only lived there a few days, yet her absence turned it to an entirely different sort of place, her bicycle abandoned by the gate, the windows shuttered.

Cecilia wondered if she should just leave the house to its mourning, yet Anne Price had sent a note at breakfast asking if she could call if she came to the village. Cecilia only had the morning hours before she would be missed, since she had promised her mother she would help with the infernal bazaar that afternoon.

She stepped back onto the garden path to study the upstairs windows, where the bedrooms lay. They were all shuttered, blank, and she thought maybe the Prices had already departed. But they surely couldn't leave until after the inquest, and Anne *had* asked her to call.

She was just about to knock again, when the door opened suddenly. Nellie stood there, her hair loosely pinned under her cap, eyes reddened.

"Oh, Lady Cecilia," Nellie sniffled, giving a crooked bob of curtsy. "I'm so sorry if you've been waiting, I was just—just packing a few things upstairs."

Packing away Mrs. Price's belongings, no doubt. No wonder the poor girl looked so distracted. "I'm sorry if this is a bad time. I had a note from Miss Price and thought I would come by while I was in the village."

"She's just gone out. That sergeant with the crooked nose came to fetch her."

"Sergeant Dunn? Did he say what he wanted?"

"Just had a few questions, I think. She shouldn't be long, Lady Cecilia. Would you like to wait in the sitting room?"

"If it's not too much trouble. Thank you." Cecilia followed Nellie through the foyer and down the narrow corridor. She glimpsed the dimly lit staircase and tried not to remember how Mrs. Price had looked lying there, like a broken doll. And now she seemed to have left a broken family and Union in her wake.

The sitting room looked as if no one had been there at all since Cecilia last sat there with Anne. The table was spread with wineglasses and loose papers, the fireplace in ashes. The air smelled stale and close.

"Is Miss Black still in residence?" Cecilia asked. "I would have thought everyone would want to stay until the whole matter is, well, resolved."

"So they do. Miss Anne just wanted me to get a head start on the packing, for when it's all solved at last. Miss Black is asleep upstairs. She couldn't sleep at all last night. Miss Price called Dr. Mitchell to give her a draught this morning. We had hoped she was feeling better, but now . . ." Nellie waved her hand in a helpless gesture.

"I'm sure she will feel much better once she can return to her own home," Cecilia said, and she wondered where that was.

"The inspector says we have to stay for the inquest."

"Of course. Has Mrs. Winter been back to Primrose Cottage?"

Nellie laughed humorlessly. "Her? Not today. Mr. Winter came around last night, trying to take Mrs. Price's pearls. For safekeeping."

Mr. Winter didn't seem to waste any time, then. "I suppose they have to stay, as well. The Winters."

"I guess so, but you're quite right, Lady Cecilia—we'll all be better off when we can leave and go home."

"Where is your home, Nellie?"

"Kent, once upon a time, but I've lived in London since I started to work for Mrs. Price. It's wonderful there, so much happening all the time! Especially with a mistress like Mrs. Price, you know, never a dull moment." Nellie smiled wistfully.

"Have you been with her long?"

"Almost five years now. Since before she moved to her own flat, back when she and Mr. Price lived together."

Cecilia was quite sure Nellie had many fascinating tales to tell about the Price ménage, and the Union's work. "So the whole family lived together back then?"

Nellie shook her head. She unlatched the window and let in a breeze of fresh air, waving away the stale stuffiness. "Mrs. Winter was just married and gone, and Miss Price was getting her own flat after she finished school. It's a good thing, since she and her father quarreled all the time."

"I suppose he didn't approve of the suffrage work."

Nellie snorted. "He worries about the gossip, like Mr. Winter. That's all they care about. What people think of *them* and their careers." There was a sudden thud upstairs, as if someone was walking on the old floors. "I should look in on Miss Black."

"Yes, of course. I'll be fine waiting here, Nellie."

As the maid left, Cecilia plumped the cushions on the settee by the window and studied the room. She noticed Cora's cards on the table and wondered if maybe she had tried to contact Mrs. Price using her medium skills. She went to straighten them and saw that no one had yet cleaned away the torn papers strewn on the tablecloth: . . . *regret this . . . never tell . . . improper dalliance . . .* she read on the papers.

Improper dalliance. Fascinating. Cecilia studied the scrap and saw that the handwriting was dark black and straight, the paper cheap. There was the faint whiff of some kind of scent, not the heady roses Mrs. Price wore, more grassy and green. The edges were roughly torn.

She glanced back at the fireplace, which hadn't been properly cleaned out and relaid. There were scraps among the ashes, too, and she remembered how Anne had stirred up the fire on the day Mrs. Price died. She herself had glimpsed some papers in the ashes that day.

She heard the squeak of the garden gate and looked out the window to see Anne walking toward the door. She wore a purple walking suit, a black band around the sleeve, and her head was ducked beneath a narrow-brimmed hat, as if she was deep in thought. Cecilia wished she could stuff the papers into her handbag to show Jane later, but she had left her bag across the room on the settee, and she didn't want to be barred from Primrose Cottage for snooping. She rushed to put the scraps as she found them back on the table and sat down on the nearest chair, her hands folded in her lap.

"Oh, Lady Cecilia," Anne said, unpinning her hat as she stepped into the sitting room. "Thank you for calling. I'm sorry to keep you waiting."

"Not at all. I haven't been here long," she answered. "Nellie told me Sergeant Dunn came for you. Is there any news?"

"It seems some well-known thief was found with Mother's ruby ring, and I was asked to identify it. Perhaps there was merely an interrupted break-in, after all."

Cecilia thought of the man Mr. Talbot thought he saw walking by with the sack. "Was the ring the only thing they found with him?"

"Yes, from here anyway. I suppose he didn't have time to take anything else."

"So is there still to be an inquest?"

"Colonel Havelock insists on it, as it was a suspicious death. I suppose that's part of why I needed to speak to you, Lady Cecilia."

"Because I may be called on at the inquest?"

"Yes, but also to invite you to a memorial we're going to

have for Mother at the Guildhall. Most of the Union ladies have returned to their homes, but some of us must stay until things are resolved, and we want to do something to keep us occupied, to continue Mother's work."

"That sounds like a wonderful idea. Of course I'll be there. Do you need any assistance? I could make arrangements with the florist's shop here in the village. They do beautiful work and can get a wide variety of blooms in very quickly."

"That's very kind of you, Lady Cecilia. I also wanted to ask if you might like Mother's bicycle."

"Her bicycle?" Cecilia said, thinking of the way it wobbled and swayed under her when she first tried to ride it. Could she conquer it in the end, in honor of Mrs. Price?

"Yes. I know you're just now learning to ride, but having your own vehicle for practice will surely help. And she'd like that so much. I hate to think of it going unused."

"I will certainly ride it! And think of your mother when I do. Thank you, Miss Price."

Anne gave a small smile and nodded. "Now, I am sure I asked you to call me Anne."

There was the sudden roaring sound of a motorcar coming to a stop outside the open window. "Are you expecting someone?" Cecilia asked.

"Not at all," Anne said with a puzzled frown. "In fact, I'm quite sure everyone who can wants to stay far away from us right now."

Cecilia followed her to the window and went on tiptoe to peer over the taller woman's shoulder. She took a surreptitious sniff of Anne's perfume. It wasn't her mother's roses, nor the green-white scent of the letters, but something almost citrusy, like her own mother's scent. It didn't seem to be the smell left behind on the torn fragments of letters.

Outside the garden gate, a new Renault motorcar had just come to a halt, dust clouding around it. A uniformed chauffeur emerged and opened the back door for a tall, lean man in a perfectly tailored gray cashmere overcoat and black silk hat. He tilted back his head to study the cottage, and Cecilia saw he was quite handsome in a hawkish way, with sharp cheekbones, a blade of a nose, and a graying mustache.

"Who is that?" Cecilia said, watching as the man unlatched the gate and strode up the path as if he owned it.

Anne's lips tightened. "That," she muttered, "is my father. Mr. Henry Price, Esquire."

❧

Several minutes later, Cecilia herself hurried along that same walkway to the garden gate. The chauffeur leaned against the hood of the car, smoking his cigarette as the village rushed past on its own errands. It was a fine, cloudless autumn day, but she shivered a bit after the chill Mr. Henry Price seemed to carry around with him.

He had been everything that was polite when he heard her name, but it was clear her presence was not needed in Primrose Cottage any longer that day. Even Anne, who had begun to relax a bit, had gone rigid again, her cheek carefully turned up for her father's pecking kiss, her eyes full of caution. Cecilia had a hard time picturing Amelia Price with such a man at all. Surely, it was no wonder they had gone their separate paths in life.

Yet Nellie had said Mr. Price hated all the gossip. He did seem a thoroughly conventional sort, and if he had built his career on service to the royal family, he would be very careful of his reputation. Would he have become so angered by his wife's work, her public life, that he would do away with her? Cecilia had heard too many tales of men doing just that with unsatisfactory wives.

But the police had arrested the thief with Mrs. Price's ring. Surely, that would put an end to any other avenues of investigation. Maybe a theft *was* the answer, though it seemed such a small and ridiculous fate for a grand, larger-than-life woman like Mrs. Price.

Cecilia turned at the end of the lane and headed toward the village green, and then the rows of fine brick and stone houses behind iron gates just beyond. She didn't have much time before she had to return to Danby, and she wanted to call on her grandmother. Her father had said the dowager would remember the gossip about the long-ago Season when Mrs. Price was the Diamond of the debs. Cecilia was sure that was true; her grandmother never forgot anything at all, even when one wished she would.

The dower house was at the end of the lane, a fine old Georgian place with white shutters at the windows and a large, beautiful garden around three sides. Two gardeners were working on the very last of her grandmother's prize-winning roses for the season, harassed by Sebastian nipping at their heels and growling. The butler greeted her at the door and led her toward the drawing room at the back of the house, where she could hear voices.

So her grandmother wasn't alone. The Bateses' lawyer, Mr. Jermyn, was with her, some papers spread on the alabaster table in front of them. They sat on a pair of Jacobean tapestry chairs her grandmother had taken from Danby when she left, along with carved cabinets, porcelain ornaments, and Dutch still-life paintings. It was all very grand, very old-fashioned, very intimidating—much like her grandmother herself.

"I'm so sorry, Grandmama. I didn't realize you had a caller," Cecilia said.

"It's only Mr. Jermyn, my dear, come to have me sign some papers, and I insisted he stay to explain them to me," her grandmother said as Cecilia kissed her powdered cheek. She smelled of old-fashioned violets. "I cannot keep it all straight in my mind now, you see. Old age."

Cecilia and Mr. Jermyn exchanged a small smile. *Nothing* ever escaped her steel trap of a mind, and everyone knew it.

"Indeed, I was just leaving, Lady Cecilia," Mr. Jermyn said, gathering up the papers and tucking them neatly into his valise. "I must take some of these into Leeds myself by the late train."

"Mr. Jermyn's office has been so terribly busy of late," the dowager said, clucking in sympathy. "I am sure Mrs. Jermyn worries about you being so run off your feet."

Mr. Jermyn grimaced. "She has expressed a thought or two in that direction, Lady Avebury, but I don't mind the work in the least. We may have some relief in the office soon, at any rate."

"How so?" Cecilia asked. "Are your clients becoming less demanding?"

He laughed. "What do you think, Lady Cecilia?"

She laughed, too. Not with her own family as his chief clients. "I fear it is too much to hope."

"No, we may have another attorney soon to take on some of the more junior clients. I just received a letter from a man called Mr. Montgomery Winter asking about a position. Though his last place was with a larger London firm, so I'm not sure why he is seeking a change to the north."

"Mr. Winter?" Cecilia said, surprised. The Winters were looking to leave London and stay in Danby?

"Do you know him?" Mr. Jermyn asked.

"No, not at all. That is, I've met him, but not for any length," Cecilia said. "I've spoken with his wife, and I would also be surprised to hear they wanted to settle so far from Town. Mrs. Winter seems very, well, London-fied. She is Mrs. Amelia Price's daughter, you see."

Mr. Jermyn's brow rose. "Amelia Price? Is Mrs. Winter a suffragette, then?"

"Oh no. The very opposite, I would say."

"Well, I am looking forward to meeting with the man, anyway. A bit more time at home would not go amiss with Mrs. Jermyn, if there were someone competent to lighten the load at the office. Good afternoon, ladies."

"Good afternoon, Mr. Jermyn, and thank you," her grandmother said. She waved Cecilia to his abandoned seat. "Now, my dear, do stay for some tea."

"I can't linger very long, Grandmama. Preparations for the church bazaar are at a fever pitch at Danby."

Her grandmother chuckled. "Oh yes, I do recall those days. I do not envy your mother. Are you hiding out here, then?"

"Yes, I must be. But I also wanted to ask if you remembered the Season before Papa married Mama."

"Of course I remember it. The year Lord Frederick Cavendish was murdered by those wild Irishmen, so dreadful. And the Football League; it was all the men could talk about, tiresome at dinners. And the Married Women's Property Act, which set off this wildness we have now. Why do you ask?"

"Papa says that Amelia Price was quite the deb of the Season then. She was Miss Merriman then, I think."

"Miss Merriman? Oh yes! She was very pretty, I'll give her that, but quite the minx, even then. Drove her own phaeton in the park! And let Lady Bryanston's monkey out of its cage at a party, such a to-do that was. Your father did dance with her once or twice more than I would have liked, and I admit I was a bit relieved when his attentions turned elsewhere."

"To Mama?" Yet Cecilia remembered the tales that her grandmother had not quite taken to the slightly middle-class Emmaline at first.

"Not quite yet; there was Lady Muriel Repton-Smythe-Smythe first. Now *there* was a girl with a steady head on her shoulders. But she married Lord Merton and hied off to India, and then your mother came along."

Cecilia was fascinated by the glimpse of her parents' long-ago past, but she knew she had to get home soon. "And then Miss Merriman married Mr. Henry Price?"

"I suppose so." Her mother's lips pursed as she remembered. "I do recall now it all happened quite quickly, and was rather a surprise. Everyone said she had a viscount or some such on the hook, and then she married an attorney instead. Of course, the man *did* come to be a very trusted adviser to Queen Alexandra, but at that time no one had heard of him. It was probably her father's misfortune that took her there."

"Her father's misfortune?"

"He had lost most of the Merriman money, you see, in some absurd Brazilian silver mine scheme. The family had done quite well for themselves before that, and with her looks and dowry everyone thought she would do well. Then—pfft! It was gone, and the girl married off. It was said Mr. Price had to pay the dowry rather than the other way 'round." The dowager shook her head. "I am very glad your grandfather never engaged in such nonsense. Left my dower in the five percents, very sensible."

Yes, and now those "sensible" investments meant Patrick had to marry an heiress. But Brazilian mines probably wouldn't have been the answer, either.

"And then she turned suffragette, I suppose, and got herself killed in our very own village," her grandmother concluded, with a dismissive thump of her walking stick on the Axminster carpet. "Typical. Let that be a lesson to you, Cecilia."

Cecilia wasn't sure *what* sort of lesson it could be, unless it was "don't marry for money, or decades later you will be killed." Or "don't invest in dodgy mines."

"Of course, Grandmama. No mines."

"Now, tell me more about the bazaar. Has your mother figured out how to keep everyone from each other's throats this year?"

Chapter Fourteen

The day of the inquest was gray and drizzling, battering down the last of the summer flowers in the garden. Cecilia wiped at a foggy spot on the car window with her gloved hand and peered out, thinking that the day was quite appropriately gloomy for the backdrop to an inquest. She wished Jack could have come to give her some comfort, but cats wouldn't be allowed in official inquiries.

"Oh, look, you've left a spot on your glove," her mother clucked. She took Cecilia's hand in hers and brushed futilely at the navy blue suede, just as she had when Cecilia had mussed herself in the garden as a child.

"I don't think the coroner's jury will be looking at my gloves, Mama," she said, though it *was* true that she had dressed carefully for the day in a suitably somber dark-blue dress and coat and an unadorned gray velvet hat. She had never attended an inquest before; it was equal parts terrifying and interesting.

"I don't know why Colonel Havelock asked you to be there anyway," Lady Avebury tsked. "To think—an earl's daughter at a public inquest! What is the world coming to?"

Cecilia thought her mother was beginning to sound quite a lot like her grandmother. "I was there soon after the body was found," she answered. "I'm sure they just want as much information as possible, in the circumstances."

"Cec is quite right, my dear," her father said. "They must be thorough whenever there is a suspicious death, and we don't want uncertainties hanging over Danby's head in any way. Better to get it over and done with. And luckily, there wouldn't have been the chance of going out shooting today anyway, not with this beastly weather."

"Oh, don't remind me," Lady Avebury groaned. Once the bazaar was over, a shooting party that included the Duke of Strenton was expected at Danby, and Cecilia's mother was already going into a whirlwind planning it.

"Anyway, I'm sure Cecilia will do wonderfully," Lord Avebury said. "She has a good, cool head on her shoulders, just like her mother. Don't you, Cec, dear?"

"I'm not sure about that right now," Cecilia murmured. She did feel rather sick to her stomach at the thought of speaking to the room.

"She could have just written them a letter to be read out before the coroner," her mother said.

Collins brought the car to a stop near the Crown and Shield, where the inquest was to be held. Other motors, as well as a few horses and carts, were already parked in the gravel driveway.

Cecilia smoothed her gloves one more time and followed her parents into the pub, where she had so rarely been before. But she had only a moment to avidly study the dimly lit interior, the polished bar, the array of glasses behind, the tables arranged next to the hazy, old-glass windows, the smoke that lingered in the air, before they were ushered up the stairs to a room at the back of the building.

It was a plain but very large room, usually called into service for meetings and dances, which was good, as it was packed full that day, rows and rows of chairs lined up in the dusty light under the heavy smell of damp wool and smoke from the fireplace at one end.

At the other end were two tables set up facing the rows of chairs. Colonel Havelock and a tall, portly, gray-haired man who was probably the coroner sat at one, papers spread before them, and the jury sat at another long table off to the side of the room. As Cecilia and her parents took their seats near the front, she studied the crowd for familiar faces. Mr. Jermyn the attorney soon joined them, in case she was in need of any advice, and Mr. Brown sat behind them with a reassuring smile.

She saw Anne Price, sitting with Nellie, Harriet Palmer, and Cora Black, their mourning clothes like shadows as they whispered together. Behind them sat the Winters, Monty seeming quite distracted as Mary fiddled with the fringes on her black velvet jacket. Henry Price sat next to them, handsome and austere, but also seemingly in his own world, far away with his own thoughts. Mr. Talbot sat at the back, where Collins joined him after parking the car. Cecilia waved at them.

Lord Elphin was there as well, sitting by himself in a back corner, his arms crossed, his red face thunderous. She wouldn't have thought he would be interested in the death of Mrs. Price, unless it was to dance about the demise of a dreaded suffragette. Maybe he had been summoned because of the behavior of his men after the rally? Cecilia was just glad he didn't have his bully-band with him now.

"Mr. Jermyn," she whispered to the attorney before the proceedings could begin, "is that Mr. Winter over there, the one who applied for a position with you?"

He glanced over and nodded. "Yes, indeed. We are to have tea with him tomorrow and gauge his suitability."

"Do you remember the name of the office where he worked in London?"

Mr. Jermyn tapped his chin thoughtfully. "Bird and Wither in Middle Temple."

"Good morning, everyone," Colonel Havelock said, bringing the hushed murmur of the room into silence. "Thank you for taking the time to render assistance in these terrible circumstances. Remember, this is *not* a trial, merely an occasion to pose additional questions to clarify and expand any previous statements made. The jury will then render a judgment on whether this death was natural or suspicious so we may move forward. Now, this is the county's coroner, Mr. Lancing, who attended at the scene."

Mr. Lancing shuffled his papers and cleared his throat. "The deceased, Mrs. Amelia Price, was of good health, aside from some scarring of the liver. Upon examination, I determined she had been dead for approximately four hours when she was found. The cause appears to be a contusion to the head, leading to a broken neck and various cracked ribs upon landing at the foot of the stairs, we assume. There was bruising to the left side of the torso, and the fingernails were torn on the left hand, as if she reached for the railing of the stairs. There were also score marks on the wooden rails."

Cecilia remembered how Mrs. Price's sash was torn away on the left, as if someone had grabbed it to pull her close—or push her away. Where had that scrap gone?

"What we must determine today," Mr. Lancing continued, "is if Mrs. Price died of an accident, or by misadventure or unlawful killing."

"To begin, the court calls Miss Anne Price to the stand," Colonel Havelock said. Anne rose and made her way to the stand, or rather the table, that was laid out for witnesses. She did not look left or right, just moved with a careful, quiet dignity.

She was calm and composed as she answered questions about her mother's last night. The rally, returning to Primrose Cottage, everyone retiring except her mother, who usually did stay up later to go over what had happened with her speeches. Anne's room was at the back of the house; she had heard nothing out of the ordinary. Her sister and brother-in-law had visited briefly, but she thought she heard them leave soon after, and no one else came to the cottage. Nellie was called next, and confirmed Anne's account, as well as stating that yes, Mrs. Price did sometimes have a nightcap of wine or brandy when she went over her speeches.

The maid trembled a bit and fumbled over words at

times, as if emotions threatened to overwhelm her. But her answers were clear and firm. It was Cora who sobbed into her handkerchief, breaking the intense hush of the room. Anne nudged at her and shoved a clean handkerchief into her hand.

"We next call Lady Cecilia Bates," Colonel Havelock said as Nellie retook her seat.

Cecilia drew in a deep, steadying breath and made her way to the witness table. One of the jury members that she knew, the milliner's husband, gave her a small smile, and her mother watched her closely, worriedly. Anne nodded at her, and she knew she had to do her very best, for Mrs. Price.

"Lady Cecilia," Mr. Lancing said, "you were at Primrose Cottage the day of these events, were you not?"

Cecilia smoothed her gloves carefully. "Yes. I had been to Mrs. Price's rallies, and she asked if I would call on her. I didn't know what had happened until I arrived at the cottage."

"Do you know why she asked you to call?"

Cecilia thought it was probably to recruit an earl's daughter to the Union, but she shook her head. "Not really, no. But the Prices seemed quite nice—Mrs. Price offered to teach me to ride a bicycle. And I was in the village that day, the— the day Mrs. Price died, so I went."

"What did you observe when you arrived?"

She forced herself to remember the chaos, the tears, the uncertainty. "Mrs. Price was at the foot of the stairs. Sergeant Dunn and Colonel Havelock were already there, so I sat with Miss Price to see if I could be of any help at all."

"Did you know Mrs. Price well?"

"Not well," Cecilia answered, though she did feel as if she

came to know her more and more all the time now that she was gone. "We had met a few times since she arrived in Danby Village. I did like her."

Mr. Lancing frowned. "What sort of person did she seem to you?"

"She was . . ." Cecilia paused to consider. What sort of person *was* Amelia Price? What did she really know about her, beyond her public face? "Very energetic, and magnetic. Perhaps not—always practical? Very intelligent."

"And she got along with people around her?"

"I didn't know her long enough to be able to say. I would imagine that anyone in public life cannot be liked by everyone." She glanced at Lord Elphin.

Mr. Lancing gave a discreet little cough. "I should think not indeed. Back to the morning you arrived at Primrose Cottage during the—incident. Did you notice anything odd, out of place?"

Cecilia shook her head. "I saw that Mrs. Price's ruby ring was missing, but was told everything else in the household appeared quite as it had when I visited before." She remembered the papers scattered on the table, the wineglasses. All had indeed looked the same.

She answered a few more questions, inconsequential things about timing, before stepping down. Mary Winter was called next.

"Were you close to your mother, Mrs. Winter?" Colonel Havelock asked.

Mary dabbed at her eyes with a lacy handkerchief. "Not

recently, no, I am very sad to say. I don't agree with her work at all, and it is—was—all she really wanted to talk about."

"But you came to visit her here at Danby Village?"

"Well—yes. She *is* my mother, after all. She still had a duty to her children, and I had wanted so much to have her more in our lives. Family is so important."

Cecilia wondered if that was true. Mary Winter had been apart from her mother for a while; why this yearning for family now, of all times?

"Was this the first contact with her recently, then?" Mr. Lancing asked.

Mary's face twisted. "I—I wrote to her. She didn't answer."

Cecilia remembered those scraps of paper on the table at Primrose Cottage. Could they be from Mary, then? They hadn't sounded like a search for reconciliation.

"What did you write to Mrs. Price?"

"Oh, just expressions of affection. Asking if we could meet soon. Filial devotions, you see. My heart cannot stop loving her, no matter what."

Cecilia thought of the letters. *Forced to take action . . . hope it does not come to this . . .* They didn't sound like "devotion," but then no one would admit to threatening a dead woman.

"Er—quite," Colonel Havelock said doubtfully. He only had sons; maybe he knew nothing of "filial devotion." "But you had not seen her in London? Only here in Danby Village?"

"Yes, that is so. We are so busy in London, you see. Social duties."

"And your purpose in seeing Mrs. Price here was only to express your devotion?"

"Indeed. A vain hope, sadly." She sniffled and dabbed at her eyes again.

"When was the last time you saw your mother?"

"It was the night she—she died." The sobs came harder. "Though I could not have known it would be the very *last*!"

"Indeed not," Colonel Havelock said kindly. "What did you talk about that night?"

"Oh—just life things, I suppose. Monty and I called on her at Primrose Cottage after her rally. We spoke of the future, our hopes of seeing each other more often. My hopes that my family could be reconciled. Then we left, I had my cocoa at our lodgings, and I went to bed. It was rather early, but I was quite tired. I was plagued with terrible dreams that night! Perhaps I had a premonition."

Cora looked up sharply, and Cecilia wondered if the two of them might come to be rival mediums.

"And Mr. Winter?" Mr. Lancing asked.

"He went with me to see Mother. He does urge me to keep the connections with my family, so solicitous of my feelings."

"And he retired with you?"

Mary frowned as if in thought. "No, he usually has a brandy before he retires, and as I said, I was quite tired. He brought me my tea in the morning."

"Did your mother seem unhappy in any way that evening? Anxious or melancholy?" Mr. Lancing said.

"Mother, anxious? Never! She was always as cool as winter snow. I am quite different, you see. I feel things so deeply."

Colonel Havelock nodded, and after a few more short questions, Mary was released and Henry Price called. As Mary collapsed in tears on Monty's shoulder, and he awkwardly patted her back, her father answered a few questions. He looked all that was proper for a purported widower, solemn and serious, careful with his answers, but he could be of very little help. He had not seen his wife for some time and he hardly knew of her activities. He himself had been occupied with his own work much of late and only came to Danby when he heard the sad news. He wanted to be there for his daughters.

Anne made a little scoffing snort of a noise.

Mr. Price shot her a narrow-eyed glance. "My wife's life was not compatible with mine, Colonel, I am sad to say. I knew close to nothing of her friends or activities lately, so I fear I cannot help now. I am sorry it has all come to such a sad place." He was quickly dismissed, though Cecilia pondered whether or not he was telling the whole truth. Would a man like that really let his wife go on her way, not caring what she did next? And he had arrived in Danby Village shockingly quickly after Amelia's death.

Mr. Talbot then took the stand, to speak of the man he thought he saw coming from the direction of Primrose Cottage on the night in question. Yes, he said, it had been too dark to identify him, but he seemed tall and quick, perhaps carrying some sort of sack. Mr. Talbot had been sure to double-lock his shop afterward.

"Was this possibly the man you saw, Mr. Talbot?" Mr. Lancing gestured to Sergeant Dunn, who quickly left the room and returned leading the thief Georgie Guff. The man looked rumpled and grubby, cringing in the sergeant's grip, and Cecilia thought he looked like a picture-perfect culprit. When had they brought him in? How did they find him?

Mr. Talbot adjusted his spectacles and closely studied Mr. Guff. "I could not say. It was rather dark, and I did not get a detailed look. Perhaps he is about the same height and build, or perhaps he is a little too thin."

Colonel Havelock consulted his notes. "And it does seem a ruby ring was discovered in Mr. Guff's lodgings. Along with a Georgian silver wine cooler, which it appears did not come from Mrs. Price's house."

"It weren't me!" Mr. Guff cried in a shrill, dry tone. "I'm a thief, sure, so nick me for that. But I'm not a murderer, and I never took no lady's ring!" He tried to wrench away from the sergeant, who gave him a stiff shake.

Mr. Perkins, landlord of the Crown, rose with a timid wave of his hand. "I feel I must say—I don't think this man really could have done it, depending on the timing. I saw him drinking downstairs that night, in the snug for hours. He still owes me for three pints. I doubt he would have been in any fit state to see straight when he left, or be at all stealthy. Unless he's a good actor."

"What time did he leave, Mr. Perkins?" Colonel Havelock asked.

"We had to throw him out after last call. Past midnight."

The coroner made a note. "And the deceased died at approximately two in the morning, give or take. So Mr. Guff *might* have done it, but it's a faint possibility if what Mr. Perkins says is true."

Colonel Havelock pursed his lips and shook his head, and Cecilia was sure he must be thinking how easy and convenient it would have been to put all this down to a robbery gone awry, committed by a villain who didn't even live in Danby Village. But at last he sighed, admitting the web had not yet entirely unraveled. "Indeed. Yet that still leaves the question of how Mr. Guff acquired the ring, not to mention the wine cooler."

Guff shook his head, sobbing. "I didn't take that ring. I do swear it."

"And what about Mrs. Price's torn sash?" Mr. Lancing asked. "Was that perhaps found in Mr. Guff's rented room, wrapped about the ring or elsewhere?"

Sergeant Dunn answered. "Nothing like that was found there, sir."

"Very well, Mr. Guff is no longer needed here," Colonel Havelock said. "But he will be held for questioning on the stolen items. Mr. Talbot, you may step down. May we call Miss Nellie Pryde for a few more questions?"

Nellie looked terribly nervous and trembled as she made her way back to the stand. Strangely, Cora also looked more agitated, her head twisting this way and that as if she looked for something, and Mrs. Palmer took her hand in a gentle grip and murmured in her ear.

"May we ask you again about your employer's habits before retiring?" Mr. Lancing asked. "Would she have removed her rings, perhaps to wash, and thus misplaced them?"

Nellie's eyes widened like saucers, and Cecilia wondered if she worried that they would try to pin the robbery on her. "She—she did sometimes have a bath of an evening, and would put her jewelry in a little box on her dressing table. Otherwise she wore her rings, and a pair of pearl and diamond earrings, all the time. Along with her imprisonment badge to pin her sash at the shoulder. But that night she hadn't gone to her chamber. She was still wearing her evening gown when she sent me to bed, with her sash and all her jewelry."

"And her other evening habits?"

Nellie looked confused. "Such as what, sir?"

Colonel Havelock gave her a patient smile. "It has previously been said that Mrs. Price enjoyed a drink before she went to bed. Was this still a habit of hers?"

Nellie glanced at Anne, who was carefully studying her gloves. "I—sometimes. She said it helped her sleep; she was often very energetic after a speech. She did know ever so much about wine, especially after we went to France."

"She also bought a few bottles of brandy from me," Mr. Perkins added.

Colonel Havelock smiled again at Nellie. "Is it indeed possible that Mrs. Price lost her footing on the stairs after an evening brandy? We have been told she's stumbled before."

"I—yes, she had fallen before," Nellie stammered. "But I don't think . . ."

"Fallen before due to an excess of wine?" Mr. Lancing asked, and Cecilia recalled that Mrs. Price's liver had been found to have scarring.

There was a loud guffaw, and everyone twisted around to

see Lord Elphin laughing in a most unseemly way. Cecilia knew what he and no doubt many others were thinking. Only a drunkard could be such an *unnatural* woman as to not only seek the vote but urge others to do the same.

Cecilia glanced at Henry Price, who seemed to be biting back a smug smile. Anne looked appalled and somewhat disgusted, but if at the laughter or at her mother's behavior, Cecilia wasn't sure. Mary Winter gave a loud sob and buried her face in her husband's shoulder.

"No!" Cora suddenly shouted. "It wasn't like that at all. I—I did it. It wasn't Mrs. Price's drinking. It was me."

Cecilia was shocked, and a startled silence fell heavily over the room. Cora adored Mrs. Price! Why would she have pushed her down the stairs? In a laudanum haze, perhaps? Sleepwalking?

"Miss Black," Colonel Havelock said slowly, "do you mean to say that you are confessing that *you* are responsible for Mrs. Price's death?"

"Yes. It was me." She rose to her feet and stumbled to the stand, looking so pale Cecilia feared she might faint. Nellie hurriedly gave her the chair and hovered over her protectively.

"Did you deliberately push Mrs. Amelia Price down the stairs?" Colonel Havelock asked.

Cora turned even whiter, and Mr. Lancing quickly passed her a glass of water. She gulped it down. "Not—not deliberately, no. We just had a quarrel, and she—she stepped back and fell. She had *not* been drinking. She never drank to excess. She was a strong and intelligent lady, a—a perfect leader." She swayed as if she would tumble out of the chair.

Eliza Casey

"Tell me, Miss Black," Colonel Havelock said gently. "What did you and Mrs. Price quarrel about?"

Cora swallowed the last of the water and seemed a bit steadier. "I—well, the Union, of course. The Women's Suffrage Union."

Cecilia glanced at Anne and Harriet Palmer, who watched Cora with careful intensity.

"What about the Union?" Colonel Havelock asked.

Cora shook her head. "Just what we should do now. How things should be run. An organization cannot stand still. We had different ideas on a few things, you see, and had argued about it before."

"And the quarrel turned violent?" Mr. Lancing said.

Cora flushed. "I—might have pushed her. I don't remember. I didn't mean for her to fall!"

"Perhaps you will show me how you pushed her, which way she fell," he said. Cora nodded, and Nellie helped her to stand. Mr. Lancing came to stand before her, and Cora thought for a moment before she gave his shoulder a half-hearted shove. Then she demonstrated how Mrs. Price tumbled backward.

Mr. Lancing took his seat next to the colonel again, and they conferred in low voices. Finally, Colonel Havelock stood and said, "Thank you, everyone. We shall adjourn for the day and hear the jury's verdict later. Miss Black, you may go."

"What do you mean?" Cora cried. "Aren't you going to take me into custody? This is all my fault!" She swayed and almost fell, until Nellie caught her. Cecilia instinctively leaped up and ran to them, helping Nellie lead Cora back to her chair and pouring her more water. Anne also came to their side, searching through Cora's handbag for a medicine bottle.

"We know where you are lodging, Miss Black," Colonel Havelock said in a very sad tone, filled with pity. "You do not look well. Please, do go home and rest, and we shall speak again later."

"I certainly will want to speak to you, as I did not have the opportunity today," Inspector Hennesy said sourly. "Such irregular doings here, I must say."

Cecilia and Anne each took one of Cora's hands and led her through the shocked murmurs of the crowd, Nellie hurrying behind them. "It wasn't Mrs. Price's fault," Cora said with a sob. "She was not like that. It was all me."

"Of course," Cecilia murmured softly. She glanced at her mother as they passed and saw that, far from the disapproval she thought to see on her mother's face, Lady Avebury looked concerned. "Don't worry, Mama, I can find my way back to Danby. Don't wait for me."

"Cecilia, my dear, what are you . . ." her mother began, but the crowd closed between them.

"You needn't come with us," Anne said. They led Cora outside into the fresh air, hoping it might revive her as she sagged against Anne's shoulder.

"I don't mind at all," Cecilia said. "Better than driving all the way home with my parents and listening to their scolding." She was sure they would have much to say about "keeping the wrong company" today.

"I do understand the feeling. Parents are not always the

most sympathetic," Anne answered with a crooked smile. They led Cora down the lane toward Primrose Cottage. For a moment, Cecilia was afraid Cora might break away and run back into the inquest, but in the end she went with them quietly. Cecilia feared she felt too ill to protest.

At the cottage, Nellie had run ahead, and led them up the stairs to Cora's chamber. It was a small room at the back of the house, looking out onto the meadow that stretched behind the cottage, plainly furnished but quiet and cool. Nellie turned back the bedclothes and took Cora's hat and shoes, and Anne and Cecilia helped her sit back against the pillows. Cora lay back with only a small murmur of protest.

"Nellie, I'll fetch some tea, if you can help me? Can you sit with her for a moment, Lady Cecilia?" Anne said.

Cecilia nodded. Anne did seem very good in a crisis, but maybe not as patient as needed to sit at a sickbed. "Of course." Cecilia put away Cora's kid boots and hat, took her jacket, and tucked the blankets around Cora's shaking shoulders. She seemed so different from the efficient Union secretary who had first arrived in Danby Village. What had happened? Had her illness simply become worse? Had something spooked her? "Where is your sleeping draught, Miss Black?" The draught that had made her unable to hear anything strange on the night Mrs. Price died.

Cora gestured to the dressing table, where Cecilia found a brown, heavy glass bottle next to an ivory-backed hairbrush, a carafe of water, and small scent bottle. Cecilia took a quick sniff—lilies of the valley.

"But surely I should wait," Cora said. "They said they would have more questions."

"I'm sure they won't bother you until you have had a chance to rest," Cecilia said. She measured out a dose into the water and pressed it into Cora's hand. She drank it down and sank back farther against her pillows. "Miss Black, are you quite, quite sure that is how Mrs. Price died?"

"Of course," Cora answered, her voice already turning blurry at the edges. "It was my fault, not hers. The women of the Union must believe that, must remember Mrs. Price as— as she was."

Cecilia wasn't so sure they would. *She* did not entirely believe it herself. It made sense that Amelia might fall, if she'd had a nightcap too many. But would Cora ever push her? Could she even be able to do that, have the strength for it? And then wait until the inquest to say so? Cecilia was not so sure.

"I saw her, you know," Cora whispered. "Last night. Standing in the doorway. She wanted to tell me something, but she couldn't. Then she just faded away."

Cora saw Mrs. Price's *ghost*? Cecilia was startled, but before she could ask more about such an extraordinary sight, Cora's eyes drifted shut and Nellie returned with the tea tray. Cecilia realized she needed to say goodbye to Anne and return to Danby before her mother became too angry. She paused at the top of the stairs, looking down at where Amelia Price had landed after her fatal fall. The space was narrow and dark, and the staircase itself was old and rickety. Could

Cora really have stood here and watched her friend fall to her death? Then keep it a secret until today?

When Cecilia made her way back to the high street, she saw that the crowd around the Crown and Shield had thinned out considerably. To her relief, she didn't see her parents or their car anywhere, so hopefully they had long since returned home. She needed someplace quiet, where she could sit down and write some notes about what she'd learned at the inquest to tell Jane later.

The Moffats' tea shop looked rather busy as she peeked in the pink-draped window, and Mr. Hatcher's bookshop was locked. Disappointed, she studied the street and decided to go back to the Crown. She'd never been there by herself, but it was 1912, not 1712. Surely, no one could be scandalized if she had a ginger beer and sat in the snug for a few minutes. It was a bit of a thumb in the eye to men who were afraid women would take over the pubs, men like Lord Elphin. And then she could try to find out if Georgie Guff had indeed spent the whole evening drinking unpaid-for pints.

She marched across the street and into the pub, her head high with a boldness she didn't quite feel yet. It was quiet after the inquest, with just a few customers whispering together over their ale. Mr. Perkins and his daughter Daisy were working behind the bar.

"Lady Cecilia," Daisy said in surprise. She was almost the same age as Cecilia, though she had been working at the pub for years, a pretty girl with lustrous brown hair and a shrewd gleam in her hazel eyes. "We thought you had all gone back to Danby."

"I had a few errands to run first," Cecilia answered. "And I do find myself quite thirsty from all the excitement. Could I have a ginger beer, please?"

"Of course, my lady," Mr. Perkins said. "Maybe a sandwich as well? We have some nice tomatoes today, probably the last left of the season. Or Daisy could cook you up some fish."

Cecilia's stomach rumbled at the suggestion, and she remembered she had been too nervous to eat much breakfast. "Thank you, a sandwich would be most welcome."

She found a quiet seat, half-hidden from the rest of the common room. She took her notebook and pencil from her handbag and tried to recall everything she would have to tell Jane. Cora's confession, the ghost sighting, Mr. Guff and the ring . . .

Daisy brought her drink and sandwich and arranged them on the table in a careful way Cecilia imagined the more regular customers didn't always get. "Thank you very much, Miss Perkins, that looks lovely."

"Ma makes the bread herself, Lady Cecilia," Daisy said. "It's always very popular, fresh every day."

"I would imagine so. Do you run out of food quickly on busy evenings?"

Daisy laughed. "Five minutes flat sometimes. I'm always run off my feet in the evenings."

"Do you remember, Daisy, if it was very busy on the night of the rally? The night Mrs. Price died?"

Daisy frowned in thought. "It was, yes. Lord Elphin and his group had been in earlier; they're always a handful. They never want to pay up all they owe at the end, and they do get handsy sometimes."

Cecilia cringed, imagining that rough crowd who pushed Mrs. Price on the Guildhall steps grabbing for her. "That sounds terribly unpleasant."

Daisy laughed. "I know how to slap them down quick enough. But it's a nuisance when we have lots of customers to serve and not a moment to lose."

"Do you remember Mr. Guff here that night?"

Daisy glanced back at her father, who was talking to a customer as he pulled a pint. "The one they say is a thief? The tall man who smells a bit skunkish?"

"I think that would be him, yes."

"I do remember him early on, but it got so busy later I'm not sure. Dad might remember."

Cecilia recalled that Mr. Perkins had said Guff was indeed there, in the snug. But if it was busy, surely Mr. Perkins wouldn't have noticed him from the bar? "Was your father here all evening, too?"

"Oh yes. Nowhere else to go on nights like that. He did go down to the cellar for a while; there was a problem with one of the barrels. Ma pulled the pints then."

Cecilia wondered if Guff had left then. "Did you see anything strange at all? Maybe people you didn't know coming in, or something on the street when you were closing?"

"I went straight to bed when we closed, too tired to do anything else. I glanced out the windows upstairs, but everything was quiet. The only light I could see was above Mr. Hatcher's shop, but he often stays up all hours." She tapped her blunt fingernails on the table. "There *was* someone here that night, a toff sort. Tall, had a goatee. A fancy coat."

"Was his name Mr. Winter, by any chance?"

"I'm not sure, but he did order an expensive port and still owes us for it, I think. Dad said he saw him at the inquest today."

"Daisy!" Mr. Perkins called out. "Those glasses won't wash themselves, and Lady Cecilia needs to eat."

"Coming, Dad! Hold on to your horses, then," Daisy shouted back to him. "Anything else I can get you, my lady?"

"No, everything looks lovely, thank you." As Daisy walked away, Cecilia considered what she had discovered. Georgie Guff *had* been at the Crown but could have left while Mr. Perkins was seeing to the barrels. And how did he get the ring? And the Winters were in the village on the fateful night. If Monty Winter was at the pub, then Mary was alone. Before or after they called on Mrs. Price? Then there was the letter Mary said she wrote to her mother, which didn't correspond to the fragments left on the table at Primrose Cottage. Who *had* written it, then? And what was it about? As she ate her sandwich, she took her notebook and jotted down a few thoughts to share with Jane.

The clock over the bar chimed, and Cecilia looked up, startled that so much time had already passed, over an hour. She would be missed at Danby soon, surely. She gulped down the last of the ginger beer, jotted one more idea before she tucked her notebook away, and rushed out of the pub, waving to Daisy. The high street was crowded at that hour, people finishing their shopping and hurrying home to start their tea.

"Lady Cecilia!" someone called, and she turned to see Mr. Brown hurrying toward her. His brown, glossy hair was rumpled by the wind, as he took off his hat to keep it from blowing away, and he looked quite handsome that way. Less polished than he did in the pulpit, younger. He smiled and waved.

"Mr. Brown," she said. "How nice to see you again today. Are you on your way to evensong?"

"Oh no, my curate has agreed to take the service today. I was invited to tea at Danby by your mother and just saw you walking past. Can I escort you home?"

Was her mother matchmaking again? "Oh, I just had some errands here in the village I'm finishing up. I wouldn't want to take up your time . . ."

He shook his head, his smile widening. For the first time, Cecilia noticed he had rather an adorable dimple in his cheek when he did that. "Believe me, Lady Cecilia, it is hardly an onerous chore. A walk on a lovely autumn afternoon, now that the rain has cleared, is a treat."

Cecilia had to admit it would be nice to have the company on the walk home, with everything so uncertain in the village. "Then—thank you. It's most kind."

They made their way out of the village, talking of the bazaar, of village matters, of books and music. Once out on the mostly empty lane toward Danby, she relaxed a little more, free of the watching eyes looking at them strolling together, the gossipy interest she knew would follow and make its way to her mother.

Mr. Brown, too, seemed easier with just the trees and

hedgerows to watch them. He laughed more, talked more freely. They climbed the slope of a hill to study the landscape around them, the patchwork of dark stone walls and fields, the curl of smoke from chimneys in the distance.

"How beautiful it is here," he said as they paused to take in the view. "I never get used to it, no matter how long I've been here. It always catches me by surprise somehow."

Cecilia remembered the stir of excitement when he first came to St. Swithin's. The previous vicar had been elderly, set in his ways. A new, handsome young man was something quite different, something to energize the village. And so he had, in his gentle way. "Where was your last parish, Mr. Brown?"

"Not in a lovely place like Danby. I was in Manchester, quite in the city's center near mills and factories."

"Manchester!" Cecilia exclaimed. "How interesting that must have been. We must seem terribly quiet and dull to you here. Just church bazaars and flower-arranging committees, things like that."

He laughed, and it made him look younger, more carefree. "I like the church here, and the people. My last place was a poor parish, and I did feel I was starting to do some good there. I was surprised when the transfer order came from the bishop. When I was at university, I imagined I might be a missionary one day."

"A missionary?" Cecilia tried to imagine him in the dust and the heat. She wondered if his viscount uncle put paid to that, sent him to a proper country living.

"Doing good works in India or Africa. I was ridiculously idealistic, quite insufferable. When I didn't want to be a missionary, I thought I would be a poet! Can you imagine? But good works must be done everywhere, and I am liking my place in Danby more and more every day." He gave her a gentle smile. "And it hasn't been so very *quiet* here lately, has it?"

"Indeed not, I'm afraid." Cecilia took his proffered arm, and they walked on. "May I ask you something, Mr. Brown?"

"Of course, Lady Cecilia. Anything."

"Lying is quite wrong, I know."

He looked rather discomfited. "Er—yes, indeed."

"But what if it was meant to be kind, to—well, to save another person, in a way?"

"I imagine that often a lie does begin in such a way. I do believe most people want to be kind, want to avoid injuring another's feelings. Yet the lies almost always end badly."

Cecilia nodded. She thought of Cora and her protective instinct for Mrs. Price—and how that instinct might hinder finding the real culprit. "By inadvertently covering up something worse? Or accidentally protecting someone who doesn't deserve our kindness?"

"Considering that I don't know the specifics of what you speak, I would rather tend to agree. Lies usually don't end with the first one spoken, but pile in upon themselves. With unfortunate, unforeseen consequences. There's a reason for that hoary old saying 'honesty is the best policy.' But I also think God sees the truth in our hearts and forgives our kindly meant mistakes."

"I do hope so, since I am quite sure we all make them."

They came to a low, crumbling stone wall, and he took her hand to help her climb over it. His touch was warm through their gloves, strong, and Cecilia felt a rather surprising little thrill at the feel of it. *How extraordinary*, she thought.

His smile turned shy, and he ducked his head under the brim of his hat. "Things have seemed rather topsy-turvy here of late, with poor Mrs. Price and the inquest and all," he said. "I hope you know I am always here to listen, if you need assistance with anything at all, Lady Cecilia."

"That is very kind, Mr. Brown. Thank you."

They turned through one of the side gates into Danby's park and made their way along the pathway in silence, but it was a comfortable sort of silence, companionable. Cecilia found she quite enjoyed his steady, quiet presence next to her, his certainty in things she could never feel certain about herself. She still was rather doubtful she could make a good vicar's wife, but if she *had* to marry a clergyman, she could certainly do far worse than the handsome, kind Mr. Brown.

Redvers opened the door before they even reached the marble steps of the front portico. His expression was, as always, unreadable. "Lady Cecilia. Mr. Brown. Her ladyship is expecting you. Tea is being served in the White Drawing Room. I do hope you are still joining us, Mr. Brown? Mrs. Frazer sent up your favorite raspberry curd with the scones."

"How kind of her," Mr. Brown exclaimed. "I do seldom get such treats in my bachelor rectory, Redvers."

Cecilia bit her lip. The White Drawing Room. They seldom used that grand chamber for family tea, preferring the cozier music room, or even the terrace on nice days. What was her mother planning now? "Thank you, Redvers, we will go there directly. You *can* join us as planned, Mr. Brown? I haven't kept you too long from your duties?"

"Not at all. I couldn't miss Mrs. Frazer's raspberry curd, could I?" he said with a flash of that dimpled grin.

Chapter Fifteen

It was a somber group that set out from Danby to the memorial service at the Guildhall. The car was filled with silence as they jolted along the lane. Cecilia and Jane were joined by Bridget, who was allowed the afternoon off to go with her aunt, Mrs. Palmer, to the service. Their dark clothes matched the gray day outside, and even Jack stayed in his basket and was quiet, after his clamoring to go with them. Jesse, who sat up front with Collins, had also come along to assist them.

The day seemed stage-set perfect for mourning, the sky low and heavy with rain, the air full of a strange, electric tension. Cecilia smoothed her black suede gloves and wished it was over and she was back home in front of the fire with a good book. On the other hand, this was possibly her last chance to see all the suspects in Mrs. Price's death in one place.

The village was quiet as they drove to the Guildhall, the shops blank behind their closed windows, only a few intrepid walkers on the rainy green. Cecilia knew many of the Union ladies had already left the village, but there were still several gathered on the Guildhall steps, handing out black-bordered copies of Mrs. Price's eulogy. Their white dresses and purple, green, and gold sashes were bright against the dismal day, except for the black bands on their sleeves and their tear-streaked faces. Whatever Mrs. Price's private shortcomings may have been, her inspiration would be so much missed.

As Cecilia stepped from the car, she noticed a few people gathered on the walkway, watching the proceedings. One of them was Lord Elphin, who seemed strangely shrunken and gray. No disdainful laughter today. He held his hat in his hands, and she didn't see any of his bullyboys backing him up, so hopefully he had come to make some peace.

"Isn't that the unpleasant fellow who was here on the night of the rally, my lady?" Jesse asked quietly.

"Lord Elphin. Yes." She remembered how he and his men had behaved on that night, when one of them shoved Mrs. Price and the anger ran high. "He seems quiet enough today, I think."

"He doesn't have his gang to back him up," Jesse said, watching Lord Elphin with narrowed eyes. "Do you think *he* had something to do with Mrs. Price's death?"

She had wondered the same thing, many times. Would such anger, such hatred at the thought of women living their own lives cause him or one of his ilk to lash out like that? "I don't know. He certainly seemed furious that anyone *not* a landed, white male might demand rights. Perhaps he followed her back to Primrose Cottage to argue with her?"

"Shall I talk to him, then? See what he says after a pint or two at the Crown?" Jesse asked. "I'm not landed, but I am a white male. Maybe if I hinted that I might share his views . . ."

"How clever, Jesse! It's quite true that he'd be sure to tell you things he would never tell someone like me."

Jesse nodded grimly, and strode off toward Lord Elphin, who watched him warily for a moment. But when Jesse spoke to him he finally nodded, and the two of them headed to the pub.

"What is Jesse up to, my lady?" Jane asked, lifting up Jack's basket in her arms. He peeked out with his bright-green eyes, as if studying the scene.

"He's going to buy Lord Elphin a pint and see what the old ruffian might have to say," Cecilia answered. "Just as we have to find out what Mrs. Price's family and coworkers might have to say."

Jane tilted her head as she studied the ladies in white arrayed on the steps. "So you don't think she fell?"

"I do think it rather unlikely. Where's the torn scrap of her sash? How did her ring get into Guff's possession, if he didn't take it himself? And why would Cora make such a confession?"

"To protect Mrs. Price's reputation, surely," Jane said. "Mrs. Price is a martyr for suffrage now; that's what the newspaper said. If she was remembered as just a clumsy drunkard . . ."

"Quite." Cecilia remembered her conversation with Mr. Brown, about kindly meant lies. "I am sure Cora *does* want to protect Mrs. Price. But is Mrs. Price the only one she is protecting? Maybe Cora knows someone else did it and is covering up for them?" She shook her head in confusion.

One of the ladies in the doorway rang a bell, a slow, mournful pattern, and Cecilia took Jane's arm to turn toward the Guildhall, where Bridget was just going in with Mrs. Palmer. Mrs. Palmer looked rather pale in her dark gray suit, but dry-eyed, and Cecilia remembered the rumors that Mrs. Palmer was not entirely happy with how Mrs. Price ran the Union. Could she really want to take it over for herself? How far would she go to do that?

Inside, all was hushed and solemn, except for one lady in white who played a long, slow, soft passage from the Mozart *Requiem* on her violin atop the dais. The platform was draped not in black, but in white with magnificent wreaths of white carnations and blue irises from Mr. Smithfield's florist's shop. Anne greeted guests at the head of the aisle, and she smiled as she saw Cecilia.

"Lady Cecilia, Miss Hughes, how kind you are to come today," she said. She looked sad but composed in her black silk dress and hat, and even smiled wider when she saw Jack's basket. "And you brought Sir Jack!"

"I hope he won't be in the way; he simply yowled and howled when we tried to leave him behind," Cecilia said.

"Not at all. Mother would have enjoyed him. Do let me show you to some empty seats. Perhaps you would like to come to Primrose Cottage after? I can give you the bicycle then. We'll be returning to London as soon as possible. We can aid the inquiry from there, I'm sure."

"Of course," Cecilia said, but she knew not *everyone*

wanted to go back to London. The Winters seemed to want to stay in Danby permanently. She studied the faces of the crowd as they followed Anne toward the front. Mary Winter was sniffling into her handkerchief, while her husband looked rather bored by it all. "Where is Miss Black? Is she still ill?"

"I fear so," Anne said, her tone unreadable. "Your excellent Dr. Mitchell was with her when we left. I'm sure he will give her some laudanum; she keeps talking about Mother's ghost and it makes her quite agitated." She led Cecilia and Jane to some seats near the front and to the side. "Forgive me, I must greet the rest of the guests. Thank you again for coming; it's so kind."

Cecilia and Jane settled into their seats, Jack in his basket at their feet as they listened to the music, the hushed whispers. Had it only been a few days since the excitement of Mrs. Price's rally, her stirring speeches? It seemed ages; everything was so different now.

"My lady?" Jane asked. "What do you think he would want here?" She gestured to Inspector Hennesy, who hovered near the door, hat in hand, looking rather uncomfortable.

"I suppose he wants to see if anyone does anything suspicious," Cecilia said. "In the novels, don't the villains sometimes come to funerals to gloat?"

"Well, Sergeant Dunn told me once I should take care and not go out in the evenings alone. Maybe they know something we don't."

"Interesting," Cecilia murmured.

There was a small stir of latecomers at the door, and to Cecilia's surprise, Henry Price walked down the rows and sat down beside her. He looked all that was proper for a widower, a black band on his arm, his face composed in solemn lines, perfectly polite but perfectly distant.

"Lady Cecilia," he said with a bow of his head. "I hear that you befriended my wife and elder daughter in recent days. That is most kind of you to take the time for them. You must have many duties at Danby Hall."

His tone struck her as coolly condescending, like her mother at some of her charity benefits. And of course, he was quite wrong. Her duties at Danby helping her mother write invitations and trying to play the piano were not exactly onerous. She would probably be even less busy when Patrick and Annabel married. It seemed quite silly next to the Union's work.

"Not at all," she said. "They have been very kind to *me*. I enjoy their company; their conversation is most fascinating."

"Indeed?" Mr. Price looked doubtful. "I am not sure about Anne, but yes, my wife could be quite charming when she wished to be."

"Were you much in love once?" Cecilia remembered Miss Merriman and all her suitors.

Mr. Price frowned. "When I was younger, and quite foolish, I may have imagined myself so, Lady Cecilia. Amelia was beautiful and vivacious, where I was terribly sunk into my work. But beware the whirlwind passions of youth, my dear. They do lead a person quite astray."

Cecilia thought of her own distant romantic prospects and nodded. "And you were—led astray?"

He laughed wryly. "In a manner of speaking. Our views

of life, our wishes for the future, proved to be quite incompatible. Family life should be a haven of peace."

She wondered if he did have a prospect of a "new" family now, as the rumors of his love life in London said. Did he need to get rid of his wife to move forward into a haven of peace?

There was no time to say more, as the memorial service began. As a young lady in her white gown and sash played the violin, more Union members came onstage bearing wreaths, and Anne rose to deliver a eulogy. All the while, Mr. Price sat next to Cecilia in quiet watchfulness, his hands folded serenely on the handle of his silver walking stick.

❧

"Shall I find Mr. Collins and tell him we're ready to go back to Danby, then, my lady? I think he's waiting at Mr. Talbot's shop," Jane asked as they emerged from the sadness of the hall into the gray day. Anne and Nellie had already vanished, and Monty and Mary were walking away toward their own lodgings. Jack seemed to be snoozing quietly in his basket, but Cecilia could see the gleam of his bright eyes between the wicker slats. He was watching everything, too.

"Yes, of course. Would you mind waiting at the shop with Mr. Collins, Jane? Have some tea, see if there's anything new on the shelves. I have to go by Primrose Cottage to fetch the bicycle, and then I will come and find you." She also had to find out if Jesse had learned anything from Lord Elphin at the Crown.

"Yes, my lady. Come along now, Jack, and be on your good behavior at Mr. Talbot's shop with all those breakables."

Cecilia watched Jane take up Jack's basket and walk away, and she turned toward Primrose Cottage. She still felt sad after the service, and worried about the Prices. The cottage looked as well as could be expected. The shutters were open to let in the pale-gray light, and smoke made a silver spiral from the chimney.

As Cecilia knocked on the door, she found it was ajar, and she pushed it open. There were trunks and hatboxes stacked in the small foyer, as if Anne was ready to fly at the first available moment. Nellie came hurrying down the stairs, a valise in her hands, but Cora was nowhere to be seen.

"Oh, Lady Cecilia, do come in!" Nellie called, adding her case to the pile of luggage. "Would you care to wait in the sitting room? Miss Anne won't be long. I'll bring some tea in just as soon as I finish carrying down these boxes."

"No hurry, Nellie. I am quite fine waiting," Cecilia answered. She made her way into the sitting room, which had a cheerful fire crackling in the grate but didn't seem to have been tidied anytime recently. Luckily, she found the table still cluttered, with the scraps of paper scattered amid the glasses and cards, and she snatched one to tuck into her handbag and examine later.

"Oh, Lady Cecilia," Anne said, rushing into the sitting room. She tucked a stray lock of dark hair back into its braided knot and brushed some dust off her black skirt. "The bicycle is ready, but it seems we needn't hurry quite so much after all. Inspector Hennesy has left a message to ask if we can stay a little longer, which is such a nuisance as we're nearly packed. I've told Nellie she can leave on the evening train, though, as she is so eager to return to London. I have the feeling she would quit my employ rather than stay here a moment longer. There isn't much for her to do around the cottage. I was so sure I could help with any inquiries from my own home now."

Cecilia thought of the inspector's warnings. "That must be a great inconvenience."

Anne frowned. "Indeed. There is a lot of work to be done in London now, to make sure the Union is kept on a steady course. Now Mrs. Palmer will have to run the office for a few days."

"Is Mrs. Palmer allowed to leave, then?"

"It seems so. But Cora must stay until everything is made clear."

"What of your sister and her husband?"

Anne shook her head. "I haven't spoken to them. I would imagine Monty will be anxious to get back to his work, unless he thinks he has some inheritance to be hanging about for. Really, I am not entirely sure why *any* of us must stay. It's just London, a train ride away, not Abyssinia."

"I am sure you have so much work to be done in London."

"Yes, especially with Mother gone and so many decisions to make about the Union. It is my responsibility now, and I think . . ." She paused with a short laugh. "But you do not need to worry about such things. Come, let me get the bicycle for you. Do we have time for a quick riding lesson?"

Cecilia made her way downstairs early for dinner, long before the last gong, hoping to find Jesse and have a quiet word about what he'd found out from Lord Elphin. Luckily, he was alone for the moment, putting the final touches to the dining table. Silver epergnes of fruit gleamed in the faint light, while the crystal he carefully placed at each spot glittered.

"Lady Cecilia," he said calmly, quite as if he was expecting her, as he put the polish to the silver fruit bowl in the center of the table and made sure it was straight on the white damask cloth.

Cecilia tiptoed closer and whispered, "What did you talk about with Lord Elphin today, Jesse? I didn't see him again after the service."

Jesse grinned. "I ought to be due hardship pay, my lady, for listening to the old boor for so long."

Cecilia laughed. "Indeed so. Above and beyond."

He rearranged the pears and hothouse peaches in the bowl. "He's certainly not happy with ladies like the Prices. Railed on and on about how they're ruining the fabric of society and causing unhappiness in the family, though I'm not exactly sure how that affects *him*. Maybe there's something about his own wife? No one seems to know much about her. Maybe she was an independent sort, too. After a measure of Mr. Perkin's finest lagers, Lord Elphin's conversation isn't the most coherent, I must say."

"There was really a Lady Elphin, then?" Cecilia cried, surprised.

"Did you never meet her?"

"Not at all. I've never heard of her. But then, I seldom see Lord Elphin in a social capacity. He tends to stay on his own estate, unless he's haranguing ladies for wanting the vote. What did he say about this Lady Elphin?"

Jesse shrugged. "Just that they were happy once, until she decided to start reading. And women who go beyond their natural spheres are ruining the treasured social order that made England great. You abandon your children, let your households starve because you won't attend to the kitchen . . ."

"We drink in pubs?"

Jesse gave her a mock-stern glance that made her giggle. "That's the worst thing of all, my lady."

Cecilia laughed. "I did have a ginger beer the other day at the Crown. It wasn't as thrilling as I expected. But if I don't think I've heard of a Lady Elphin, I have definitely never heard of an Elphin Junior. Maybe if he did have a wife, she left him ages ago, before there were any children to neglect by demanding the vote. Good for her then, whoever she is."

"I could ask my aunt if she ever knew any Lady Elphin, or any old scandals there."

"Good idea, Jesse." Mrs. Mabry and her late husband had owned the greengrocer's shop for decades; nothing in the neighborhood would have escaped her notice.

"I did get the sense that, whatever bee he has in his bonnet, it does have to do with the Prices," Jesse said, turning a wineglass so it faced the right way, the engraved crest at front.

"The Prices? He does seem to dislike them, but they're London people."

Jesse shrugged. "I'm not sure, but he certainly detests them. Says they're leading the innocents of this district astray in their quest to do all that fabric-of-society destroying." He smiled at her over the gilded edge of the glass. "Are you being led astray, my lady?"

"I should hope so. What fun is life without a little straying?"

"Daisy did say . . ."

There was a note of familiarity in his voice when he said that name that gave Cecilia a rather uncomfortable twinge of—could it be *jealousy*? Certainly not. "Daisy, is it?"

"Miss Perkins, the landlord's daughter. A very nice girl, very observant. She said Lord Elphin likes to complain about modern Delilahs like Mrs. Price whenever he's in his cups. Women of the London stews of iniquity."

Cecilia sniffed and pushed away an image of Jesse flirting with Daisy over the bar. "I think I might need a small visit to a London stew myself, just to see what I can find about the Prices' past."

"You need to go to London, my lady?"

"Yes, it seems that is where Mrs. Price did most of her work, and her home is there as well. Maybe the mysterious Lady Elphin is there, too. And who knows what else." Like Mr. Winter's law office, which he seemed to be so keen to leave. And the Union headquarters. "Yes, I need to ask a few questions in London."

Jesse smoothed the tablecloth with a concerned frown. "I hope you'll be careful there."

"Careful?" Everyone seemed so intent on warning her lately. First the inspector, now Jesse. And she was more inclined to listen to Jesse.

"One lady is already dead. And the situation does seem—complicated. Someone might not like questions being asked, you know."

Cecilia was touched he cared what might happen to her. "I do promise I'll be careful. I'll be much less noticeable in London than I would be here, anyway." The last gong sounded, a brassy echo through the cavernous rooms of Danby, and Cecilia realized everyone would be downstairs in only a few minutes. "I should go. Thank you so much, Jesse. You have been such a great help."

He grimaced. "I'm afraid my questions only made things murkier."

"I do have the feeling lots of those puzzle pieces won't appear to fit together at all—until suddenly they do."

She waved at him one more time and hurried to the Yellow Music Room. She was sitting quietly by the window, her mother's new copy of *The Lady* in her hands, when her parents appeared. Patrick and Annabel followed them, and Redvers with his tray of sherry glasses.

"You're early tonight, dear," her mother said, smoothing her kid gloves and straightening the yellow lace of her sleeves.

Annabel sat down beside Cecilia and gently turned the magazine right side up in her hands. "These fashionable coiffures might look a little better this way, Cec."

Cecilia felt her cheeks turn hot. "Oh. Yes. I did wonder how to get curls to land that way."

"It was lovely seeing Mr. Brown at tea the other day. I do hope he can come again soon," Lady Avebury said, carefully casual. "So kind of him to make sure you got home safely, Cecilia! He is such a charming young man. St. Swithin's is lucky to have him."

"Yes, indeed. He is very nice," Cecilia answered warily.

"By the way, Mama, I had a letter from Aunt Maggie last week." Mrs. Margaret Solent had been Lady Avebury's best friend since their school days, and Cecilia quite adored her. Even though Aunt Maggie and her mother had been debs together, Aunt Maggie had married an army officer with a large family inheritance when Lady Avebury married her earl, and then was widowed after only a few years. She had spent her time since traveling the world and sending back thrilling accounts of her adventures to Cecilia.

"How is dear Maggie?" Lady Avebury asked. "I hadn't realized she was back from Persia yet."

"Oh yes. I was thinking I should visit her for a few days in London, help her settle in at home again," Cecilia said, trying to be breezily convincing. "I could also order a new dress for the bazaar. Nothing I have seems quite right."

"London?" her mother said doubtfully. "But we haven't been back at Danby long, and the shooting party is coming up after the bazaar."

"I could go with you," Annabel said. "I would love to look at some of the new hats at Madame Millier's salon. Perhaps we could go to the theater, as well? I was sad to miss that new show *Buzz-Buzz*; it sounded like such fun."

Cecilia was suddenly thrown into a panic. Having Annabel along on her sleuthing trip was *not* part of her plans! "Oh, I am really such dull company . . ."

"You give yourself too little credit, Cec," Annabel said with a light little laugh. "Besides, surely we should get to know each other better now?" She glanced at Patrick, who ducked behind his botany book.

"Well," Lady Avebury said slowly, "I suppose if Annabel goes with you, and it's only for a few days . . ."

"Yes, let them go have a little fun, Emmaline," Lord Avebury said, rattling his evening papers. "Surely, seeing a play and buying some new hats can't do any harm."

"And I will help Cecilia pick out a lovely new dress for the bazaar," Annabel said. "I'm sure Mr. Brown would appreciate that."

Lady Avebury sighed. "Very well. But only for a few days. You must be back in time to help me set up the bazaar."

"Will you go, too, Patrick?" Lord Avebury asked.

Patrick glanced up from his book, startled. "Me? My experiment is at a delicate place right now. I couldn't possibly leave it for even a day."

Cecilia sighed with relief. At least her entire family wouldn't be there for her to escape.

"You would only get in the way of our lovely shopping anyway, Patrick dear," Annabel said with a laugh. "So, it's settled. Cecilia and I will just jaunt off to London for a few days."

Cecilia made herself smile—and resolved to write to Aunt Maggie right after dinner and beg her to accept some unexpected guests in a good cause.

Chapter Sixteen

Only once the train gathered speed, launching out of Danby Village station toward London, could Cecilia really take a deep breath. Her mother had seemed reluctant to let them go until almost the last minute, until Aunt Maggie's letter saying they would be most welcome and Annabel's insistence she must have a new hat convinced her they couldn't get into too much trouble.

It was a good thing Lady Avebury didn't know about the notebook in Cecilia's handbag, the lists of suspects and clues and ideas concerning Mrs. Price's death. Nor did she know that Cecilia's main goal in Town was to ask more questions.

The train compartment was small but comfortable, with room for Cecilia and Annabel on one velvet-cushioned seat and Jack's basket and Jane facing. The small fold-down table between them was lowered to hold refreshments and cards.

As the train flew through the countryside, parkland giving way to moors and then fields, Annabel unpacked the hamper Mrs. Frazer had sent for them, spreading out a linen cloth and arranging the cold chicken and ham, salads, and fruit tarts on porcelain plates. She passed Jane a platter of hothouse strawberries and opened the silver flask of wine.

As she poured it out, she said, "Tell me, Cec. What is our real errand in London?"

Flustered, Cecilia stared at Annabel, trying to study her pretty face beneath the large, silk-rose-laden lace hat. "I—to find a new dress, of course. None of mine seem quite right for the bazaar."

Annabel waved away this excuse with her manicured white hand. There was no heirloom Bates sapphire ring there yet, but Cecilia was sure it was only a matter of time, and then this secretly observant woman would be her sister-in-law. "Cec, you have plenty of new frocks from this last Season. I'm not sure you've even worn them all yet, and I do remember you ordering them."

Cecilia remembered, too. Visiting the fashion salons and milliners with Annabel seemed like a military campaign in its precision and ruthlessness. One dared not walk out with nothing. "I just thought . . ."

"And somehow I doubt you are quite as eager to impress that sweet Mr. Brown as your mother is. In fact, you wouldn't really have to do anything but crook your finger to bring him running, if that's what you wanted."

Cecilia frowned and glanced over at Jane, who shrugged helplessly. "Why do you think that?"

Annabel gave one of her silver-bell laughs. "Because one

thing I do know, Cec dear, is men. Mr. Brown is gaga for you. It would be the simplest thing in the world to bring him up to scratch, if you wanted."

Cecilia remembered what little she knew of Annabel's rumored past, lots of romances, maybe even a thwarted elopement, before she came to Danby. Maybe Patrick was simply too dull for her. "I'm not really sure what I want at the moment," she admitted.

"Very wise. No matter what your mother says, there is no hurry. It's a terribly big decision, and you must be sure to make the right one. Mr. Brown *is* very handsome, and Lady Avebury says he's quite respectable. Well-connected, and sure to be a bishop someday." Annabel took a thoughtful sip of the wine. "But if I was an earl's daughter, I might set my sights a mite higher. A duke or something. Are there any eligible princes left? You don't seem interested in all that, though."

"I'd make a worse duchess than I would a vicar's wife," Cecilia said. She took a drink of her own wine, savoring the sharp-fruity bite of it as she thought about Annabel's words. It *was* a big decision, and of course marriage was what she was raised for. But meeting the Prices made her feel restless for something else, something more. "I suppose I *do* have enough dresses, you're right. The white-and-purple one would certainly do for the bazaar."

"Or the blue silk with those lovely new pagoda sleeves," Jane said, and Jack made a loud "mrow" from his basket. He did like sleeves with swing to them, all the better for his sharp little claws to grab.

"Quite so," Annabel said. "I have just the hat to go with it, too, that cunning little toque with the velvet violets. I could loan it to you. But if we truly aren't going to London to shop, why *are* we going? Not that I'm complaining. A trip to the city after all that boring shooting party talk is always welcome."

"You'll just have to get used to shooting parties when you run Danby," Cecilia said.

Annabel gave a little catlike smile. "*If* I decide to run Danby. I admit I may have had some, shall we say, overly romanticized ideas of English country life back in California. But that doesn't matter one jot now! Tell me, why are we going to London? It must have to do with this terrible suffrage business."

Cecilia sighed and exchanged a long glance with Jane. It was clear that not everything could be hidden from Annabel. She had seemed all frothy whipped cream when she arrived in Danby; now Cecilia knew her shrewdness could not be underestimated.

"Well, yes, I suppose it does," Cecilia admitted. "It's all so very strange, and I can't quite put all the puzzle pieces together. Since Mrs. Price was from London, I thought things might look a bit clearer there."

"Fascinating," Annabel said, and her eyes gleamed with the truth of that. "You don't think she really fell in a drunken stupor, *or* that Miss Black pushed her?"

"Maybe the fall," Cecilia said. "But definitely not Miss Black. And I do wonder if she *could* have tripped, really. That bit of her sash is missing, and it looks as if someone might have snatched at it to shove her, or maybe to try to keep her from falling. And Miss Black only wants to protect her mentor's reputation now."

"And so many people disliked her or had arguments with her," Jane said. "Her family, the other ladies in the Union, Lord Elphin . . ."

"Well, then," Annabel said decisively. "If you do think Mrs. Price was murdered, we must do what we can to discover the truth. That poor Miss Black can't be allowed to take on the burden."

"We?" Cecilia asked in surprise.

"Well, of course. Don't you think I could be of some help, Cec dear? I am terribly good at ferreting out gossip, you know. It's like mining for secrets. And a family like the Prices is sure to have a mother lode of *those*." She clapped her hands together in delight.

"I thought you didn't believe in women's suffrage," Cecilia said.

"I don't. We ladies have our own kind of power, you know, and we get what we want through that. I don't think we should give that up. But a lady like Amelia Price, who forges her own path with such panache—I've got to admire that. She deserves to have the truth known, don't you think? And I admit I do enjoy a little intrigue after so long in the countryside." She poured out more wine. "Now—tell me about everyone you suspect."

Cecilia told her about the Union, Cora, Miss Palmer, and their new ideas; Anne wanting more responsibility; the Winters moving to Danby; the ruby ring and Georgie Guff; the cold Mr. Price, who was separated from his wife and didn't seem to greatly mourn her.

"Is Mr. Price having an affair, then?" Annabel mused.

Cecilia was chagrined she hadn't made more of that idea. "I—well, I'm not sure. I feel quite foolish saying I hadn't considered that enough."

"Oh, it's the first thing we should consider," Annabel said. She leaned over to hand Jack a morsel of ham. "He's handsome for his age. And he must be rich, too, don't you think? Working for Queen Alexandra and all that. He had a wife who left him and was certainly embarrassing him. Or did he leave her? Either way, he'd be a catch if he was single. Able to marry a pretty, socially connected little thing, maybe even have a son."

"He did seem disapproving of his family," Cecilia said, remembering Mr. Price at the memorial service. So distracted and cold.

"And the married daughter. What's her name again?"

"Mary Winter. Mr. Jermyn says her husband was looking for work in Danby Village, though he's been a solicitor in London."

"Very odd indeed to change careers like that. And the suffrage daughter? Miss Anne?"

"I think she was rather exasperated by her mother. Anne seems very no-nonsense, practical. I think they had some disagreements about how to run the Union going forward."

Annabel sighed. "So—the Price family was at odds, as well as the famous Union. What a turbulent life Mrs. Price led!"

"Yet she didn't seem at all ruffled by any of it," Cecilia said, thinking of Mrs. Price's serene good humor.

"Good French wine will do that for people." Annabel laughed. "There won't be very much going on in London at this time of year, will there?"

"No. Almost everyone will be in the country. But I'm sure Mr. Winter's law office will be open, and maybe Union headquarters. I have a letter from Anne introducing us to them. Aunt Maggie will know where else to go. Maybe the ladies at her club will have met Mrs. Price. It's a lovely place anyway, full of women who live to travel as Aunt Maggie does. And, as you said, there's the theater."

"Maybe we could find a tea party, or a dance or two. Getting all the Town gossip can't hurt." Annabel sat back with a happy smile. "Well, that has certainly livened up my week no end. More wine, ladies?"

❧

Aunt Maggie's house was in Ebury Street, which Cecilia couldn't help but remember was also where the Winters lived, though it was a very long street and it seemed the Winters lived at the less-palatial end. Aunt Maggie's house was a quiet, respectable, substantial redbrick and cream stone Georgian town house in a row of identical houses, four stories tall, muffled with yellow satin draperies. As they stepped out of their cab, the black-painted door opened and Aunt Maggie rushed out to greet them.

Tall, with sun-burnished dark hair, glowing pink cheeks, and dark eyes that saw everything, Maggie always exuded energy and health and enthusiasm. "Cec, my dear! How wonderful to see you. I was so excited to get your message. And Miss Clarke, what a lovely surprise. Do come in. I just rang for tea."

Jane followed the housekeeper upstairs to the bedchambers, carrying Jack with her, and Cecilia and Annabel made their way with Aunt Maggie through the small, black-and-white-tiled foyer to the drawing room. It was a bright, comfortable room, scattered with yellow-and-white-striped chairs and settees and marble-topped tables on a pink-and-blue-flowered Axminster carpet. There were signs of her travels everywhere in paintings from France, mosaics from Persia, filmy embroidered draperies from India, Italian porcelain and Egyptian alabaster statues. The tea table was laid out by the fire, silver and gilt-edged china gleaming.

Aunt Maggie waved them to chairs across from her and poured out the tea into antique Florentine cups. "Your mother sent me a message, too. She seems quite relieved you decided to leave Danby for a few days. It seems there is some sort of drama happening right now?" She laughed and pushed a loose strand of hair back beneath the red-and-gold silk scarf that bound it back. "I always thought of Danby as an unchangeable island of peace, but first Mr. Hayes and now this? Whatever is the world coming to?"

"Yes. Mrs. Price, the president of the Women's Suffrage Union, died at Primrose Cottage in the village," Cecilia answered. "I had attended her rallies."

Maggie clucked her tongue sadly. "Oh yes, of course. Your mother did tell me about that, so shocking. Mrs Price has been quite the cause célèbre here in London."

"Have you attended any of the Union meetings, Aunt Maggie?" Cecilia asked, taking another slice of seedcake from the tray.

Aunt Maggie shook her head. "I'm seldom at home these days; there's not time to get involved in anything. But of course I support Mrs. Price's cause. It's about time women had some freedom to lead their own lives."

Cecilia thought Aunt Maggie was one of the *freest* women she had ever known. But she was that rare, lucky creature—a rich widow of youngish years, whose husband had left her all his unentailed property free of restriction. "I did wonder if perhaps Mrs. Price was a member of your club."

Aunt Maggie nodded. "She was, and her daughter Miss Anne Price, as well. We do have all sorts of members, women of a modern way of thinking. But I didn't meet them often at all."

"Perhaps someone else there might have been a particular friend to the Prices?"

Aunt Maggie narrowed her eyes as she studied Cecilia closely. "Why, Cec darling. Never say you are *investigating* Mrs. Price's death?"

Cecilia laughed nervously. "Not investigating, really. Just asking a few questions, since the authorities don't seem interested in doing so. Mrs. Price's secretary, Miss Black, said she had pushed her, but I don't think that's true. I think she is trying to protect Mrs. Price. I'd like to help her, if I can."

"Why is that? Perhaps the poor girl *did* push her. I'm sure people would like to do that to annoying employers all the time."

Cecilia shook her head. "Not Miss Black. She worshiped

Mrs. Price. I think she's afraid the Union will be damaged if Mrs. Price is remembered as a drunkard. And plenty of other people had quarrels with Mrs. Price."

"Interesting. Of course, we can visit the club if you like, though not a great many members are in Town right now. And I had an invitation to a little dance at Mrs. Trentworth's tomorrow night. She's very interested in suffrage; I'm sure she must have met the Prices. You'll enjoy her anyway; she's quite the artistic bohemian, and she attracts absolutely everyone to her salons."

Annabel looked doubtful. While Cecilia knew that Annabel had a skeleton or two in her own American closet, she doubted anything "bohemian" had ever entered Annabel's orbit. "Are there many ladies' clubs in London, Mrs. Solent? I never heard of any at home in San Francisco."

"Oh, do call me Maggie, please." She refilled the tea and passed the cake plate. "There are indeed several ladies' clubs in Town now, though I admit the idea might have shocked my mother, rest her conventional soul. She thought women should only socialize at home. Like men's clubs, they are usually centered around certain interests. Literature, science, things like that. My own attracts ladies who enjoy traveling, like myself. A bit like a female Travellers Club."

"Was Mrs. Price much for travel, then?" Cecilia asked.

"Only around England lately, I believe, giving her speeches. And speaking tours to America, France, things like that." She took a thoughtful bite of a strawberry. "When she was younger, I believe she did travel a bit in the East."

"With Mr. Price?" Cecilia said, surprised.

Aunt Maggie frowned. "I'm not really sure. She was a bit older than me, and we didn't run in the same circles at all back then. I would imagine not. Henry Price is famously busy with his work, and he doesn't seem the exploratory type, does he?"

"No," Cecilia murmured. Mr. Price seemed like an Englishman through and through. "The Prices have another daughter, one who is quite against suffrage. Mrs. Mary Winter. I think she and her husband live on this street."

Aunt Maggie tapped her fingertips on the carved arm of her chair. "Winter—Winter. Oh yes, I know who you mean. They live several numbers away, at the end of the lane. I met her at a tea or garden party or something of the sort. She's pretty, but I think considers herself rather sickly. Not much interesting conversation, I'm afraid. And he's a rather po-faced attorney, seems to want to make himself into his father-in-law's image, but without the talent for it."

"Yes, that sounds like them," Cecilia said with a laugh.

"I'm afraid I can't tell you much about them, but my staff might. They are here more than I am, and they do seem to hear everything. Do you think Mrs. Winter might have done away with her mother? How shocking."

"I don't think they got along very well. Their lives are so very different. And it seems Mr. Winter is having some career troubles. He is trying to get a position with Mr. Jermyn in Danby."

"Good heavens," Maggie exclaimed. "And here I thought coming back to England would be dull!"

Once they'd finished their tea and were making their way

Lady Rights a Wrong

upstairs to their chambers, Annabel asked, "What *does* one wear to a bohemian dancing party? Or to a ladies' club?"

"I'm not really sure," Cecilia admitted, secretly delighted that even Annabel, who always seemed to know everything perfectly in Society, didn't know this.

"Maybe there will be time to shop as well as snoop tomorrow," Annabel said. "I must say, England is proving to be more fun than I thought."

Fun, Cecilia mused as she shut her chamber door behind her and found Jack asleep on her pillow. She wasn't sure that was the word she would have used. But it all was certainly rather intriguing . . .

❧

"So what do you think of a London household, Jane?" Cecilia asked, as Jane brushed and plaited her hair for bed. Jack was exploring the room behind them, crawling under the white-painted, pink toile–draped bed looking for stray objects and stalking across the flowered carpet. Once in a while he would jump up on the pink-cushioned window seat to "mrow" at the busy street outside.

"It's different from Danby, isn't it, my lady?" Jane said. Cecilia knew Jane had worked for an elderly lady in America, and then at a hotel, and now a large country house at Danby, but never a town house. "Just a cook, a kitchen maid, two housemaids, a butler, and one footman. Plus the lady's maid, Miss Bleeker. And they say Mrs. Solent isn't even home very much, she just travels with her own maid, so there isn't much for them to do except keep things clean. The cook says that when

211

Mrs. Solent *is* home, she only has informal receptions and a few musical evenings. The butler seems a bit let down by it all! But they say the pay is very good, and there's lots of free time."

"Would you prefer a place like this, then?"

Jane seemed to think this over as she tied off the end of Cecilia's plait. "I might like the musical evenings, my lady. The housekeeper says all kinds of artists and writers attend, and they have string quartets and opera singers. But it must be boring most of the time. Danby is never boring."

Cecilia laughed. "You just haven't been there long enough. Wait until after Christmas, when there is nothing at all happening. But I admit it's not dull right now."

"Did Mrs. Solent know anything about the Prices, then?"

Cecilia picked up a ribbon to dangle for Jack, who pounced and rolled on the scrap of blue silk. "Sort of. Mrs. Price belongs to her club, and the Winters live just down the street. Not that they're Aunt Maggie's sort of people; they're too conventional and worried about their status. Aunt Maggie said Mr. Winter was 'po-faced,' which sounds about right from what I've seen."

"Are all English widows like Mrs. Solent, then? So—free and happy? The lady I worked for in New Jersey was rich, but she liked to sit around complaining about the lapse in morality these days and never went out. But then, she *was* old."

"Not many English ladies are like Aunt Maggie, no. Mama has been friends with her since they were schoolgirls, and Mama says Maggie always went her own way, followed her own calling. I think maybe Mama admires that, deep down inside, and wants to be friends with Aunt Maggie to be a vicarious part of her adventures! Aunt Maggie fell into a terrible mourning when Mr. Solent died so young, but travel seems to have revived her spirits entirely." Cecilia trailed the ribbon for Jack, thinking of how things must have been when her mother and Aunt Maggie were girls, how they were now. "I do wonder how my own daughters might live. I'm sure the world will be very different for them."

Jane gave her a teasing smile as she handed her a flannel for her face. "Are you going to have lots of daughters, then, my lady? With Mr. Brown, maybe?"

Cecilia laughed and pretended she was going to give Jane an indignant swipe. "Then they would have to be properly behaved vicarage children, wouldn't they? I can't quite picture it . . ."

She went to the window and studied the scene outside in the gathering darkness, the flare of gaslights, the cars and carriages rattling past. It was never still here, never quiet. Always something happening.

"Would you want to live in London, then? Like Mrs. Solent?" Jane asked as she picked up the discarded dinner dress and shook it out.

Jack rubbed against Cecilia's foot, and she picked him up to cuddle his warm, purring body close. "It would be exciting to have my own house, I think. And to see the world, as Aunt Maggie does. But I like the country, too. One can't get in a real gallop here, even in Hyde Park, and the air always has the most appalling smells."

"I'm not sure the country is any safer than the city these days," Jane said.

Not with so many murders happening near Danby. Cecilia sighed. "Quite so. But surely the seeds of whatever happened to Mrs. Price were planted here."

"So where do we look first here in London?"

"Aunt Maggie says Mrs. Trentworth is having a dance party; she might know some of the gossip. She is famous for her bohemian salon. And since Mrs. Price was also a member of Aunt Maggie's club, we can ask around there. We don't have much time, of course, but a visit to the Union headquarters seems in order, and a stop at Mr. Winter's place of employment. I want to find out why he's really looking for a position in Danby Village of all places."

"Maybe I could find an excuse to talk to the servants at the Winter house, since it's just down the street? They're still safely away."

"Good thinking, Jane!"

"And you'll have to find a dress, or won't your mother wonder what you were doing here?"

Cecilia sighed. "You're right. Very well, then. Mrs. Trentworth's dance, Mr. Winter's office, Union headquarters. And the modiste. Madame Handley is sure to have something ready to go soon. And we'll ask around to anyone who might have known Mrs. Price at all."

"Just be careful, my lady," Jane said with a frown.

"Careful?"

Jane shook her head. "Someone killed once, yes? I doubt they'd worry about doing it again."

Chapter Seventeen

Mrs. Trentworth's house was in the Bloomsbury neighborhood, one Cecilia never had the opportunity to visit with her parents but which she knew was filled with artistic and literary sorts, and she had always been curious to venture there. She felt a tiny bit disappointed to see it looked just like any other respectable neighborhood, with rows of tidy houses, small gardens, nannies pushing prams along the walkways for one last evening airing.

The Trentworth residence was tucked back on a small, quiet lane, Barbon Close, a narrow, tall, dark redbrick home. The windows and the open door radiated a warm, glowing golden light that silhouetted the laughing crowd making its way up the polished stone steps. Cecilia glimpsed bright cashmere shawls, loose-fitting frocks in Liberty-patterned cottons, velvet jackets on the men, all that she had imagined.

She smoothed the skirt of her coral-colored silk dress,

trimmed with fluttering sleeves of dark-gold lace, and hoped she might look quite artistic enough for such a crowd. She certainly knew she didn't compare with Aunt Maggie, who wore the latest French fashion from Patou of pale-rose chiffon and satin harem pants below a bodice banded in silver-and-gold embroidery. The shawl tossed over her shoulders was a turquoise-blue cashmere from India. Even Annabel, in her usual ultrafashionable style with amber velvet and tulle, looked a bit fusty in comparison.

"I do think we must do some shopping while we're here," Annabel whispered. "Just look at *that* gown over there!"

Cecilia looked and had to agree that the Ballets Russes–inspired tunic gown of various shades of green, from deepest emerald to palest seafoam, was amazing. The lady who wore it tossed back her head of auburn curls and laughed with her companions as if she hadn't a care in the world. And standing next to her was a man so beautiful that Cecilia couldn't help but stop and gawk just a bit. He was tall, lithe, golden haired, a veritable Apollo. Did people look like that in real life?

The inside of the house was no less impressive. It could have been a perfectly conventional foyer, with a parquet floor and a staircase winding up to the noise and light of a drawing room, but it was hung with antique tapestries of a Tudor hunting party and lined with blue-and-white Chinese vases on marble plinths. The scent of incense hung in the air, smoky and sweet, and two sinuous Italian greyhounds greeted the guests with a twinkle of their beaded collars. As they made their way up that staircase, she saw the blue silk–papered wall was lined with bright, vivid French paintings, all bold brushstrokes and movement, and Cecilia began to think that Jane's suggestion of a life as an independent, modern London lady would not be so terrible at all. A house like this, voyages to Italy and Greece, Egypt once in a while, sounded quite enticing. All she needed now was an independent income like Aunt Maggie's.

"Maggie, darling! I was so happy you had returned to Town just in time for my little soiree," a lady cried from the head of the stairs. She was tall and very thin, in a draped caftan of green-and-blue peacock-like silk, a matching feathered turban on her head. She held a dog under her arm, a snapping Pomeranian with an amber-and-topaz collar to match the lady's earrings.

"Mariah, I could never miss it," Maggie answered. She exchanged air-kisses with the lady, who left a cloud of some spring-sweet, exotic perfume in the air.

"Mariah, this is my goddaughter, Lady Cecilia Bates, and Miss Annabel Clarke. They're visiting me for a few days. I do hope you don't mind my bringing them," Maggie said.

"Certainly not! The more the merrier, especially when they are such beauties," Mariah Trentworth said with a loud laugh, leaning down to kiss Cecilia and Annabel in turn. She put the dog down before it could bite anyone, and it scampered off. "Bates, Bates—are you from the Danby Hall Bateses, by any chance, my dear?"

"Yes, Lord and Lady Avebury are my parents," Cecilia answered. "And Miss Clarke is our guest at Danby, all the way from America."

"America! Oh, how thrilling." Mrs. Trentworth fitted a cigarette into an amber holder, and one of the passing gentlemen guests lit it for her. She exhaled a silvery plume of smoke and smiled. "Do you know how to round up cattle, Miss Clarke? Or have you ever lived in a teepee? I would so like to try that myself."

Annabel frowned. "Not at all, I'm afraid, Mrs. Trentworth. My father is one of the richest men in San Francisco, quite a large city. I'm too enamored of hot running water in the bath to try a teepee."

Mrs. Trentworth squinted through the smoke. "Oh? What a pity. I did have so many questions about buffalo." She took another inhalation. "Wait a minute, my darlings—isn't there something quite shocking going on at Danby now? A cold-blooded murder or some such thing."

"I am afraid that is true, Mrs. Trentworth," Cecilia answered. "Mrs. Amelia Price, the suffragette, just died in the village."

"Of course! That was it. Appalling. Mrs. Price was so extraordinary; she'll be much missed. One does think of the countryside as being all verdant silence, but one can be thought safe nowhere these days."

"Are you a member of the Women's Suffrage Union, then, Mrs. Trentworth?" Annabel asked.

Mrs. Trentworth gave a pealing laugh. "Oh no, I am much too busy with my own Theosophical and artistic pursuits."

"You are a spirit medium?" Cecilia said, thinking of Cora Black's ghostly interests.

Mrs. Trentworth's expression turned solemn. "I am not so gifted myself. My place is to seek out and assist those who are, as well as finding talented artists and musicians who just need a soupçon of help to find their audience." A new crowd flowed up the stairs, and she waved them through. "Oh, but do go into the drawing room, my dears, and enjoy yourselves! Dance, my darlings, dance, dance—it is what youth is for, I say."

As Mrs. Trentworth greeted more newcomers, Aunt Maggie led them through a narrow passage, the walls painted sea green and lined with more paintings almost from floor to ceiling. More French landscapes, a few portraits, and strange images of brightly colored shapes and squiggles that seemed to portray nothing at all. Cecilia thought they were fascinating.

"What an interesting woman," Annabel mused. "Can one really make a career in England of finding new artists and sponsoring spirit mediums?"

"And poets and playwrights. Mariah isn't choosy about her patronages," Maggie said with a laugh. "Of course, one can make a career of anything one likes, Miss Clarke, as long as a lady has an inheritance first. Mrs. Trentworth's father was the head of a large shipbuilding firm in Belfast, and her husband invented some kind of electric heater contraption."

Cecilia was impressed. How fast the world was changing! When she was a child, she would never have met anyone artistic or in "trade." She wasn't really sure her mother would approve of it now, but it was all terribly fascinating.

They emerged at the end of the corridor into a large drawing room, crowded with people. The tall windows were open, letting the breeze catch at the silk and gauze curtains. The furniture of white-painted chintz and brocade upholstered chairs and sofas was pushed against the flower-papered walls to make room for a dance floor in the middle of the space and a long table laden with refreshments and bottles of wine. A phonograph played a waltz for the couples who already circled the floor, and the air smelled even more of incense and expensive perfumes.

"How marvelous it all is," Cecilia breathed.

"Indeed," Annabel said, smiling at a handsome young man nearby, who blushed at her gaze. He reached for her hand, quite without being properly introduced, and whirled her into the dance. They soon disappeared into the kaleidoscope of ever-shifting color and light and movement.

Aunt Maggie led Cecilia to the refreshment table, where they took two silver Turkish goblets of punch. "Now, do go slowly, Cec dear," she said. "Knowing Mariah, there could be almost anything in there."

Cecilia took a sip. It seemed light, fruity, sweet, but her tongue immediately went numb and her head swam. "Yes, I see what you mean. You do know the most fascinating people, Aunt Maggie."

Maggie laughed. "Just don't tell Emmaline I brought you here. She would never let you out of Danby without a guard again."

Cecilia shuddered to think of it. The world's door just now seemed to be creaking open for her. She couldn't bear for it to slam closed again.

She studied the crowd over the silver rim of her cup, the daring fashions, the laughter, the free chatter. "Do you really think any of these people knew Mrs. Price?"

"I'm sure they must have," Aunt Maggie answered. "Suffrage and other radical political ideas often go hand in hand with artistic experimentation, and Mariah is famous for her painters and sculptors and poets, you know." She studied the swirling dancers with narrowed eyes. "You may want to talk to Lady Stonely over there. I think her son used to be a law clerk for Henry Price before he decided to be an artist of social protest collages instead."

"Mr. Price makes collages?" Cecilia gasped, unable to hear very well with the noise of the room.

Aunt Maggie laughed. "Of course not, though a little artistic expression might do his stuffy heart some good. Lady Stonely's son. I think he lives in Pigalle in Paris now, but his mother might know some gossip from his old job. Or Miss Reade, the young lady in the eau de Nil tunic gown. She used to go about with Mary Winter, before that lady was married."

"Margaret, my love!" a man in an aubergine velvet jacket called, and Maggie disappeared with him into the crowd.

Cecilia got a refill of the punch, which was indeed a titch heady but quite delicious, and made her way around the edge of the room, listening to snatches of conversation about new paintings, the narrow-mindedness of the Royal Academy, the state of upheaval in Russia, Parisian ballet. At last she glimpsed Lady Stonely, the mother of the law clerk turned artist, sitting on an emerald velvet settee near the windows. Plump and silver haired in her bronze-colored silk, she looked like every other matron Cecilia saw at London parties, but her smile was kind.

"Would you mind terribly if I joined you?" Cecilia asked.

"Not at all!" Lady Stonely said with a wider smile, and

patted the space next to her. "Dear Mariah's parties are entirely delightful, but one's feet do get weary of dancing. I'm Lady Stonely."

"Thank you. I'm Lady Cecilia Bates. I'm visiting my godmother, Margaret Solent."

"Oh yes, dear Maggie. I am quite aching to hear all about her latest journey. Are you a traveler yourself, Lady Cecilia?"

"Not yet, I'm afraid. Just a little country mouse. My home is at Danby Hall in Yorkshire."

"Danby, Danby. Now why does that sound so familiar?" She fluttered her lace fan faster, as if it would help her thoughts. "Oh yes. Oh, dear me. Didn't Amelia Price recently meet a most unfortunate end near there?"

Scandalous news *did* travel far and fast. "Yes, sadly. In the village. I had just attended her rally and found it very inspirational."

Lady Stonely clucked in sympathy. "And you had to escape to London to leave the sadness behind. You poor dear."

They sat in silence for a moment, watching the whirl of the dancers as the music grew louder. Cecilia glimpsed Annabel at the refreshment table, surrounded by three admirers. "I understand your son worked with Mr. Price?"

Lady Stonely's serene smile flickered. "Only for a short time. It was my dear late husband's wish that Samuel might pursue a career in the law. He obtained the position for Samuel, you see, but Sammie always wanted to be an artist. He has quite an extraordinary talent. When Lord Stonely died, Samuel left Mr. Price's office and went to stay in Paris. Dear Mariah has purchased several of his works."

"Was it only the love of art that drove your son away from that office, then?"

Lady Stonely shook her head sadly. "My dear, how perceptive you are. Are you one of Mariah's spiritual adepts, then?"

Cecilia smiled. "I fear not. Just a nosy parker."

Lady Stonely laughed and fluttered her fan faster. "Well, you are correct. It was not merely art, though law would never have made Sammie happy. I rather wonder if a more sympathetic employer would have made the work less an anathema to him. Mr. Price, though quite esteemed in the profession, was—well, rather set in his ways. He ruled with an iron fist. And since his son-in-law was working with him then, there was not much room for anyone else to advance. Though I did hear that Mr. Winter left his father-in-law to take a position elsewhere. Most strange."

Cecilia did like Lady Stonely; she seemed so open and friendly. "And do you think Mr. Price ruled his family with just such an iron fist?"

Lady Stonely sighed and shrugged. She took drinks from a passing footman's tray and handed one to Cecilia. "Don't so many men do that, my dear? Such insistence on being sole master of their house. My own dear Stonely was kind but had the same tendencies at times. I can't imagine a man like Henry Price would even bother with the kindness. If he wouldn't even help his son-in-law in the end . . ."

"Perhaps Mr. Winter was unsatisfactory at his work?"

"Or stole from the till. One does hear of such things happening." She leaned closer to whisper to Cecilia, "Henry

Price is a rich man, with the highest caliber of clients. Yet they do say he may have had some financial reverses lately."

Cecilia whispered back, "What sort of reverses?"

"Some unfortunate investments. And, of course, his wife leaving him to be a suffragette—that couldn't have done his professional reputation any good. The gossip has been thick as the fog about that, I tell you, my dear! *Thick.* And things might be changing in a house like this one, but a man like Mr. Price . . ."

A man like Henry Price wouldn't take kindly to his wife making a laughingstock of him. Or an embezzling son-in-law. The Price family drama just grew larger and larger. But could Henry Price have been in Danby Village on the night his wife died?

"I do beg your pardon," a low, rich voice said. "I know this is terribly bold, but would you do me the honor of a dance?"

Cecilia turned—and froze. Standing before her was the Apollo she had glimpsed on the way in, and up close he was even lovelier. And he was looking at *her.*

"I . . ." she began and trailed off, not sure what to say. They had not been introduced, after all, but Mrs. Trentworth's didn't seem the place to worry about such niceties.

"Go on!" Lady Stonely whispered, giving her a nudge. "If I was twenty years younger . . ."

"Yes, thank you," Cecilia managed to say, and she reached for his hand. Whoever he was, she found out he was an exceptional dancer as he twirled her into the crowd. For a moment, she was dizzy with it all.

"I don't think I've seen you at Mrs. Trentworth's before,"

he said, whirling her around and around until she laughed with giddiness.

"I've never been here before. I'm just visiting my god-mother for a few days, and she's friends with Mrs. Trentworth. I've heard such exciting things about her salons."

"I thought you might be one of her new artists. Or an opera singer, or trance medium. She's had several of those here lately, quite amusing."

"Are there séances here often, then?"

"Sometimes, yes. Disembodied voices, tables shaking, even some ectoplasm once. My old mates at Oxford would certainly laugh to think I attended."

Cecilia remembered Cora's "gifts." "Has a medium named Cora Black ever been here?"

His handsome face turned thoughtful. "That name does sound familiar. Ah yes, a thin lady, with frizzy reddish hair, quite intense?"

"Yes, that sounds like her. Did she summon up any spirits, then?"

"She did take on a very weird voice, said she was chan-neling an ancient Indian guru. But then she fainted, and the séance was quite over. She didn't seem well, I'm afraid. I saw her home in my car, and she was very quiet, seemed al-most feverish, poor lady. Are you quite sure you're not a me-dium, too?"

Cecilia laughed. "Quite, quite sure. I'm just a country lady. Though they do say my family's home has a ghost. The Blue Lady. I'm not sure I'd *want* to talk to her; the rumor is that she only appears when tragedy is about to befall the family."

He spun her in a wide circle, and she clung dizzily to his shoulders to keep from falling. He didn't *feel* like someone who spent all his days at louche salons, but rather someone who hunted and shot and fished. She wondered who he was. She *knew* he was a distraction from her purpose in London. "Do you remember if anyone was with Miss Black that night?"

He frowned in thought. "Yes, there was. We all thought she was some sort of assistant, but I must say she didn't look at all ethereal. A very stolid, middle-aged sort of matron in a dark-blue suit."

It sounded a bit like Harriet Palmer, but Cecilia couldn't figure out why that lady would attend a séance. From her appearance, and what her niece Bridget had told Jane, Cecilia wouldn't have thought she was a séance sort.

"So," he said as he led her through another twisting, dipping movement of the dance, his touch light, "if you aren't a medium, could you be an artist? Maybe an actress? You do have a rather Shakespearean look about you, if I may be so bold. Ophelia, or Juliet."

Cecilia laughed and felt her cheeks warm with a blush. "Not at all. I'm—well, not much of anything yet."

"Now that I cannot believe."

"Maybe I just haven't found my path yet. What about you? Are you an artist?"

"The merest dilettante, I'm afraid. I do appreciate art, though, so Mrs. Trentworth takes pity on me and invites me to her soirees."

The music changed then, to a fashionable tango, which Cecilia hadn't been allowed to learn. She stepped back from her handsome partner, feeling rather breathless. "Thank you for the dance. I did enjoy it."

He smiled, a piratical, bold white slash that made her feel out of breath all over again. "As did I. I hope you'll partner me again later."

Cecilia nodded and hurried away to find Annabel with her admirers near the open windows, a champagne glass in her hand. "Cecilia, you clever thing! Dancing with the Marquess of Eversham. They say he is the most eligible of eligible bachelors."

"What!" Cecilia cried. She scanned the crowd for her erstwhile partner, so handsome and mysterious, but he had vanished. She had heard of the marquess, of course—who had not? All the other debs had giggled over him during the Season, hoping he would show up at a ball or reception, but he never did. Mysterious as well as rich and titled. "I thought he was an artist or something."

Annabel laughed. "Oh, Cec! For an earl's daughter, you *are* a funny one. He seemed quite smitten with you, too."

"I am sure that's not true. And anyway, he seems to have disappeared."

"Oh, never mind that. He's sure to find you again, anyway." Annabel took Cecilia's arm and strolled with her along the edges of the room, leaving her admirers looking after her sadly. "I heard the most delicious gossip about the Prices from Mary Winter's old friend Miss Reade. It seems Mr. and Mrs. Price did not separate just because of Amelia Price's suffrage activities. Neither of them was faithful at all. And they say Mr. Price might indeed wish to marry again."

"Really?" Cecilia found she was not very surprised to hear that. She had had an inkling and was curious to find out more. The Prices definitely did not seem devoted to each other. "Any word on who they were cheating with, then?"

"Not a solid name, but just leave it to me. I'm good at ferreting out gossip, you know."

Cecilia was certainly coming to realize that. Annabel was shrewd and pragmatic, giving nothing away while her charm invited confidences from others. She knew she would have to be very careful once Annabel was her sister-in-law. "I suppose Henry Price could be with a typist from his work, or a dancer or actress. And once he's out of a respectable period of mourning, I'm sure he could find some young deb to marry. But who would Amelia Price have been with?"

"She was a lovely woman, for her age," Annabel said. "And smart and fun, from what everyone says. This crowd quite adored her. Most unlike what I would have imagined from a suffragette! They are usually so—humorless, aren't they? So stern. It could be anyone, really. How delicious." She took a drink from the refreshment table and took a sip with one of her catlike smiles. "Oh, Cec. I am enjoying England more and more."

Chapter Eighteen

M y word, Lady Cecilia!" Jane gasped as she stared out the bus window at the London streets flying past, the Houses of Parliament and the river in the distance looking like a picture postcard, the crowds swarming the streets. "Do this many people really live here in London?"

Cecilia laughed, studying a group of businessmen in their somber bowler hats trying to keep the chapeaux from blowing away in the wind. "Most of them, probably. But surely there were even more people in New York? They say the streets there are so crowded no one can ever cross."

"That may be true in some neighborhoods, my lady. The hotel where I was employed was always busy, and we worked all hours so I hardly stepped outside. And I would always see the same people in my parents' neighborhood in New Jersey. Everyone always knew where we were, what we were doing, and they were sure to tell our parents if we stepped out of line."

"That sounds exactly like Danby," Cecilia said. People who had always known her, who knew everything that happened to her family. "How I should love to see New York, though! Everything new and full of excitement."

"Or maybe Egypt or India, like Mrs. Solent? They do sound fascinating."

"I see Aunt Maggie's travel tales have captured you, as well, Jane." They had stayed up late into the night after returning from Mrs. Trentworth's, listening to Aunt Maggie's magical tales of the places she had seen. Cecilia and Jane had set out to explore the city early the next morning while Annabel shopped, and Cecilia couldn't help but yawn from staying up so late.

"It does sound like something from a book, my lady. Elephants and ancient temples! I never thought I would even see England. Bombay might be too much to hope for."

"Maybe not, if you stay in Miss Clarke's employ. Patrick seems like such a hermit, but he often talks about going off to some jungle to hunt for rare plant specimens. Annabel could go with him."

Jane laughed. "Can you picture Miss Clarke in a pith helmet, hacking her way through the jungle, my lady?"

Cecilia tried to imagine it, but it was indeed difficult. "It is a bit of a stretch, I admit. A Worth gown might not be so useful in the Amazon. Yet I get the sense, Jane dear, that there's more to Annabel than might meet the eye. And travel isn't always jungles and cannibals. She might be vicereine of India, if she can persuade Patrick to try his hand at politics."

"Would Lord Bellham do that, then?"

"It's hard to imagine, I know. Probably being an earl will be enough of a challenge to him. But wouldn't you like to be lady's maid at a viceregal court?"

Jane gazed thoughtfully out the bus window. "I think I like it here in England, my lady. Especially London."

"Me, too. I admit, Jane, I do sometimes wonder what it would be like to live on my own here in London. Not like at my parents' house, pouring tea and never going out alone, but my own flat. Maybe a job of some sort. Or university, like my friend Maud Rainsley. She does love it there." Cecilia let herself imagine it, just for a moment. Books and studies, friends her own age. "That sounds silly, doesn't it?"

"Not at all, my lady! When I lived at home, my brothers were always yelling and getting into my things, my mother handing me chores. I could never go out to a dance or even for a walk. I imagined my own home, too. A room that was only mine."

"Why is such a simple, human thing as wanting our own space, to do as we like, so impossible for us women?"

"Is that why you went to hear Mrs. Price's speeches, then?"

"Perhaps. There *are* alternatives out there, Jane. We are living in the twentieth century now. Things are changing every day. Maybe we just have to be brave enough to reach out and grab them." Yet reaching out for her own life had not ended well for Mrs. Price.

They were silent for a long moment, watching the city streets go by.

"Oh, my lady! Is that grand place the National Gallery?"

"And look over there, the church of St. Martin-in-the-Fields."

Jane sighed happily. "My mother will never believe I've seen such things."

"Even above seeing things such as murder, Jane?"

Jane frowned. "Well, my lady—what my mother doesn't know won't hurt her."

Cecilia laughed. "An excellent motto for us both."

They rode the bus until they reached Tudor Street in the City, an area Cecilia knew little about compared to Mayfair and Belgravia, since she did little business. It would hardly cause gossip if she was seen there, but the wide, bustling streets were lined with banks and law offices, not a lady's usual purview.

Mr. Winter's law office was at the end of a smaller side lane, next to a gated garden. The nondescript, old brick building had polished marble front steps and a brass plaque at the door: "Bird and Withers, Law."

"I think this must be it," Cecilia said. She marched up the steps with a confidence she didn't quite feel—an earl's daughter seldom had business with London attorneys, after all. She was quite glad she had worn what she felt was her most businesslike, albeit stylish, attire, a new bronze-brown wool and velvet suit and matching wide-brimmed hat.

The front office was not large, but most efficiently yet comfortably furnished with leather-upholstered chairs, landscapes and hunting scenes on the walls, and dark-green curtains casting the deep-burgundy carpet into shadow. A lady sat at the polished mahogany desk behind a typewriting machine. She was neatly dressed in a navy blue suit, her graying hair tied back in a tight knot. As the bell on the door rang, she peered at the newcomers over her spectacles, watchful and warily welcoming. Cecilia wondered if she led the independent London life Cecilia and Jane had speculated about.

"May I help you, madam?" she asked, her fingers poised over the typewriter keys.

"Yes." Cecilia took out one of her calling cards from her handbag. "I am Lady Cecilia Bates, daughter of Lord Avebury of Danby Hall. I'm looking for a Mr. Montgomery Winter? He's an associate here, I believe."

The lady's expression softened as she studied the card. "Do you have business with Mr. Winter, Lady Cecilia?"

"Not myself, precisely. Our family's attorney, Mr. Jermyn, said Mr. Winter wrote to him seeking a position. Mr. Jermyn, of course, deals with a great deal of—sensitive information working for my family. I am sure *you* understand, working in the profession yourself, Miss . . ."

"Miss Smythe, Lady Cecilia." A small smile touched her lips. "And yes, I do understand. A family such as yours . . ."

"Quite so. I happened to be in London for a few days and agreed to make some discreet inquiries. One cannot be too careful these days."

"Indeed not. You are quite wise." Miss Smythe waved them to a pair of leather chairs in front of her desk. "I'm afraid Mr. Winter is out of the city, and Mr. Wither is in court today, Lady Cecilia, if you would care to make an appointment with him?"

Cecilia wasn't sure. She didn't want word to get around that she had been there. "I would, certainly, though I would hate to take up his time. He must be terribly busy."

Miss Smythe sighed wearily. "Especially since Mr. Winter's departure. This is a very old office, and we have many clients who rely on us."

"And you have worked here long, Miss Smythe?"

"Since I left secretarial school years ago. I was just filing then, but I worked my way up to personal secretary to Mr. Wither." She smiled proudly.

"Then I am sure you must know just as much about what happens here as Mr. Wither himself." Cecilia leaned forward to whisper confidentially, "Probably more, I would say."

Miss Smythe glanced around. "It is true Mr. Wither and his partner Mr. Bird are not often here. Court appointments, you know. But I am always at my desk."

Cecilia studied the closed office doors around them, all in close proximity to Miss Smythe's desk, and realized she must be able to hear much of what happened daily. "What was your opinion of Mr. Winter when he was here?"

Miss Smythe leaned forward. "We did have high hopes when he arrived, Lady Cecilia. He came recommended by his father-in-law, and Mr. Price is highly respected in the profession. At first, all seemed to go well enough, if not quite as well as Mr. Wither hoped. Mr. Winter did not bring in the clients it was imagined he would."

"Law did not—prove to be Mr. Winter's passion?"

Miss Smythe shook her head. "He even *lost* some of his

clients. And then there was the gossip about his wife's mother. You do know about Mrs. Amelia Price?"

"The suffragette, yes, of course." Cecilia decided to feign ignorance of the family and Mrs. Price's sad end. "Did Mrs. Winter follow in her mother's footsteps?"

"Certainly not! Quiet as a little mouse, on the rare occasion we saw her. Mr. Winter could not be blamed, of course, for his wife's relations, and if he was merely discreet about them, I am sure Mr. Wither could have overlooked it all. Times *are* changing, and there are all sorts out there. Look at Lady Constance Lytton!"

"But Mr. Winter was not quiet about the connection?"

Miss Smythe pursed her lips. "He did not like his mother-in-law, no. But really it was the matter of the Cartwell case. It was terribly bungled and cost us a lot of business."

"Indeed?" Cecilia said. She remembered vaguely the Cartwell case but didn't know Monty Winter was involved.

"After that, Mr. Wither had no choice but to dismiss Mr. Winter. Mr. Cartwell insisted on it, and of course he has a great deal of influence with many other clients."

"And did Mr. Winter go discreetly?"

Miss Smythe shook her head. "I do fear not. We are accustomed to working with gentlemen here, Lady Cecilia, and I confess I was rather shocked by it all. He became quite angry about it all, even shouted! I do think he might have blamed his mother-in-law once. Most odd." She sighed sadly. "The poor man. I thought a physician might need to be called for; he turned quite purple and nearly smashed that lamp on the cabinet over there. And it is eighteenth-century, very rare."

Cecilia remembered seeing those little flashes of Mr. Winter's temper toward his wife while at Danby Village. "Shocking indeed."

"He had to be shown out quite forcefully by two of our clerks. Mr. Wither could barely speak for half an hour. And now we must find a new partner. I daresay Mr. Wither will be far more careful in the future."

"I'm sure he will."

"And I hope, Lady Cecilia, you will discreetly warn your Mr. Jermyn? If he writes to us for a reference . . ."

"Of course I will tell him, in the strongest language I can," Cecilia answered. "You need not fear hearing any more about Mr. Winter from us, Miss Smythe."

"Thank you." Miss Smythe opened her appointment book. "Do you still wish to schedule time with Mr. Wither, Lady Cecilia?"

"Oh no, I'm sure I have all the information I require. You have been most helpful, Miss Smythe. Mr. Wither is very fortunate to employ you."

Once back out on the street, Jane said, "Well, that was hardly surprising, was it, my lady? After the way Mr. Winter behaved in Danby Village."

"Not surprising, no." They turned toward the bus stop, Cecilia ignoring the men in their businesslike suits and bowlers who watched them walk past. "Mr. Winter certainly doesn't seem the sort of man to build a career at a place like Bird and Wither. I'm sure Mr. Price was mortified."

Eliza Casey

236

"If he can behave like that at his work—how does he act with his wife?"

Cecilia shook her head. "Yes. Poor Mary Winter. He must bully her, too."

"Yet she does seem quick to defend him, to take his side against her own mother and sister."

"What choice does she have? According to Miss Smythe, it sounds as if Mr. Winter thinks his mother-in-law's notoriety cost him his position, not his own actions."

"Of course he would think that, wouldn't he? Men like that always blame everyone except themselves."

"I fear you are too right, Jane. Is Mr. Price a man like that, as well? Maybe he blames his wife for creating scandal and gossip in his venerable career." Cecilia glanced at the little enameled watch pinned to her velvet lapel. "We should find the headquarters of the Women's Suffrage Union, before it grows too late. Even thinking about a man like Monty Winter gives me a headache. Shall we find a tea shop first?"

"Excellent idea, my lady. And the dressmaker. Remember?"

Cecilia sighed. "How could I forget?"

❧

The Union headquarters, where mostly officers of the organization met to plan strategy, seemed like some wonderfully mysterious temple, Cecilia thought, guarded by vestal virgins, pillared halls holding on to secret oaths. But it was nothing like that at all. It was a large, factorylike room above a printer's shop, lined with plain pine desks and filing cabinets, the walls hung with corkboards covered with notes and pamphlets. Typewriters clicked, and the air smelled of stale coffee and chalk dust and ladies' rosewater scent. The flowery sweetness was nothing like the perfume on the letters at Primrose Cottage.

The only color was a large "Women's Suffrage Union" banner of white, green, purple, and gold hung on the far wall and a portrait of Amelia Price draped in black crepe. Cecilia tilted her head to study it, the painted image just as beautiful as the real woman had been, but more serene.

"You're not a reporter, are you?" a lady asked loudly. She came from around a table where she had been studying a large document, the cuffs of her shirtwaist stained with ink, her brown hair sliding from its pins. "Because we still have no comment on Mrs. Price's tragic passing."

"Not at all," Cecilia answered, taking Anne's letter from her handbag. "I'm Lady Cecilia Bates, of Danby Hall in York-shire, and this is Miss Jane Hughes. We met Mrs. Price shortly before her death, and I was so much moved by her words. I wanted to pay my condolences. I have here a letter from Miss Anne Price."

The lady scanned the short note, and her face softened in a smile. "Lady Cecilia. How do you do? I am Miss Wheeler, vice secretary of the Union, but trying to keep matters mov-ing forward here until Anne or Mrs. Palmer returns. It is no easy task; as you can see, there is much grief." She gestured to the busy, noisy room behind her. "Please, do follow me."

She led them into a small, windowless office in the corner of the space and poured out cups of thick, bitter coffee. "Please, Lady Cecilia, Miss Hughes. How are matters *really* progressing in Yorkshire? We hear only snatches of news here. Is Cora truly ill again?"

"I'm afraid so. She's taking Mrs. Price's death quite badly."

Miss Wheeler rubbed at her eyes, as if weary or sad. "Of course she is. She quite idolized Mrs. Price. We all did."

"And I think confessing at the inquest to pushing Mrs. Price down the stairs has not helped her state of mind."

Miss Wheeler snorted. "That's all nonsense, of course. Cora would never have touched Mrs. Price in anger. And with the TB, she would hardly have been able to shove a cat."

"TB?" Jane said sharply. "Is that what's wrong with her, then?"

"She seemed quite energetic when she first arrived in Danby Village," Cecilia added. Though the flushed cheeks and bright eyes, the manic energy followed by collapse she had seen in Cora, did point to such an illness.

"Yes, Cora Black is certainly one of the most ardent workers for the cause," Miss Wheeler said. "She will do anything at all she thinks might help. But the last hunger strike she went on severely weakened her constitution."

"Has she ever used her spirit medium gifts in aid of the Union?" Jane asked.

Miss Wheeler shrugged. "She does card readings for us on rainy afternoons sometimes. I am not a believer myself, but I certainly have no reason to curtail the amusements of others. And Cora has brought much comfort and enjoyment to so many of our ladies."

"So you don't think she could have harmed Mrs. Price?" Cecilia said.

Miss Wheeler firmly shook her head. "They were staunch allies in our war for freedom. I admit Cora sometimes took medicine that gave her terrible dreams, even caused sleep-walking once or twice, but . . ."

"She wasn't that strong even under the influence of those dreams?" Jane said.

For the first time, a touch of doubt flickered across Miss Wheeler's expression. "I shouldn't think so. But I haven't seen Cora in some time, as they've been on a speaking tour. Perhaps her condition has changed."

"What about any enemies?" Cecilia asked.

"Mrs. Price had many, of course." Miss Wheeler busied herself tidying papers on the desk, tapping them into piles. "This office and her flat are often vandalized, paint and rotten eggs, things of that sort, and poison-pen letters. She was knocked unconscious once on a march. And, of course, her marriage didn't end well. A man like Henry Price could never bear a wife who thought for herself."

Cecilia nodded, remembering the rumors of infidelities. "Was her London home kept secure? Anne said her mother had valuable jewels she always wore."

"She did have a contingent of ladies who were a body-guard of sorts, and had taken lessons in Eastern martial arts. But Mrs. Price never seemed much concerned. Were things stolen from her cottage?" Miss Wheeler's face contorted, as if she struggled to hold back tears. "How awful it would be for such a great lady to meet her end through common robbery!"

Or through a drunken fall. No wonder Cora wanted to protect Mrs. Price's reputation when all else was lost. "No one is really sure what happened yet. Where will the Union go now with their officers?"

"There will be a vote for a new president in due course. I am sure Anne will stand for it, as might Mrs. Palmer."

"Would Mrs. Palmer continue on as Mrs. Price has?" Cecilia asked. She recalled rumors of quarrels over the state of the Union, differences in opinion as to where the cause should go next.

Miss Wheeler frowned. "It's impossible to say at this point. Things are so very uncertain. But we will certainly continue the fight, one way or another. Perhaps you might join us, Lady Cecilia?"

"Yes," Cecilia said. "Yes, I think I just might."

❧

Aunt Maggie's club was on the top two floors of an exclusive hotel in Mayfair, all elegant white and gilt paint, comfortable chintz settees, desks for letter writing, and shelves and shelves of books, mostly about exotic travel destinations and travel memoirs. Large doors opened to a library, a cardroom, a dining room set with heavy silver and large flower arrangements, no need spared. Maggie and Annabel were already having tea in the palm court, a string quartet playing discreetly behind the potted plants, light streaming from the glass-domed roof.

"Oh, my dears, there you are at last!" Aunt Maggie called. "Do sit down and have some of the club's delicious crab salad sandwiches. Tea, or perhaps something bubbly? You do look exhausted to bits. A busy day?"

Jane paused, looking quite awed as she studied the opulent space, but Cecilia nudged her into one of the cushioned wicker chairs and handed her a teacup. Aunt Maggie waved her hand to order a bottle of champagne.

"We visited Mr. Winter's office—or should we say his former office. And the Women's Suffrage Union headquarters, not to mention a couple of ateliers to order a new frock. All on buses!" Cecilia gestured to the ribbon-bound box at her feet, which contained a lovely white lace gown one of Madame Handley's clients had ordered but canceled, and happened to fit Cecilia quite well. She wiggled her aching toes in her kid boots as she told Maggie and Annabel all they had learned from Miss Smythe and Miss Wheeler.

"We had quite an interesting day ourselves, didn't we, Annabel?" Maggie said. She waited for one of the maids in her crisp white cap and apron to pour out the wine and leave more cakes before she went on. "We went to Madame Haya's Turkish baths."

"The Turkish baths!" Cecilia cried, delighted to imagine Aunt Maggie and the highly elegant Annabel wrapped in towels and sitting in clouds of steam. "Did you use a hookah? See disreputable ladies?" She sighed happily as she sipped at the champagne and let the bubbles tickle her nose. An independent London life of champagne and baths would be quite delightful.

"Oh, Cec, no one but your grandmother would ever think such a place scandalous now," Maggie said with a laugh, straightening her large, sapphire-blue velvet hat. "Even Queen Mary has visited Madame Haya's. And it's the best place to hear all the gossip."

"It seems Mr. Price *is* hoping to marry again, and might even have a specific young lady in mind," Annabel said. "And Mrs. Price was seen with some unknown young man at the park and theater. *Ages* younger than her, they said, but no one knows who he is. Delicious."

"We met old Lady Fermoy," Maggie said. "She was at your debut ball, remember? She always wears those old Victorian bonnets. But she has the most prodigious memory I have ever encountered; she remembers every betrothal, affair, divorce, babies who looked nothing like their putative fathers . . ."

Annabel took a sip of champagne and giggled. "I daresay she was bridesmaid at the wedding of Princess Charlotte and King Leopold, she was so ancient! When she dropped her towel . . ."

"Oh, pish, Annabel. Victoria and Albert's wedding, maybe. But then, none of us is getting any younger." Maggie patted at her abundant, sun-streaked hair.

"But maybe she remembered Amelia Price when she was Miss Merriman?" Cecilia asked, recalling that her own grandmother had said Amelia was the belle of the Season then.

"Oh yes. It seems that Miss Merriman had her pick of suitors. She was engaged at least three times before Mr. Price. And one of them was . . ."

"That dreadful Lord Elphin!" Annabel cried.

"No!" Cecilia gasped. "Lord Elphin was once engaged to Mrs. Price?"

"I'm sure he couldn't always have been a reclusive gargoyle," Maggie said. She refilled everyone's glasses. "Lady

Fermoy even said he was rather handsome, if a quite shy man. Everyone was surprised when Miss Merriman accepted him."

"But it didn't last long," Annabel said with a sad sigh. "And then Lord Elphin left London, never to return. They say he did marry later, but somehow it ended quickly. Maybe he was pining for his true love."

"It's more likely she died, poor lady. Miss Merriman married Henry Price at the end of the Season, after Mr. Merriman suffered some sort of financial reversal," Maggie said.

"But why did her romance with Lord Elphin end?" Cecilia mused.

Maggie shrugged. "Even Lady Fermoy didn't know for sure. It was all very hush-hush. I shall have to ask around a bit more."

"Oooh, does that mean another visit to the baths?" Annabel clapped her hands. "I could quite get used to it. And having champagne in the afternoon."

Cecilia realized she was starting to really like Annabel Clarke. "Maybe Lord Elphin still nurses a defeated love for Mrs. Price. Maybe it's festered in him all these years, and that's why he was so hostile to her Union."

"And he was so overcome by his emotions when he saw her again he just had to kill her?" Jane whispered.

"Just like in a penny dreadful story," Cecilia said. "And he gave her ring to Guff? Or had Guff steal it for him?" She wondered if it was Lord Elphin who gave her that ring in the first place.

"Then maybe he also still has that torn scrap from her sash," Jane said.

"Oh, good thinking, Jane!" Cecilia said. "But then how do we find it?"

"I know a way," Annabel said. "The church bazaar."

"The bazaar?" Cecilia asked, confused.

"We need donations for the bring-and-buy tent, right?" Annabel said, wafting her glass. "We could go to his house and ask for one of those donations."

Cecilia shivered at the thought of Lord Elphin's ramshackle house. "I don't even know anyone who has set foot on the Elphin estate in years, except for his workers and cronies who heckled us at the rally."

Annabel used her glass to wave this away. "Pooh! He doesn't scare me. I bet he lives there like—oh, who was that character in that one book? With her old wedding cake and moldering veil?"

"Miss Havisham?" Cecilia asked.

"Yes. Pining away for his lost Miss Merriman. Kissing the scrap of her sash." Annabel sounded delighted by the macabre idea, and Cecilia found she liked her even more. "We'll call on him when we get back to Danby, have a little peek around. I can distract him while you search his desk, or whatever. Now, shall we order another bottle of champagne? Is that allowed in your club, Margaret?"

"Oh yes," Maggie said cheerfully. "It is most definitely allowed."

Chapter Nineteen

When Annabel had suggested they try to get Lord Elphin to make a donation to the church bazaar, it had seemed like quite a good idea. In London, anyway, after all that champagne at Aunt Maggie's club. Now that the task was actually before them, Cecilia wasn't quite so sure of it all.

She stared up at Lord Elphin's manor house from the seat of the governess cart. Annabel and Jane, squashed close next to her, were just as silent. Even Jack, in his basket under the seat, was quiet. While the Elphin house had never been as grand as Danby, or as modernly elegant as the Byswater estate, it had always had a respectable place in the neighborhood. Built in the Jacobean era by a family of prosperous farmers and added on to over the years, it had always been known as the seat of an old name and good English husbandry.

Now the paint was peeling, the chimney cracked, the

shutters banging loose from the old mullioned windows. The gardens around the house were long desiccated, but Cecilia knew the farm still had respectable yields, thanks to Lord Elphin's loyal bullyboy tenants. None of them seemed to be around today, though.

"It looks like the houses in the old ghost stories my granny used to tell us when we were kids," Jane said softly.

Cecilia laughed. "I think I might prefer to talk to a ghost rather than Lord Elphin."

"Oh, pooh!" Annabel said, but even she sounded a bit doubtful. "He might be a dreadful Neanderthal of a man, but he *is* just a man. And once, at least, he had the good taste to fancy a lady like Mrs. Price, right?"

"Until she rejected him, and he took to heckling women who just want to live their own lives," Cecilia said. But Annabel was right—Lord Elphin *was* just a man, and the sooner they knocked on his door, the sooner they could leave. She climbed down from the cart, tethering the mare to one of the peeling columns that supported the portico, and marched up the cracked stone steps. Annabel and Jane were right behind her.

There was no bell, just a crusty old lion's head knocker. Annabel pounded on the door with it, and they waited silently for so long that Cecilia began to wonder if Lord Elphin was fortuitously absent.

But finally, they heard the sound of a rusty lock being peeled back, and a tall, cadaverously thin, balding man in a dark butler's coat peered out at them. A dog snarled behind him. The man looked rather surprised and quite annoyed, emotions Redvers would never have betrayed at the sight of visitors.

"Yes?" the man said, pushing the dog behind him.

"How do you do? I am Lady Cecilia Bates, from Danby Hall, and this is Miss Annabel Clarke and Miss Hughes," Cecilia said, in the haughtiest voice she had learned from her mother. She took a card from her handbag. "We are on the committee for the St. Swithin's Church bazaar and wondered if perhaps Lord Elphin, as a most esteemed member of this neighborhood, might like to make a small donation to the cause. Is Lord Elphin at home, perhaps?"

The man looked quite startled. "I will ascertain." He took her card and disappeared back into the house, shutting the door. They could hear the echo of the dog barking.

"How very charming," Annabel said, her tone indicating it was anything but. She straightened the large, yellow silk and tulle hat she had bought in London. "I'm sure I'll find lots of tips for running a most proper English household here."

They waited another moment before the butler returned. "Follow me, please. His lordship will be down presently."

The inside of the Elphin house seemed just as ramshackle as the outside, with wallpaper much in need of replacing, faded carpets, scratched furniture that hadn't seen a lemon polish in many years, cobwebs around picture frames. Yet Cecilia could see that once it must have been rather lovely, and perhaps could be again. Like a castle in a fairy tale coming back to life.

The butler left them in a drawing room, closing the door behind them as he left. Cecilia was glad; they had a little privacy to snoop. And they did, each of them wandering into a corner to examine the faded furniture, the piles of dusty books and old letters.

"My heavens!" Annabel suddenly gasped. "Cec, Jane, look at this."

Cecilia and Jane hurried over to where Annabel was examining a portrait hanging near the soot-stained fireplace. Though in need of a good cleaning, Cecilia could tell it was a Frith, an image of a beautiful lady sitting on a garden bench beneath a shady, summer-green tree, a spaniel at her feet. Her dark hair was piled high in an elaborate Victorian coiffure of curls and waves, a skirt of pink-and-white lace spread around her as she studied a book in her hand.

And on her finger was a large ruby ring.

"Is that the same ring that was stolen from Mrs. Price?" Annabel asked.

"Yes," Cecilia murmured. "I used to think it was her engagement ring from Mr. Price. Anne said her mother never took it off, even though she was separated from her husband."

"But was it from Lord Elphin instead?" Jane said. "They did say she changed her mind about marrying him all those years ago. But what if she was *forced* to refuse? Like in *Lady Emily's Secret.*"

"Lady Cecilia," they heard Lord Elphin say in his gravelly voice. The three of them spun around guiltily to find him standing in the drawing room doorway, his gray hair standing on end, his necktie hastily fastened, his tweed jacket frayed. He scowled at them. "What do you want? I don't have time for visitors here. Especially not of your sort."

"My sort?" Cecilia choked out.

"Suffragette types."

Annabel gave him her most charming smile and hurried forward in a rustle of yellow silk ruffles to gently touch his arm. "How wise you are, Lord Elphin. We ladies have our own duties in the world we must see to, our proper sphere, which we were created to fill. It is quite important for us. We were, in fact, just admiring that exquisite portrait of beautiful ladyhood."

Lord Elphin actually seemed to soften a bit at her cooing words. "That is my mother. She died many years ago, and yes, she was beautiful. Always so gentle and sweet. A true lady."

"And such lovely jewels. Family pieces, I am sure," Annabel said. "Those pearls, and that ruby . . ."

"Her engagement ring," he said gruffly. "Now sadly lost, just like her. Such an unworthy world we live in."

"How very, very sad," Annabel murmured, patting his arm. "Oh, Lord Elphin, I do apologize for us taking up your time when you must be so very busy with your important estate work."

"Hmph," he snorted. "My butler says you've come about the church bazaar or some such thing."

"Oh yes, indeed," Cecilia chimed in. "We are collecting donations to help raise money for the new church roof, and everyone would be sure to bid wildly on anything you could contribute."

Lord Elphin scowled and shuffled his feet. "Well—I suppose I could donate a painting or something of the sort. My mother *did* love that church, and she is buried in the nave. Can't have the roof falling over her, I suppose."

Cecilia was startled it had been that easy. She had never dreamed he might actually make a donation! "How very kind of you! We are gathering the donations at Danby, if you would like to have it delivered, or I am sure Mr. Brown could arrange for it to be fetched."

"Not necessary," Lord Elphin said. "I will send it. In my mother's name."

"And we do hope you will join us at the bazaar," Annabel said. "It should be a lovely afternoon for everyone to gather together, so consoling after such a terrible ordeal for the village."

Lord Elphin coughed and shuffled his feet again. "I— well, yes, perhaps. If I am not too busy on the day."

"That would be a shame if you missed it," Annabel said. She gently touched the frame of the portrait, her glove coming away dusty. "You know, Lord Elphin, you have such a lovely and historic home here. So much older and more elegant than *anything* where I came from in America! A lady's touch could do so very much for it, as I am sure your mother would agree. I do know two or three charming widows who will be at the bazaar. They would so love to meet you."

To Cecilia's amazement, Lord Elphin blushed a bright pink. "My marrying days are long past, Miss Clarke."

Annabel giggled. "Oh, I am sure that cannot be true! Or—oh dear. Perhaps you *were* married once, and your true love was carried away tragically young? Have I made a great faux pas, Lord Elphin?"

"I was married briefly, very long ago. I'm sure you must know that; old Lady Avebury knows all the neighborhood gossip. But when I was young and foolish—things were quite different."

Annabel laid her gloved hand over her lace bodice. "I knew it! You do have a star-crossed true love in your past. I can always tell such things about people, being a romantic myself. One must never give up hope!"

Lord Elphin coughed and shuffled his feet again. "Maybe once I fancied myself in love, but I am no Romeo, nor ever was. Such things aren't meant to be for some of us, thankfully. Now, ladies, can I offer you some tea before you leave?"

They declined, pleading other errands, but he saw them to the door in polite enough fashion. Cecilia was astonished.

"You see, Cec," Annabel said with a bright, satisfied smile as they climbed into the cart. "Charm is always effective. You should tell that to your shouty suffragette friends." As they drove away, she turned and waved to Lord Elphin, who stood in the doorway, a strangely lonely figure. "A woman doesn't need the vote to get what she wants."

❧

The Moffats' tearoom was not very busy at that time of day, with only a few pink-skirted tables occupied with groups of ladies and a couple or two gossiping and laughing over the strawberry cakes and currant scones. But Monty and Mary Winter were seated in a shadowy corner. A tray of sandwiches and tarts sat between them, but neither seemed to be eating. Mary looked as if she had just been crying, and Monty's face was tense.

Cecilia and Jane exchanged a glance, and Cecilia wondered if Jane was considering what she herself was—Annabel's words about how charm worked far better than arguments. If only Annabel had not gone back to Danby instead of coming to tea with them!

"Mr. and Mrs. Winter," Cecilia said, approaching their table with a smile. "I'm quite surprised to see you still here in our village. I'm sure you have many duties in London waiting for you."

Monty gave her an obviously forced smile, a rather intimidating rictus under his mustache, and Mary dabbed surreptitiously at her eyes. Jane handed her a handkerchief.

"We couldn't think of leaving while arrangements are still being made for my poor mother-in-law," Monty said. "And despite the sadness of the occasion, we are finding Danby quite charming. Are we not, Mary my dear? The country idyll one can never find in wretched London."

"Oh, indeed," Mary said faintly. "Charming."

Cecilia thought of the job he once held at Bird and Wither. "Perhaps we could persuade you to stay a little longer, then. At least until after our annual church bazaar, which is always held in the gardens at Danby Hall. It's our last little celebration before winter, and we would certainly love for you to attend."

Mary looked a bit more cheerful at that. "Oh! We would be honored to attend, Lady Cecilia. Such a fine chance to meet more kind neighbors."

"Wonderful! We do love to see new faces; we get so bored with each other all the time." Cecilia leaned closer and said quietly, "This might sound terribly presumptuous, Mr. and

Mrs. Winter, but the church is always so grateful for any donations for the bring-and-buy tent. I'm in charge of it this year, and I fear St. Swithin's roof is in shocking condition. So many people adore finding treasures to buy to benefit the fund! Last year, there was even a duchess who purchased every tea cozy she could find and was utterly delighted." Appealing a bit to snobbery never hurt.

"A duchess." Mary sighed.

"We would certainly be happy to make a donation to such a worthy cause. Would we not, Mary darling?" Monty said.

"Oh yes," Mary cried. "What would your neighbors enjoy, Lady Cecilia? A nice lamp, perhaps? Or I could sew something . . ."

"Anything is most welcome," Cecilia said. "Just send it to Danby, or maybe bring it with you? Just be sure there is a label saying you were the kind donors. You are much too kind to help us at such a difficult time. I'm afraid we've kept you from your tea for too long; do forgive us." There, now—she would soon have examples of both Lord Elphin's and the Winters' handwriting to compare to the scraps from Primrose Cottage.

Mary smiled and handed Jane back the handkerchief. She looked more cheerful, and as Cecilia walked away, she glanced back to see them finally eating their sandwiches. She and Jane sat down at their own table near the window and gestured for a serving of lemon cake to fortify them until Danby dinner.

Jane passed Cecilia the handkerchief under the table, and Cecilia took a quick sniff of the muslin folds. Mary had previously worn a heady, white-flowery scent, but today it smelled sharper, greener. Maybe more like the scent on the torn notes? Perhaps, then, Mary *did* write those letters after all, though it was hard to tell. Cecilia just knew she had to find more samples of the notes, maybe ones she could piece together.

❧

A black crepe wreath was on the door of Primrose Cottage even a fortnight after the death, the draperies drawn over the windows as Cecilia and Jane made their way through the garden gate. But the door opened quickly to their knock, and Nellie stood there, pale and red-eyed in her black dress. She smiled when she saw Jack's basket in Jane's arms. He had insisted on coming after waiting in the cart at Lord Elphin's.

"We are certainly sorry to disturb you at such a time, Nellie," Cecilia said. "Is it a bad moment for a call?"

"Not at all, my lady. In fact, I'm glad you're here." Nellie stepped back to let them in, and Cecilia saw that luggage was still piled high on either side of the narrow entrance corridor. "Maybe you can talk some sense into Miss Black. She insists she's going to hold a séance!"

"A séance?" Cecilia said, intrigued. She had never attended such a thing before. "What for?"

"To talk to Mrs. Price, of course. Come with me, my lady; she'll tell you about it herself."

Cecilia and Jane followed Nellie to the sitting room, where Anne and Cora sat by the empty fireplace. Anne looked tired in her black silk gown, and Cora was swathed in shawls, her face very pale as she gestured emphatically to make some point. Nellie took the pillow behind Cora's back and gave it an energetic plump. Jack leaped out of his basket and started exploring under the tables.

"Oh, Lady Cecilia, Miss Hughes," Anne said, stirring herself from her chair. She smoothed her hair back into its knot and tried to smile. "You're back from London. How was the city? I do so envy you. I can't wait until Mother's body is released to us at last and we can go home. Oh, do sit down. Nellie, could you fetch some tea?"

Cecilia and Jane sat down in two straight-backed chairs near the cluttered table. "When does the coroner think that will be?"

"Very soon, he assures us, though no fixed date yet," Anne said, her lips tightening. "Mrs. Palmer has gone back to London just this morning. I'm sure she is planning to implement her ideas for the Union, when it is *my* place as a Price to assume the leadership."

"Mrs. Price will tell us what we must do. I am sure of it," Cora said hoarsely. "And then I will drive us directly back to headquarters to follow her instructions."

Anne shook her head. "The doctor says you should not drive yet, nor excite yourself. You should rest and plan a visit to Switzerland soon. They say the clear air has enormous recuperative powers."

Cecilia gave Cora a gentle smile. "Nellie says you are planning a séance?"

Cora nodded eagerly, her cheeks glowing pink. "I am quite sure she will come through to us now. She's surely still close by."

Jane looked puzzled. "What do you expect Mrs. Price to tell you, Miss Black? Besides how to run the Union, that is."

"She thinks Mother will tell us what really happened," Anne said shortly. "Colonel Havelock has called on us and told us that no one believes Cora's tale of pushing Mother down the stairs."

"She *will* tell us," Cora cried. "I am sure of it. But we need enough people. Will you come, Lady Cecilia? Miss Hughes? Mrs. Price did like you so much. I am sure she will tell us if you're here."

Cecilia had never been at all sure she believed in ghosts, despite the tales of the Blue Lady. She'd never seen one herself and sometimes rather envied her debutante friends whose mothers had let them attend a fashionable séance or two. It sounded intriguing, strange, and doubtful—and also just the tiniest bit terrifying. What if Amelia Price *did* appear? Or worse, some malevolent entity?

Yet Cora looked so fiercely determined, and Cecilia was so overcome with curiosity that she nodded. She could tell her mother she was helping set up something for the bazaar. "Yes, of course. Who else will be here?"

"Nellie and Anne, of course," Cora said.

"Someone has to make sure you don't do yourself an injury," Anne said with a sigh.

"And Mary Winter," Cora added.

"Mrs. Winter?" Cecilia said, surprised. Mary Winter didn't seem like the sort to go in for séances, especially without her husband and with people she had little affection for. But maybe she also sought something from her mother.

"I saw her when I went to fetch some scones from the tea shop, and I asked her if she would make up the numbers," Cora said. "She seemed quite eager, though a little timid, of course."

"Maybe she's afraid of what Mother will say about her precious Monty, if she's not here to defend him," Anne said.

"Then when shall we meet?" Cecilia asked.

"Here, tomorrow evening," Cora said. "Spirits prefer the darkness."

Cecilia nodded. Maybe Amelia would not appear; but surely, having so many of the suspects in one place could reveal many things. It was too bad Lord Elphin was probably not into spiritualism very much.

As Nellie brought in the tea, Cecilia noticed Jack climbing out from under a desk, a few papers caught under his tail. She scooped them up and tucked them in her handbag before anyone could see, though Jack seemed terribly put out at having his treasures taken. She put him on her lap and gave him a pat in apology.

Chapter Twenty

Cecilia was quite sure she'd landed in a novel scene, or maybe in the black-and-white flicker of a newfangled moving picture, not in the real world at all. Not the world of church bazaars and suffrage rallies and betrothals. It was disorienting, dizzying, amazing.

The sitting room at Primrose Cottage had been muffled in black and dark-blue draperies, shutting out even the wavers of light from beyond the old windows as the sun vanished outside. The only light came from the glow of the fireplace and a circle of candles set on top of the heavy, round table draped in a white cloth. The candles flickered in the draught as the door opened and closed. An array of chairs was placed around the table, and Cora sat in the largest armchair, her cards spread before her. A red cashmere shawl swathed her head and shoulders.

Cecilia and Jane were the last to arrive. Her parents,

along with Patrick and Annabel, had gone off to a dinner at the Byswaters' estate, and Cecilia pleaded a headache to stay home. They'd had to wait until Danby was quiet before they could sneak down to the stables to fetch the governess cart.

Anne sat next to Cora, looking doubtful. Nellie retook her seat on Cora's other side, after answering the door. She looked very nervous, her hands twitching atop the table.

The Winters were already seated, and to Cecilia's surprise, Henry Price was there also. He kept checking his watch, his foot tapping on the old floor, and Cecilia wondered what had brought him to such a place. He didn't seem the séance sort.

"Lady Cecilia," Mr. Winter said with a bow. "I must say I am surprised a Bates would attend such a farce."

"If you think it a farce, Mr. Winter," Cecilia said with a cool smile, as she took her seat across from him and between Jane and Anne, "then why are *you* here, as well? I just want to do everything I can to help catch Mrs. Price's killer."

"But the killer *is* caught," Monty declared. "It's Cora Black over there, or that dreadful Mr. Guff. Wasn't he the one with the stolen engagement ring?"

Cecilia frowned at him. If he thought Cora was a killer, why did he want to join her séance anyway?

"It was not an engagement ring," Mr. Price said impatiently. "I gave her a diamond when we were first betrothed, the height of fashion. She just always wanted to wear that old ruby; who knows where it came from? I assume her father gave it to her before he was disgraced."

"Grandfather would never have given anything so vulgar,"

Anne scoffed. "He was quite old-fashioned; it was all cameos set in pearls. Perhaps Mr. Guff was some old admirer of Mother, as it seems that strange Lord Elphin was. I heard gossip about it at Mrs. Mabry's shop, most odd. Who would have ever thought such a thing? So droll." She burst out laughing, but no one else could even smile. "Do you think Lord E has been concocting an evil plan to get Mother's ring all this time? Or perhaps we should ask why Mother wore it at all."

Nellie went to kindle the fire in the grate, a clammy chill suddenly drifting into the room. Everyone grew silent, the atmosphere tense and strange. Cecilia gave Jane a nervous glance and saw Jack hidden under her chair. He was grooming his paw in a most unconcerned manner. Ghosts and family quarrels did not seem to bother him.

The clock on the mantel tolled the hour, slow and ponderous.

"Shall we start, then?" Cora said. "Everyone hold hands, lay your right hands flat on the cloth and place the left one atop your neighbor's. Don't let the circle break open. We want no dark spirits escaping into our world."

"No *more* dark spirits, you mean," Mary murmured. She seemed quite frightened, her hands shaking, and her husband offered her no comfort.

Nellie blew out half the candles, and the room suddenly seemed like it was filled with shifting shadows, blown like scarves over the walls and ceiling. The air smelled of smoke and mingled flowery perfumes; the hands Cecilia held felt damp and cold.

Cora closed her eyes, her face very white and intent. She

breathed deeply, the only sounds in the perfect silence of the room besides the tick of the clock and the pop of the fire. A branch scraped at the window, and Mary gasped.

"For heaven's sake, Mary, don't be such a goose," Monty muttered.

"Quiet, please," Cora said. She drew in another breath. "Amelia, our departed dear friend, are you with us?"

Cecilia held her breath until her chest felt tight, hardly daring to move as the darkness closed around her. What if they *did* see a ghost? Then again, what if they didn't? What was that brushing against her foot?

Jack suddenly darted out from under the table and leaped onto her lap, his green eyes filled with laughter that he had scared her.

"Not funny, Jack," she whispered, and he blinked at her in perfect innocence.

"Amelia, are you there?" Cora called. Everything was silent for a long moment—then a crack echoed, like a graceful footstep on the old wooden floors.

"Amelia, we want only to help you," Cora said, her tone growing desperate. "Show yourself to us. We are your friends."

Nellie scowled at the Winters. "Unfriendly entities will make the spirits hold back."

"Amelia, we only have this one evening to reach out to you," Cora said. "Do not be frightened. Please talk to us."

The table suddenly trembled, the white cloth swaying, one silver candlestick toppling and sputtering out, leaving a smudge on the damask. Mary squealed and clutched her husband's hand tighter, and even Anne looked discomfited.

"Amelia, what was the last thing you saw?" Cora asked, her voice shaking.

"Surely, it was *you*," Monty snapped.

Everyone ignored him, focusing on the table as it swayed and swirled between them. Cecilia's stomach lurched in fear and excitement, and she held on tightly to Jane's hand as Jack huddled close to her.

The fire in the grate behind them flared up, like a red-gold-purple explosion, and Mary screamed.

"Who are you?" Cora shouted. "Is that you, Amelia? Tell us what happened!"

No voice answered, but one of the water glasses flew up from the table and lurched toward Mary's head. She ducked, suffering only a few droplets on the shoulders of her black satin and tulle gown, but Monty was splashed full in the face.

"Blast it!" he growled. He snatched his wife's hand and pulled her from her seat. She nearly tripped as he rushed to the door, knocking into Cecilia's chair as they passed and making Jack hiss. She had a fleeting whiff of some sharp-smelling cologne.

"Do excuse me," Henry Price murmured and followed his daughter and son-in-law out the door.

The heavy old door slammed behind them, shaking the floors of the cottage, and Cecilia was sure she heard a merry peal of laughter from somewhere in the rafters. She shivered and clutched at Jack's warm solidity.

"Amelia, if you are truly there, I will call out letters," Cora said, her voice shaking. "Make the table move when we spell out the last thing you saw in this earthly life."

Cora began to slowly recite the alphabet. It took some time, everyone glancing around nervously, but when she said "S," the table shook again, harder, more violently. And then there was only the crackle of the fire, the rough rasp of Cora's labored breath. Whatever had been there, it was gone now. Primrose Cottage was empty.

Cora slumped over in her chair, her face paper white. Nellie jumped up to wrap Cora's dropped shawl tightly around her shoulders. "Come, Miss Black, you should lie down now. You're exhausted."

Cora nodded weakly, as if she could do nothing else, but tears rolled silently down her face. "We were so close to finding her. I'm sure of it. But S? Who is S?"

Nellie led Cora upstairs, and Cecilia and Jane started helping Anne clear away the mess of their botched séance. Jane took the water glasses to the kitchen, and Cecilia straightened the candlesticks and folded the ruined cloth. She could see nothing under the table that would have let a person shake it. But had it really been Mrs. Price trying to contact them, making a mess of the sitting room and giving them the flimsy S clue?

"Do you think—maybe there really was something?" Cecilia asked Anne as they moved the chairs back to their usual places.

Anne laughed. "I'm a lawyer, trained to see the world as a rational place, able to be ordered. I can't see ghosts or fairies.

But if someone like Cora thinks it is so, and thinks it hard enough . . ."

"If they think that already, then it's easier for them to see what they expect," Jane said, coming back into the sitting room with Jack on her heels.

"Or hear it suggested to them," Anne said.

"But who or what could be S?" Cecilia asked.

Anne shrugged. "I can't think of anyone with that initial. But you are kind to come here and try to help. I've been quite worried about Cora's state of mind since the inquest. I hoped if she felt like she was doing something to help . . ."

"We all want to do that," Cecilia said, thinking about her own chase through London, digging up gossip both old and new. "It's terrible to feel so helpless."

"It's very late, I'm afraid, and we've kept you too long with our shenanigans," Anne said.

"Shall we see you at the church bazaar, Miss Price?" Jane asked.

"Oh yes, that reminds me—I have a donation for you. Let me just fetch it." Anne hurried out of the room, and they heard her footsteps on the stairs, solid and real and human. She seemed to take what had happened in her stride, unlike her sister's shrieks and shouts. She brought back a square box, wrapped in paper, and saw Cecilia and Jane out to their waiting cart.

"Who could this S be, my lady?" Jane asked as they made their way out of the now-quiet village, everyone tucked in safely behind their garden gates and windows. "The last thing Mrs. Price saw. Is anyone here named S?"

"It could be just as phony as the whole séance business." Cecilia ran through all the members of the Union she knew of, and Mrs. Price's family. "Not that I know, anyway. Perhaps a middle name, or a nickname? A title? Or maybe it's not a person at all, but a thing. Her sash?"

"A sheep? A glass of sherry?"

Cecilia laughed. "Maybe it was sherry she last saw. But how would it make her fall like *that*? What happened to the piece of her sash that's missing?"

"Do you suppose she might have been in love with that awful Lord Elphin all this time? It's hard to imagine, but she did wear his ring, didn't she?"

"The heart does strange things indeed, doesn't it, Jane? I never understand it. I suppose Mrs. Price and Lord Elphin could have carried a romantic memory of how they imagined the other to be. And then . . ."

"When he saw what she had really become, a suffragette and all, he stole back his ring through Mr. Guff and then killed her? Or had the thief kill her," Jane said. Jack hissed and arched his furry back.

As Cecilia drove past the Winters' rented cottage, a sudden small flare of golden light touched the darkness like a firefly. Henry Price stepped out from behind the hedge, a cigar raised to his lips. Despite all the odd things that had happened that night, and his abrupt departure from Primrose Cottage, he looked unruffled, cool, and handsome.

"Mr. Price," Cecilia said, wondering if he had overheard any of their conversation. "I'm surprised you're still out tonight."

"I wanted to make sure Mary got home safely, but then I

found myself a bit worried about Anne, as well," he said. "It has been a—rather odd evening."

Cecilia was rather sure the Prices' whole lives together had been odd. It couldn't be what a solicitor to the royal family would expect from his family. Could he have done away with his wife to protect his own reputation? To marry again without the scandal of a divorce? But he did look rather worried about his daughters, his face tensely lined in the light of his cigar.

"Anne seems a strong sort. I'm sure she is quite well," Cecilia said.

"Anne *is* strong. She takes after me, and after her mother, too." He smiled ruefully. "Now Mary—I could not say who *she* takes after, the poor girl. But not even Anne can entirely fight off grief with her strong will alone."

"No, I am sure that is true," Cecilia said. "Will you be returning to London soon, Mr. Price? No doubt you must have important business waiting for you there." And a new wife to woo.

"Yes, I'm sure I will," he answered vaguely. "There is nothing to keep me here. But don't let me keep you, Lady Cecilia. Your parents must be worried."

"Indeed," she said. "Good night, Mr. Price." She flicked the reins, jolting the cart forward and leaving him alone with his cigar and his mysterious thoughts.

Cecilia and Jane were silent for a long moment on the drive home, letting the thoughts and memories and puzzles fly out into the chilly autumn night, trying to make sense of something that seemed entirely senseless.

Jack settled onto Jane's lap, purring as if he was thinking

it all over, too. But they were all tired, all overcome by the strangeness of what had happened, and Cecilia knew there would be no answers that night.

"You had suitors in London, my lady," Jane said as they turned through the Danby gates. "Were there any you felt for as Mrs. Price once did for Lord Elphin?"

Cecilia thought of the men she had danced with in Town. "No. No one either so unsuitable, or suitable, either, caught my attention. Sometimes I think I must be destined to be a useful spinster, helping out with Patrick and Annabel's children while I molder away in my Danby rooms. But at least I won't have to make such a choice as Amelia Price did." Despite their financial troubles, Cecilia knew her parents would never force her to marry, even as they worried and fretted.

"So you've never been in love with anyone at all?" Jane said. "Or *thought* of being in love?"

"I know I've never been properly in love, like all the romances in books," Cecilia answered. But in her mind, she suddenly saw a flashing image of Jesse, laughing with her in the empty dining room, and Mr. Brown taking her hand to help her climb over a wall. The marquess twirling her around a dance floor. Perhaps there were *hints* of romance in her life. "It does seem to be all that my London friends talk about, but right now there are so many other things to worry about."

Jane sighed. "That's the truth, my lady. What with murderers and ghosts wandering around . . ."

Cecilia glanced over at Jane, who was studying the parkland around them thoughtfully as she cuddled Jack. "What about you, Jane? Have you ever been in love?"

"I've had to work too hard to be in love, haven't I? My dad's store, the hotel, here at Danby. But maybe there's someone—I mean, I just think he might be—well, a bit handsome. And interesting." Her freckled face blushed so bright pink, Cecilia could see it in the darkness.

"Jane! How delicious. Do I know him? Oh, who could it be?" One of the footmen? A shopkeeper in the village? Maybe even Sergeant Dunn, who went all tongue-tied every time he saw Jane? Or maybe Collins?

But any of them would take Jane away from Danby, except for maybe Collins, and the thought made Cecilia feel wistful. It was nice to have a friend nearby.

Jane shook her head. "It's not like that, my lady. Just a— what in America they call a *crush*."

"A crush?"

"When you secretly admire someone from afar."

"Oh, like a pash. Then I've had crushes, too. A French teacher when I was a girl, our old head gardener who used to pick the best pink roses for me, things like that." She laughed. "Luckily, none of my crushes have ever led me astray." Yet.

Chapter Twenty-One

...and the game of quoits can go over there, and the archery on the lawn," Lady Avebury said, gesturing to the stretch of grass beyond the rose beds. "And the tea tent over there, just past where they're setting up the bring-and-buy area. What do you think, Cecilia?"

"Hmm?" Cecilia murmured. She had been trailing behind her mother and Annabel all morning, but her thoughts were still in the noisy darkness of Cora's séance. What did S mean? What had really happened there?

"The tents!" her mother said impatiently. She gestured at the notebook in Cecilia's hand. "You have the plans, darling. You know that some of the booths cannot be placed near one another or there will be quarrels. What do you think of it all?"

"Oh yes, the archery on the lawn, of course," Cecilia answered absentmindedly.

Her mother shook her head. "Really, Cecilia, what will

you do when it is your own home and you must make all the plans?"

Cecilia thought of Aunt Maggie's life, traveling wherever she liked, a large London house all her own, no one asking her where the tea tent should be. "We must hope it will never come to that, Mama."

Her mother shook her head again, exasperated, and surveyed the busy garden with a wistful expression. Footmen and gardeners hurried past, putting up billowing white tents and setting up tables for games, while maids carried trays back and forth. Everything looked just as it was every year at that time, with church bazaars, shooting parties, the gardens at Danby in one last burst of color before winter. "Or fear it will never come to that. Oh no, Bridget, that cannot go there!" She snatched the notebook out of Cecilia's grasp and rushed over to supervise the placement of the newly arrived flower arrangements.

A gust of wind caught at Cecilia's hat, and she barely grabbed it before it sailed away, as she studied the scene before her. The same scene she had witnessed every year of her life, unchanging and dear Danby. It all seemed so far away from Mrs. Price, from London, as if Danby were as timeless as the old medieval tower that rose from beyond the corner of the house. Its ancient stones had watched Normans and Saxons, Roundheads and kings, through the centuries, and it watched over them still. Yet a menacing shadow hung over it all.

"Lady Cecilia," she heard Mrs. Caffey call, and she turned to see the housekeeper hurrying along the terrace with a bouquet in her hands. Pink and red roses with lilies and irises, a riot of color, tumbling free from its vase. "This just arrived for you. I thought you might like to see it."

Cecilia stared at the flowers, astonished. She had never received a bouquet quite so exuberant before, as small nosegays were appropriate for debs.

"My heavens," Annabel said. "Aren't those gorgeous? You must have an admirer."

Lady Avebury approached them, drawn by the vivid flowers. "What does the card say?"

Cecilia plucked the small pasteboard square from behind a red rose. "It—it's from Lord Eversham." She was completely astonished. They had only danced once, though he was indeed a handsome charmer. Why was he sending flowers, and *such* flowers?

"Oooohhh, that handsome marquess we met in London!" Annabel cooed. "How delightful, Cec. You must have utterly charmed him!"

"I don't think so," Cecilia said doubtfully. Though she *had* laughed a lot during their dance.

"A marquess?" her mother said sharply.

"We met him at a dance Mrs. Solent took us to in London," Annabel offered. "He did seem delightful."

"A marquess . . ." Lady Avebury murmured, her head tilted as she studied the bouquet. "Lord Eversham? Yes, I think I knew his mother when we were girls; his father died and left him the title when he was quite young, poor thing. He has a grand estate. I am sure he needs a marchioness to help him in his duties. Is he in the neighborhood now?"

Cecilia turned over the card and read the scribbled message. "He will be for the Byswaters' shooting party."

Lady Avebury's face lit up. "Then you must invite him to Danby for tea! It would be lovely to meet my old friend's son. And I'm sure your father will see him at the shooting. Oh, it is too bad he won't be here for the bazaar. He could have seen Danby en fête. How clever of you to make such a nice new friend, Cecilia."

Cecilia could definitely see how the wind was blowing, wafting up her mother's strong matchmaking instincts just on the basis of one bouquet. Was poor Mr. Brown to be forgotten, then? She felt her breath catch in her chest, making her feel she was suffocating under the weight of all these expectations. "I—I must go, Mama. I have a—a vital errand to run just now."

"An errand?" Lady Avebury cried. "We're still working on the plans for the bazaar!"

"We're nearly done, and you and Annabel have it more than in hand. I won't be gone long."

Cecilia thrust the flowers into Annabel's hands and hurried away before her mother could protest again. Luckily, she was already wearing a plain shirtwaist and sensible tweed skirt, so she only had to stop in her chamber to fetch a jacket. Jane seemed to have been there recently to leave a pile of freshly laundered handkerchiefs on the dressing table, but she wasn't there at the moment. Jack sat on one of the chairs by the fireplace, grooming his paws. When he saw Cecilia, he stood up with a bright gleam in his eyes.

Eliza Casey

"Mrow?" he inquired.

"I am sorry, Jack dear, but I don't think you'd like to go out with me now. Very soon, though. I know you must be terribly bored after all the excitement of the séance."

He sat back down with a huff and set about grooming his other paw. Cecilia quickly found her tweed jacket and pinned a boater hat to her upswept hair. She shut the door tightly behind her so Jack couldn't go wandering, like the time he got himself caught in the dumbwaiter.

She found Mrs. Price's bicycle propped next to the garage, freshly washed by Mr. Collins. She had only practiced a few times, but surely riding a bicycle couldn't be all that hard, could it? And it would carry her away from Danby faster than her feet.

She walked the vehicle out for a short way, until she was out of sight of the house, just in case she *did* take an embarrassing tumble. Once she was near the gates, she climbed onto the seat and pushed off on the pedals.

The bicycle wobbled under her, making her stomach clench, but all her old dance lessons stood her in good stead, and she was able to find her balance. As she rode along the lane, she remembered how Mrs. Price had talked about the delicious freedom of cycling. Mrs. Price was very right. The speed of it, the wind catching at her hat, the exhilaration of being on her own, was wonderful.

Thinking about all that had happened with poor Mrs. Price quite chased troublesome thoughts of marriage conundrums out of Cecilia's mind, and she considered everything that had happened in the last few days. The London gossip, the strange séance, the inquest that solved nothing. Cycling did seem to stimulate thoughts as well as legs.

A couple of cars and a horse and cart went by, the occupants waving at her, but other than that the lane was empty. She turned onto a narrow trail, lined on either side by tall hedgerows that blocked the wind. She felt closed around by a green, silent world, fragrant with autumn leaves.

As Cecilia rounded a sharp corner, narrowly avoiding toppling into the hedges, she thought she heard something on the other side of the greenery. A loud crack, a rustle. She shrugged it off and rode along, yet it seemed to move with her. When she stopped, it vanished.

"How very odd," she muttered, trying not to think of the footsteps and shaking table of the séance. She set the bicycle into motion again, trying to find her old rhythm. She rode faster and faster, coasting around corners—until she hit an unexpected fallen log in the lane.

Cecilia shrieked as she toppled over the handlebars, her hat slipping over her eyes and blinding her. Her stomach lurched with a cold terror. She landed with a hard thump but managed to roll free before the bicycle fell on her.

She heard running footsteps, just beyond where the hedges dipped past the lane. She shoved her hat back from her eyes and pushed herself up to twist around and study the path behind her.

"Hello?" she shouted. She heard another sharp rustling noise. "Is someone there?"

No one answered. The lane seemed empty. Cecilia carefully eased herself to her feet, wincing at the bruised ache in her shoulder and hip. The sleeve of her jacket was torn, which was sure to vex Jane, and her hat was quite beyond hope. She limped over to study the tree trunk she had crashed into and realized it didn't look as if it had just fallen there. There were drag marks in the dirt, and they seemed quite fresh. Had someone placed the trunk there where she was sure to topple over it? Was someone following her this whole time?

She heard the hum of a motor on the main road, and she ran through a stile to find Collins driving the Danby car. Relieved, she waved frantically at him, and the car sputtered to a halt.

"Lady Cecilia!" Collins cried as he flung open his door. "Whatever has happened? Are you hurt?"

"I was practicing cycling, and I fear I took a tumble," she said. "I must say, I was riding along quite well until I fell over a tree trunk. I'm glad you came by. I don't think I could walk all the way back to Danby."

"Let me drive you back right away."

"Thank you." Cecilia studied the lane, which seemed quiet now. "Did you happen to see anyone else, Collins?"

"I thought I saw a car driving away in the distance, but I couldn't make out what sort it was. Did *you* see anyone, my lady? Anyone who shouldn't be there?"

"Not really. Once I turned onto the side pathway, I saw no one at all. But I did think I heard something . . ."

"What sort of thing?"

Cecilia shrugged, feeling a bit foolish. All that had happened lately in Danby Village, her usually tranquil home, had obviously spooked her. "Just a rustling, maybe footsteps. On the other side of the hedge. It seemed to be following me for a while."

Collins went to where she indicated, to examine the hedges and the tree trunk she had toppled over. He came back in a few moments, his face taut with worry. He tossed her bicycle into the boot of the car. "We should get back to Danby now, my lady."

Cecilia was alarmed all over again. Collins was usually completely unflappable and good-humored. "Why, Collins? Whatever is the matter?"

"There were indeed footprints, my lady, in the mud on the other side of the hedges. And that tree trunk was cut deliberately and dragged onto the path."

"I see. My goodness." Cecilia hurried into the car, locking the door carefully behind her. Why on earth would someone want to hurt *her*?

❧

"There now, my lady, I have a nice, fresh, hot-water bottle for you," Jane said, helping Cecilia into her turned-down bed. "How are you feeling now after your bath?"

"Just a little sore, Jane, but I do think your lavender bath salts worked wonders," Cecilia said, sighing as she leaned back on her soft pillows. "No need to fuss."

"Of course there should be a fuss! Mr. Collins said someone put that tree trunk there deliberately to make you take a fall. Who would do such a thing?"

Cecilia had been asking herself that very thing, over and over again. She knew she had to organize her thoughts. She found her notebook and a pencil on the bedside table and started to make a list.

"I do fear Mrs. Price, though famous and important, was not universally liked by everyone close to her, Jane," she said with a sigh.

"No. But it seems Lord Elphin must have loved her a great deal once," Jane said, perching on the edge of the bed. Jack jumped up into her lap.

"Indeed, decades ago. Did it lead them into trouble *now*? Has he carried anger toward her this long? He and his men were such bullies at the rally."

"And he wanted his ring back. Was that how Georgie Guff got it? Stealing it for Lord Elphin?"

"Mr. Perkins says Guff was in the snug at the Crown that night, but Daisy says it was busy then and Guff could have slipped away. Or maybe he took the ring sometime earlier? Did Lord Elphin send him, as you say, or was he acting on his own? He was obviously engaged in some sort of stealing spree."

"Could Guff have really been the man Mr. Talbot saw walking away?"

"But he was in the pub that night."

"Mr. Winter was seen at the pub, too. Mrs. Winter said she slept deeply that night, after they left Primrose Cottage, and Anne said she thought she heard their car leave long before Mrs. Price fell. Did he return after Mary fell asleep?"

"Certainly there doesn't seem much love lost between Mrs. Price and the Winters. Though Mary says they were trying to reconcile."

"Hoping she would help Mr. Winter in his career again?"

"Very possibly, though I don't see how she could have, except by giving up her work, which she never would. Mr. Winter seems to blame his in-laws for his stalled career. Miss Smythe, though, said it was all his own incompetence."

"Would he tell his wife the truth, though? Maybe Mrs. Winter blamed her mother, too."

"And she would hate to see her comfortable life taken away, true."

"Maybe that was why the Winters left Miss Black's séance so fast. Mrs. Price might have told all."

Cecilia laughed and winced as her shoulder gave a painful twinge, reminding her how serious this matter was. "Maybe it was Mrs. Price's ghost who knocked me from the bicycle?"

"She might want it back."

"Well, she can't have it. Before I took such an embarrassing fall . . ."

"You were knocked down, my lady! You didn't fall."

Cecilia nodded. "I was quite enjoying it. Such a sense of freedom, riding down the lane! But what about Cora herself? She did confess, though not especially convincingly, and she had disagreements with Mrs. Price about the Union's direction."

"Mrs. Palmer also quarreled with Mrs. Price about the direction of the Union; you said Bridget even mentioned as much. And she was at Primrose Cottage for a time that night."

"Maybe she wanted to take it over entirely."

"Suffrage does make people passionate. And if Anne, Cora, and Mrs. Palmer disagreed with Mrs. Price, there must have been others in the Union who did, too."

Cecilia watched Jack as he calmly groomed his paw. "Perhaps it was an accident after all. Though then where is Mrs. Price's sash? A robbery gone wrong, her family, Mrs. Palmer, illicit lovers. I wonder if it could have been Mary Winter?"

"Mrs. Winter?"

Cecilia nodded, thinking of the threatening letters. "She wants to be seen as helpless, fluttery, feminine. Annabel says having the vote will mean women will no longer be protected by men. If Mary thinks her mother's 'unnatural' work is truly taking away her husband's career, her very way of life, she might lash out. Yes—perhaps it was Mary. But I just don't know." Jack leaped from Jane's lap onto the pillow next to Cecilia and batted at her pencil. "What do *you* think, Jack?"

But Jack just made a "mrow" and settled down for a sleep.

Chapter Twenty-Two

For an instant when Cecilia opened her eyes, she was caught up in the sticky remnants of dreams—flying through hedgerows as bicycles propelled themselves riderless through the sky, the nausea of fear as she tumbled downward to the hard ground. Then she opened her eyes, her breath tight in her lungs, and she remembered—it was the day of the bazaar, and no matter how sore she felt or how tired after such strange dreams, she couldn't linger in bed.

She groaned and rolled over to pull the satin blankets over her head. The curtains hadn't been drawn open yet, but she could see the golden glow of light between the folds of blue-and-white-striped silk. It would be fine weather, which would give her mother one less thing to fret about, but it meant plenty of work for Cecilia and everyone else at Danby. At least Mama would have no more time to lecture her about the dangers of bicycles.

She rolled back over to glance at the little ormolu clock on the mantel. Far past the hour she usually awoke. She glimpsed the lists she and Jane had worked on, suspects and nefarious motives, and the sunny autumn day seemed to lose some of its bright luster. Someone who had killed, who had followed Cecilia herself along that lane, was still out there. What if their work, whatever it was, was still undone?

The door slid open, and Jane tiptoed in with the tea tray in her hands and Jack at her heels.

"It's all right, Jane, I'm awake," Cecilia said, pushing herself up against the pillows. Her shoulder gave a twinge where she had landed in her fall. "I couldn't sleep very well with all the thoughts whirling in my head!"

"Me neither, my lady," Jane said with a shudder. She put the tray down on the bedside table and opened the curtains to let the morning light flood across the floral needlepoint carpet. Jack jumped up on the bed to settle on the rumpled sheets and groom his paw.

Jane poured out the tea and arranged the ginger biscuits. "I kept imagining I heard something outside my window, which is impossible, isn't it, it's up so high? No one could get into Danby. But then again, no one should be able to sneak around and tear down tree trunks, either."

"Do you have any other ideas about who might have killed Mrs. Price?" Cecilia took a long, fortifying sip of the blessedly strong tea. She didn't like to think someone like Mary Winter, so downtrodden and bullied by her husband, could have done such a thing, but it did look as if she was the prime suspect.

Jane glanced at their lists. "Nothing new, my lady. Poor Mrs. Price. What a confused life she led!"

"Let's just hope that, whoever they are, they don't disrupt the bazaar. My mother would *kill* them, as well."

Jane laughed. "That reminds me, my lady, Mr. Brown is expected for breakfast, and even Miss Clarke was downstairs early. I think Lady Avebury's habit of making lists for everything has rubbed off on her. She's very worried about the prizes for the baking competition."

"Then I am sure she will make a fine Lady Avebury herself one day," Cecilia said, and she wondered again what *would* happen to Annabel and Patrick. When would her brother come up to scratch?

"So, what do you want to wear? That new ecru muslin with the purple lace we brought from London? It's so lovely, it would be a shame to waste it. It's a bit breezy outside, but we can find a small hat to go with it and pin it on securely enough."

"A small hat will be necessary, I think. Didn't Annabel say she had a purple toque she could loan me? I'll be pouring tea and trying to persuade people to buy hideous knit things in the bring-and-buy tent all day long. A big, fashionable hat would just get in the way." She thought of Mr. Brown, and a future as a vicar's wife, when whole days would be filled with such matters. She wasn't sure how she felt about that.

She gulped down the last of the tea and glimpsed the flowers from Lord Eversham, that immense bouquet arranged in a crystal vase. What, then, would life be like as a marchioness? Surely, there would still be bring-and-buy stalls to be run. That seemed to be her fate wherever she turned.

As Jane laid out the new frock, which was indeed a beautiful creation of ecru muslin embroidered with tone-on-tone flowers and interspersed with panels of purple lace, with a matching purple bolero jacket, Cecilia ate the last of the biscuits and went to the window to study the activity out on the lawns. James and Paul, the footmen, were carrying trays of Mrs. Frazer's tarts and cakes to the tea tent, while archery targets and croquet sets were set up for the games. She pushed open the window and took a deep breath of the autumn morning air, still warm but with a snap of chill to it that predicted cold mornings to come. She could smell sugar and the sweetness of flowers, and something green-lemony . . . almost like the smell on those letters at Primrose Cottage. *Could* the same person who wrote them really be the one who pushed her from her bicycle?

Jack jumped up onto the ledge beside her, his striped head held high as if he, too, was investigating.

There was a frantic knock at the door, and Cecilia's mother called, "Cecilia, dear, are you quite ready? There is so much to be done! No time to be lounging in bed!"

Jane held up the purple-and-white skirt, and Cecilia sighed. "Coming, Mama."

᧠

The annual church bazaar, along with the summer fete and the tenants' Christmas party, was one of the few times of the year when the grounds of Danby Hall were open to the neighborhood, and it was always very popular. No sooner had the gates at the end of the winding drive been opened than the pathways and lawns were filled with people in their best clothes and hats, bright colors against the flowers, laughing and pointing out the statues, the fountains, the ornamental lake where rowing boats were ready to be hired out. The ancient medieval tower that rose at the end of the garden, so romantic looking.

As Cecilia hurried out of the house and down the terrace steps, pinning on the small purple toque hat trimmed with silk violets she had borrowed from Annabel, she waved and smiled at everyone she passed. She saw Cora sitting on a bench under the shade of a tree, Nellie hovering beside her as she tried to get Cora to drink some lemonade. Cora shook her head, but she did look a bit less pale, with a little smile on her face. Anne appeared to hand her a plate of cakes, and they all waved back at Cecilia.

Her mother and Annabel were hurrying along, the feathers of their hats waving, lists in their hands, luckily far too busy to notice that Cecilia was late, and her father was chatting with Lord Byswater as her grandmother settled herself in an armchair brought out especially for her by Redvers. Sebastian sat at her feet, growling at everyone. Even Inspector Hennesy and Sergeant Dunn were there, a spot of dark gray and navy blue among the reds and greens and purples.

"A lovely day for a game of lawn tennis, eh, my lady?" Jesse called, as he hurried past with a tray of lemon tarts. "I won a prize for it once before I left school. My stunning backhand, you see."

Cecilia laughed. "I would be much too good and win all the prizes, I fear, and then you would have to cut me off. I have a rather fine backhand myself."

"A challenge, then! Care to put your money where your mouth is, my lady?"

"Cecilia!" her mother called. "No dawdling."

Cecilia gave Jesse a cringe. "Later, perhaps. For now, duty calls. I think I'm meant to be selling tea cozies today."

The Misses Moffat had already set up most of the refreshment tent, long tables laid out in lines and draped in pink and white, while two village girls, along with Daisy Perkins, manned the huge silver urns and passed out the tarts and cakes. Right next to them was the bring-and-buy tent. Cecilia sighed as she studied the array of objects laid out for sale very neatly, though that would all soon change once people began rummaging. There were indeed tea cozies, porcelain cups and plates hand-painted by the ladies from the village, scarves and hats and embroidered handkerchiefs, dolls and tops and hoops, and one especially odd teapot shaped like a porcupine. She was quite sure most of the items would make a return appearance next year. The bring-and-buy was more an obligation than a joy, but it did raise money for the church roof.

"Ah, Lady Cecilia," Mr. Brown called to her. He excused himself with a dimpled smile from the three ladies he was talking to, or rather surrounded by, and they looked after him with disappointed moues. He really *was* a handsome man, Cecilia thought, with his curling dark hair and kind brown eyes, especially in his shirtsleeves. The church was sure to raise lots of money that day. "I was just repairing a table leg that fell off.

What fine weather we have for the bazaar this year! I remember my predecessor complaining of the autumn when a rainstorm blew in and knocked all the pavilions quite to the ground, leaving everyone drenched." To her disappointment, he put his coat back on.

She laughed at the memory of that particular bazaar, the tents swimming like galleons over the lawn while everyone shrieked and ran for the terrace. "Yes. It's funny to think of it now, but it was quite dreadful when it happened. You do seem to have brought us good luck, Mr. Brown."

He smiled shyly. "I hope so. Now, Lady Cecilia, can I help with anything else here? Do let me bring you an ice cream later. I can imagine it's hard work to get people to buy, er, porcupines."

Cecilia thought of the Moffats' lovely strawberry ices and sighed. Work first; bliss later. She rubbed at her sore shoulder. "That would be so kind, Mr. Brown. I think I can manage here for now. Jane, Miss Clarke's maid, is coming to help me soon. I daresay someone will take a fancy to the porcupine."

"Well, do just call if I can do anything at all. I am always at your service, Lady Cecilia." He actually gave her a little bow, so chivalrous. As he left the tent, the three ladies he had been talking to all sighed.

Cecilia turned back to the tables and rearranged some of the knitted scarves so the pretty colors could be seen. Mrs. Havelock must have made some of them, she thought; the colonel's wife always had such an eye for color, while Mrs. Mabry just used horrid old grays and muddy greens. A few browsers came in, and as she turned to greet them she noticed a new package at the end of the table, about the size of a small hat-box and wrapped in brown paper. She picked it up to unwrap and arrange.

The note attached indicated it was a donation in kind thanks for all the "lovely village" had done for his family, signed "Montgomery Winter." She started to untie the string, but something about it caught her attention. A whiff of scent carried on the breeze, citrus-green and sharp.

Suspicious, she took another deep sniff. Yes, she was sure it was that same smell. Not Mary's white-flower scent or Amelia Price's roses; a man's cologne. Just like those bits of paper at Primrose Cottage. Her stomach knotted, and she snatched the note off the package to study the handwriting more carefully. Dark and backward slanting. Also like the torn notes. Not like Mary's looping hand.

Unsure what to do, Cecilia spun around to run out of the tent to find the inspector. But then what would she tell him? That the handwriting on the package looked like that on a scrap of paper at Primrose Cottage—the cottage where Mrs. Winter's mother had lived, and thus might have received let-ters from her family there? Threatening letters from her son-in-law? It all sounded silly when she put it like that. But Mary's perfume was flowery and feminine, distinctive, and surely when she wrote her mother letters, they would smell like that and would have her girlish handwriting.

Could it be *Monty* Winter who wrote them, then? Monty, angry about his job loss, angry that women might want rights. Angry that his influential in-laws could no longer help him?

Before Cecilia could decide what to do, Lord Elphin

appeared in the tent entrance. His face was still red and florid, his suit ill fitting, as if he didn't dress for public occasions often, but he held his hat in his hand and looked almost shy as he nodded at her. He held a flat package in his other hand, and held it up awkwardly. Cecilia noticed that everyone else in the tent stopped to gawk at him, so rare a sight was he. She couldn't just run away from him.

"Lady Cecilia," he said, with a cough and a shuffle of his feet. "I did promise you and Miss Clarke a donation for the church roof. I—well, here it is, then."

"How kind, Lord Elphin," Cecilia answered, feeling almost as at a loss as he was. "I'm sure we're all quite glad to see you here at Danby today. I hope it's the start of many such visits." She opened the wrappings and saw a small portrait of a woman dressed in the low neckline of decades ago, her dark hair in elaborate curls. Her hand rested against her cheek, showing a ruby ring on her finger. Cecilia recognized her from the larger painting over Lord Elphin's fireplace. "Your mother?"

"Indeed. She was the donor of the St. Barbara window at St. Swithin's and is buried in the vault there. She would be happy to be of more assistance now. The artist was quite well-known, I think, which might be of some interest to a collector, or maybe the church might want it. Unless you think it's too worthless?"

"Not at all. If Lady Elphin was a church patroness, I am sure Mr. Brown would like to buy it himself. It was terribly kind of you to bring it." She studied the ring closer. "Lord Elphin, I know this is most impertinent, but is this the same ring Mrs. Price wore?"

His face turned even redder. "I—well, yes, I daresay."

Cecilia felt suddenly bold. Maybe it was her suspicions of the notes, maybe it was Lord Elphin's new polite demeanor, but she dared ask, "And you wanted the ring back? After all these years? Why?"

"I hadn't seen Amelia for a very long time. Just read about her in the newspapers. It never sounded like the same lovely girl I knew then at all. So angry, so—unwomanly." He scowled, as if upset at the memory that a young debutante might grow into a lady with ambitions and ideas of her own. "Then she showed up here, wearing that ring after all this time, bold as brass! I asked for it to be returned. It was my mother's, after all, and the girl I gave it to no longer existed anyway."

He suddenly looked so confused that Cecilia couldn't help but feel a bit sorry for him, as crude and foolish as he was. "And yet you let her keep it after she jilted you back then?"

"Her father lost his money! We couldn't marry then; I understood that. I admit I might have . . ." He half turned away, as if he didn't want Cecilia to see his emotions at old memories. "I didn't expect her to marry that Henry Price so fast, or that I would never see her again. But I suppose life does that sometimes, doesn't it? We have our duties."

"Yes," Cecilia murmured. "Duties." Duties to family, to home, to the past. But what of the future? Was there really no choice?

"I thought of her sometimes. She was a sweet, lovely girl back then, always laughing." He looked quite far away for an instant, maybe a young man in a London ballroom again, enchanted by a pretty girl. "And I did want to give that ring to my wife, rest her soul. But I never dreamed Amelia would go around flaunting it, bold as can be!"

"And so you sent Mr. Guff after her?"

Lord Elphin's jaw set pugnaciously. "I had heard of him once, from one of my tenants. He seemed reliable enough, for that sort of thing. I just wanted back what was mine after all these years."

And Guff had found Amelia dead and callously taken the ring from her finger? Or had it been more than that? She had fought to keep it and fallen? But it seemed in Cecilia's memory that the ring was gone before that. And Cecilia had been so sure it was Mary Winter . . . "I am quite sure Inspector Hennesy would like to hear about all this, Lord Elphin."

His expression turned from stubbornness to shock. "I had nothing to do with anything else but the ring! Nor, does Guff assure me, did he, and surely there is some honor among thieves? I had nothing to do with murder, or even with stealing anything else. Just my ring."

For a moment, he seemed so thunderous she was sure he would snatch back his painting and storm away. But slowly, gradually, the angry redness leeched from his face, and he seemed to crumple. He was just an old, pitiful recluse, who had wasted years in recriminations for a long-ago romance. "She used to be so lovely."

"Did she have other suitors back then, too?" Cecilia asked, wondering if maybe Amelia Price's colorful past had come back to haunt her in the present in some way not yet apparent.

"Of course she did. She was quite the prettiest girl in

London then. Such a waste, eh, thrown away on a man like Price."

"Because he is a lawyer?"

"Because his business practices were never honest! Everyone knew it then. No one could understand why the queen would ever trust him, but she did and now he is prosperous." Lord Elphin glanced down wistfully at the painting. "Ah well. Water under the bridge now, isn't it? Guff's in stir for his thefts, and I'll have my ring back soon. But poor Amelia." He put on his hat and started to turn away. "You see if the vicar might want that painting, Lady Cecilia. Mother would have liked to see it in the church."

Cecilia felt a bit sorry for him as she watched him shuffle away, but she reminded herself sternly that he *had* set the theft in motion, and had bullied Mrs. Price at her rally. Even if he hadn't harmed her himself, one of his underlings could have. But she didn't have long to ponder his misdeeds, as a crowd of shoppers came swarming into the tent, eager to buy the knitted scarves and painted figurines. She tucked the painting away beneath one of the tables and set about her job of selling. Her head was quite whirling with it all when Jane and Jack came hurrying in.

"Oh, my lady, you'll never believe who just arrived!" Jane whispered. "Lord Eversham! Lady Avebury is quite beside herself."

"Really?" Cecilia gasped. "A marquess, here at Danby for the church fete?" She felt a sudden tangle of emotions, excitement, trepidation, worry. What was he doing here, a man like that so obviously of Town? And what would her always-matchmaking mother make of it? She quickly followed Jane to the entrance and peeked outside.

It was indeed Lord Eversham, dressed impeccably for the country in his brown suit, his golden hair shimmering in the sunlight, laughing with her mother and Annabel as they strolled with him between the booths. Sebastian dashed past with a chicken leg in his mouth, which he had clearly purloined from the tea tent, and Jack set off in pursuit. After only an instant, he trotted back with the prize, victorious.

"Surely, he's come courting?" Jane whispered delightedly. Jack gave a disgusted "mrow."

"I am quite sure he has not. There are plenty of ladies more eligible than me." Ladies with beauty and money. Ladies like Annabel herself, who laughed and laid her elegantly gloved hand lightly on his arm.

Cecilia glimpsed Jesse, strolling past with a tray of glasses, and he raised his brows toward Eversham, as if asking if such an elegant toff could really be there at Danby. Cecilia almost giggled.

"I am sure there aren't lots of earl's daughters," Jane said doubtfully.

"There are lots of heiresses," Cecilia answered.

A sudden cry rang out, breaking the idyllic day, and Cecilia spun around to see Mary Winter collapse to the ground nearby, half-hidden by the tent, her lilac-colored dress spreading like a broken flower on the grass. Cecilia and Jane ran to her.

"Mrs. Winter!" Cecilia cried. She knelt down beside Mary and saw that the woman was chalky pale, her forehead clammy. She couldn't see Monty Winter anywhere near, but she remembered the threatening notes it seemed he had sent his mother-in-law, and she felt terribly afraid for Mary. "What's amiss? Are you ill?"

"I—just my stomach, I'm afraid," Mary whispered, clutching her hand over the crumpled silk of her bodice. Her wide-brimmed hat had come half-unpinned, and Cecilia helped her remove it. A bruise, which she had tried to powder away, was blue on her cheekbone.

"She was quite well only a moment ago," Monty said, and Cecilia twisted around to see him striding toward them. He was smiling pleasantly, but there was a look in his eyes she did not quite like. Something hard, steely.

"It *is* a warm day, Mrs. Winter," Cecilia said. "Let us find you a shady place to sit down. Perhaps Mr. Winter will fetch you some lemonade?"

His smile twisted. "Yes, of course. I am sure it is all just a tempest in a teapot, though, as usual with my dear wife. Her nerves are not strong, you know." To Cecilia's relief, he turned and left, walking toward the tea tent.

Cecilia glanced around and saw Rose carrying a fresh tray of Mrs. Frazer's cakes. "Rose, could you watch the bring-and-buy tent for a few moments while I find someplace for Mrs. Winter to rest?"

"Of course, my lady," Rose said, and handed off her tray to Bridget before she took her place at the bring-and-buy table, just in time to sell one of the Misses Moffat's tea cozies.

Cecilia and Jane helped Mary to her feet, and Cecilia realized they were quite near the old medieval tower. The rest of the garden was swarming with people, and her grand-mother held court on the terrace, where Lady Avebury was leading Lord Eversham. No place to find peace *there*. "Let's just go sit down in the tower for a moment, Mrs. Winter. It's a little eerie, I admit, as it was a place to watch for enemies back in medieval days, but it is quite cool and quiet."

"You are so kind, Lady Cecilia. I am such a bother, I'm afraid," Mary said fretfully.

"Not at all." Cecilia called back to Rose where they were going and where Mr. Winter might find them when he returned. As they made their way toward the tower, Jack joined them, his prized chicken seemingly gone. The small, round room at the foot of the tower was dusty and filled with drying leaves, so Cecilia led them up the winding, narrow staircase to the first landing. They found a bench there and sat down to watch the color and movement of the bazaar far below.

"I am always so stupidly ill," Mary said. She took a hand-kerchief from her embroidered purse and dabbed at her eyes. Cecilia caught a whiff of that strange perfume on the dusty air of the tower. "I had so hoped that this time there might be a—well, forgive my indelicacy, but a child. But your kind Dr. Mitchell says it is just grief for poor Mother."

"Perfectly understandable," Cecilia said gently. She took Mary's soaked handkerchief and handed her one of Jane's own. Cecilia saw that Mary's square of linen was embroidered with a masculine border of dark green, a small, plain M in the corner. Was it her own, or her husband's, soaked in that scent?

"Had you—hoped for long, then, Mrs. Winter?" Cecilia asked.

"I have always hoped, ever since I married," Mary said wistfully, trying to smile. "To tell you a great secret, it was why I married Mr. Winter in the first place. There was this dance one night, you see, and I drank a great deal of the champagne punch. He was so handsome in the moonlight, there in the summerhouse! In the end, I was quite mistaken, but we were already married by then. My die was cast, as they say."

So the Winters had been forced to marry. Could one of them be so angry at being stuck with each other that the rage would find a new, strange target in Mary's mother? "It must have been a wretched disappointment," Cecilia said.

"Horribly so. But I thought we would just try again. Monty was ever so furious. He—he said I had trapped him, you see. I think he might really have loved Anne back then, not that she would ever have him. She's only interested in her suffrage nonsense, not a true woman at all. And then when Monty's job at Bird and Wither came to nothing . . ." She broke into a fresh storm of tears. "It was all over then! Father wouldn't help him anymore."

She snatched her handkerchief from Jane's hand and blew her nose into it loudly.

"Mary," Cecilia asked carefully, "is that your own handkerchief?"

Mary glanced down at the now quite crumpled linen as if she had never seen it before. "Oh no," she moaned. "I must have taken Monty's by mistake! He'll be ever so angry when he finds out; he has them made specially by the dozen, infused with his cologne. I am never supposed to use his things." She glanced out the old, narrow window behind them, the swirl of the leaves on the stone ledge, the sound of the party below. "He is taking a rather long time, isn't he?"

"I'll just go see where he might be, my lady," Jane said. She and Jack dashed out of the tower, their footsteps echoing on the worn, ancient stone steps.

"So you believe your husband wanted to marry your sister?" Cecilia asked. She had a hard time imagining Monty Winter and Anne Price together at all.

"Oh, I know it. Anne is much cleverer than I am, you see, an asset to any business ambitions, and she's older, too. I've always just been the little featherhead."

Cecilia still couldn't quite believe it. "He was in love with *Anne*?"

Mary laughed. "Oh no. Not her *herself*. Not Monty. He doesn't really know the meaning of the word, if I must be honest. He's ambitious. He wanted an alliance with Henry Price. One sister would do as well as the other for that. And I was so silly. I see that now. I thought he was handsome, charming, that he could love me better than he ever could Anne. That we could have a proper marriage, not like my parents. So there was that summerhouse . . ."

"What was their marriage like? Your parents'?"

Mary frowned. "Argumentative. Before Mother moved away. Always shouting, things being thrown around." Now that she had started, Mary was obviously in a confiding mood. Maybe she had just kept it all bottled up for too long. "They both had affairs, you see. We all knew it. I was sure Monty and I would be different, that once we were married, he

would know I was the right wife for him. But we aren't different at all. I hardly see him, and when we do, he's always angry
with me for doing something wrong. And I do so many things
wrong, Lady Cecilia! It's become quite worse since he lost his
position, and Father refuses to help him any longer. Monty
says it's all my fault, and I must fix it with Father. That's why
we came here to Danby."

Cecilia was confused. Was Mary supposed to secure her
husband the job with Mr. Jermyn? "How are you to fix it?"

"By reconciling with my mother, getting her to return to
Father. By convincing Father to take her back and force her
to become a proper wife who can't ruin a gentleman's business prospects. That would never have worked, of course. Father would never have taken her back. But Monty is sure her
notoriety is to blame for losing his position. No reputable firm
wants to be associated with suffragettes. She's stolen his rightful place."

Cecilia thought of the scraps of threatening letters at
Primrose Cottage, the handwriting that seemed not quite
right. "He made you write to her here?"

Mary blew her nose into her hopelessly mangled handkerchief. "I told him it would do no good. Mother seldom answers any letters, she says she's too busy, and Father refuses
to help us anymore."

Cecilia opened her handbag and showed Mary the scraps
she had taken from the cottage. "Did you write these, then?"

Mary frowned as she studied them. "No. I did write her,
but I made sure the notes were kind, loving. Flattery was
the only thing with a chance to work with Mother. I wouldn't

say words like this, and it's not my handwriting." She lifted them to her nose for a long inhale, above the dry dust of the tower. "That's Monty's cologne, though. Like these handkerchiefs, see?"

"So this is from Monty?"

"It . . . it could be. But why would he be writing to my parents? He knows it can do no good."

So Monty had blamed the Prices, particularly Amelia, for his misfortunes. He had been threatening her, followed her to Danby Village—and when Amelia refused to even pay attention to his notes, to give up her work, had he gone and pushed her to her death?

Cecilia closed her eyes and remembered what everyone had said about that terrible night. Amelia stayed up late alone; Cora's mind was thick from medication; Anne thought she had heard voices, thought she heard the Winters' car leave, but couldn't be sure. A man walking away from Primrose Cottage. Everyone had thought it was Guff, but what if it was Monty Winter, visiting his mother-in-law late at night to try to persuade her one more time, who shoved her in a fury? What if Guff had only come upon her later, and taken the ring for opportunity? Or maybe Monty even sold the ring to him, insult added to injury.

"Mary," she asked, "was what you said at the inquest true? You went to sleep early the night of your mother's rally and heard nothing until morning?"

"Yes, of course. Monty brought me some cocoa—my stomach was delicate that night, too, after we met with Mother and she refused to help us again. I fell asleep, and next thing I knew it was bright morning. And they said Mother was dead then. Why do you ask?"

"Mary," Cecilia said slowly, careful not to frighten her. "I think maybe we should get out of here . . ."

❧

Jane couldn't find Mr. Winter at first. The Danby gardens were very crowded now, masses of people playing croquet and lawn tennis, having picnics on the grass, trying their hands at quoits, buying scarves. Lady Avebury and Miss Clarke were talking to Mr. Brown and Lord Eversham under the shade of the open-sided tea tent. Lord Avebury came up to them and pointed something out, making them all laugh. Her ladyship and Miss Clarke both stared up at Lord Eversham with wide eyes from beneath their feathered and flowered hats, and Jane couldn't really blame them. He *was* good-looking, and seemed charming. Rich, too, probably, with a big house just like Danby somewhere. Lady Cecilia could do worse, and maybe, just maybe, she herself could be lady's maid to a marchioness someday.

Jane sighed. No time for such pie-in-the-sky dreams right now. A murderer was still loose somewhere in the neighborhood, and Mary Winter was ill. Maybe Mrs. Winter was the killer herself, as Lady Cecilia speculated. Jane wondered if she should find Dr. Mitchell first, or the inspector. But then she glimpsed Mr. Winter over by the lemonade stand. She hurried toward him.

"Mr. Winter!" she called, and he spun toward her, startled, just as he was pulling some coins from his coat pocket.

Jane noticed it was the same jacket he wore at the séance, black piped in tan, unusual for the country.

Her sudden shout had made him spill the coins onto the grass—as well as a crumpled scrap of fabric, white linen handed with green, purple, and white silk, ripped apart roughly at one end. Mrs. Price's torn suffrage sash.

Jane couldn't control the horror on her face fast enough. His expression hardened; his eyes turned to shards of ice. Jack darted forward and caught the scrap in his sharp little teeth, running away with it. He disappeared into the thick stands of trees just beyond the formal gardens, his orange fur vanishing amid the fading greens and vivid golds. Jane ran after him, afraid she would lose him, and Monty was in close pursuit. She could swear she heard his heavy breathing, his crashing footfalls close behind her, and her heart pounded so loudly in her ears that she could barely hear anything else. She'd never been so terrified, not even when the ship sank underneath them coming from America.

Monty's fist caught her apron, ripping at the lace-edged tie, but she managed to slip out of it and keep running, chasing Jack's orange plume of a tail. In the old teahouse just past the lake, she saw two faces peering out in shock—Rose and her footman beau, Paul. Rose looked guilt stricken at abandoning her bring-and-buy post, but that seemed comically immaterial now.

"Find Inspector Hennesy, Rose!" Jane shouted as loudly as she could, not slowing down. She had to warn Lady Cecilia. "Send him to the old tower!"

She reached the tower several steps ahead of Monty

Winter and tried to slam and lock the heavy door between them. But there was no longer a bar or lock, as no one ever used the tower, and the old wood was thick but crumbling. She saw a fallen beam nearby and slid it across, hoping it might hold, before she ran headlong up the winding staircase, just behind Jack and his prize.

She found Lady Cecilia and Mrs. Winter in the round watch room at the landing and slammed the door there behind her. The windows in the room were glassless but a little wider than the ones above or below, for keeping watch for Saxon marauders. Dried leaves crunched underfoot on the stone floor, making Jane's boots slide. Cecilia and Mary rose to their feet, eyes wide with panic.

"He's—he's following me," Jane gasped, her ribs stabbing with pain. "He had the scrap of Mrs. Price's sash!"

Jack dropped it from his sharp little teeth, as if to demonstrate.

"What do you mean . . . ?" Mary whispered, but there was no time to say anything else.

The door slammed open with such force it became unhinged and crashed to the floor, scattering dust and leaves. Mary screamed at the sight of her husband, his stony face and icy eyes, looming above them.

Cecilia wrapped her arm tightly around Mary's shaking shoulders, and Jack picked up the scrap again as if to keep it safe. So, it was Monty Winter all along, not his wife or father-in-law, not the thief, not Cora Black and her ghosts or Mrs. Palmer and her Union ambitions.

Monty looked down at the scrap and back to his wife. His

expression seemed only mildly interested and vaguely disappointed, as if a play he'd paid a lot to see had fizzled terribly.

"I do wish you had not seen that," he said softly. "I was a
great fool not to dispose of the—thing much earlier. Now,
whatever shall we all do about this?"

❧

Cecilia scooped up the scrap from Jack before Monty could
indeed dispose of it, and dragged Mary and Jane back with
her to the side of the room, near the window. She knew there
wasn't far to go; the ruined room with its crumbling old stone
walls had only the one door to the stairs, which Monty
blocked, but if they could distract him, she could surely shout
for help out the window opening. She could hear the echo of
voices and laughter from the garden. If only she was louder . . .

"I certainly was a fool to hold on to that blasted thing,"
Monty said with a laugh. "So forgetful of me. But I did have
so many things on my mind lately, thanks to your dreadful
family, Mary dear. What a useless lot you turned out to be!
And your viper of a mother—I should have known you would
be made of the same stuff in the end. I suppose at least she
and your sister are not quite as stupid as you."

"Stupid!" Mary screamed. As if that was the worst of this
situation. "I loved you! I've always been a good wife to you."

"A good wife?" Monty said softly. "I married you because
your family was meant to be of use to me. And your mother's
insanity cost me my position."

"You cost yourself your position!" Cecilia couldn't help
but retort, remembering what she had heard in the offices of

Bird and Wither. "With your incompetence. Mr. Jermyn would never have hired you! And it was you who tried to knock me off my bicycle, wasn't it? There in the lane? You should be ashamed of yourself. You could never have been a true gentleman."

"You interfering little witch. Yes, I saw you going past on that absurd contraption and thought I could send a little warning. You should have listened," Monty said. "You're as bad as the other harpies who don't know their place, earl's daughter or not. Now you'll pay, too."

He suddenly lunged at Cecilia, who, caught by surprise, stumbled back over the hem of her dress and hit her already-sore shoulder on the stone wall. Mary wailed, and Monty's hand snatched bruisingly at Cecilia's arm.

She kicked out at him, but she tripped over a loose stone on the floor. Fear and anger made everything hazy in her eyes. Monty dragged her toward the window, her kid shoes slipping and sliding on the stone floor, and she made herself go limp and heavy. Out of the corner of her eye, she saw Jane rushing at Monty's face with her fingernails, yet she was too far away.

Suddenly, a golden-yellow streak shot upward with a yowl, and Jack twined himself around Monty's feet as he landed. He sank his fangs in deep, through his trousers and skin. Monty gave a yelp of pain and kicked Jack, sending him flying against the wall. Cecilia yanked herself free and tumbled to the floor in a heap.

But Jack had done his job well in those few seconds. Monty lost his balance, and Cecilia, on the ground, stuck her leg out as far as she could, tripping him. With a terrible shout and then a piercing scream, he tumbled back through the window, where he had intended to drag Cecilia. The shriek ended abruptly with an ominous thud—then silence, before a clamor rose up from the horribly interrupted party.

Mary ran to the window and peered out, screaming and screaming as if she would never stop.

Jane dashed to kneel beside Cecilia, her expression horrified. "My lady! Are you hurt?"

"Jack," Cecilia gasped. She let Jane help her to her feet, and they both hurried to poor Jack. He lay in a heart-stoppingly still heap of marmalade fur on the cold floor, and Cecilia had never felt such fear.

"Oh no, no," she sobbed. She gently touched Jack's soft little head—and was rewarded by a soft "mrow" and a bright-green eye blinking open.

"Oh, thank heavens, darling Jack," Cecilia said, carefully gathering him into her arms. Jane kissed him on his nose, and he settled against Cecilia with a sigh. "You are a hero, Jack!"

❧

"So, let me see if I understand this rightly, Lady Cecilia," Inspector Hennesy said doubtfully. "Montgomery Winter was the murderer."

Cecilia shivered and drew the blanket someone had brought her closer around her shoulders. They sat in the library, Jane next to her on one of the red leather settees, Lady Avebury hovering in the corner, poised as if she would run to her daughter at any moment. Anne had taken Mary, to be questioned later, back to Primrose Cottage with a sedative from Dr. Mitchell. The garden had emptied out, everyone eager to spread the gossip that a murder had occurred at Danby Hall. Again.

"Yes," she said. "Because he blamed Mrs. Price for losing his employment. Even though it was his own incompetence at his job, as I am sure they can tell you at Bird and Wither in Town. Or Mr. Henry Price could tell you. He refused to help his son-in-law any longer. Jane and Mrs. Winter also heard it all. I really do feel like such a fool!"

The inspector looked puzzled. "A fool, Lady Cecilia? And why is that? For getting trapped with a murderer in a tower? I admit it's not something I've seen before, but hardly impossible considering the criminal mind."

Cecilia sniffled. "Well—that, too. I shouldn't have taken Mary there. Mostly because I, well, I did think for a while it might have *been* Mary."

"Mrs. Winter?" Inspector Hennesy looked even more confused. "You thought a woman could have done such a murder, Lady Cecilia? Her own mother? Why?"

Cecilia glanced at her mother, who was watching her with such worry. She thought of their own relationship—such deep love, such irritation sometimes, so much bafflement about where the other one was really coming from. *She* could never hurt her mother, but she had learned that people were sometimes capable of truly dreadful things. "Because of the letters, and what she said at the inquest. She admitted she had written seeking some sort of reconciliation, but nothing like those scraps at Primrose Cottage. And she was so very opposed to her mother's work, so ambitious for her husband.

She wanted a comfortable life as a successful lawyer's wife. Surely, desperation to hold on to the life she knew would drive her do things she wouldn't ordinarily even think of. You must see such things all the time in your work, Inspector."

"Er—yes. Certainly. But not usually from ladies."

"Then you should watch carefully, Inspector Hennesy," Cecilia said. "Women have fewer options, you see. Marie Manning, for instance, or Constance Kent. But it was *Mr.* Winter this time. Who knows what might happen next?"

"Quite. I think we've learned a great deal about the feminine nature this week, have we not, Sergeant?"

Sergeant Dunn looked utterly baffled, as if he certainly hadn't learned a thing about the "feminine nature" from the whole messy Price business. "If you say so, sir."

"I'm sure you'll both be happy to get back to a nice, peaceful city," Jane said.

"I've certainly had quite enough of fresh country air," Inspector Hennesy said, snapping his notebook shut. "Do you have anything to add, then, Lady Cecilia? Miss Hughes?"

Cecilia and Jane shook their heads. "I am afraid that's all we can tell you, Inspector. Maybe Mrs. Winter can add more once she is feeling calmer."

"Very good. You can go, then. I will speak to Mrs. Winter and Miss Price later today."

Cecilia remembered how Mary looked when her sister led her away, utterly pale and shocked. "I'm not sure she can be of much assistance *yet.*"

"Nevertheless, one must do one's duty," Inspector Hennesy said.

Cecilia thought he sounded just like her grandmother. "Certainly."

She tugged the blanket closer around her, like a cloak that might protect her from those awful, flashing memories of that day, Monty Winter trying to kill her then tumbling to his crushing death. Mrs. Caffey had just come in with a tray of well-sugared tea and some of Mrs. Frazer's best raspberry tarts, and Lady Avebury busied herself pouring out the drinks and urging Cecilia to drink more of it, to eat something. It took a few minutes for Cecilia to escape and follow Jane from the room.

To her surprise, she found Sergeant Dunn waiting in the foyer while Inspector Hennesy spoke to Mr. Brown just outside the front doors. The sergeant looked quite surprisingly shy as he glanced at her.

"Yes, Sergeant Dunn?" she said. "Did you have another question?"

He glanced surreptitiously at his boss, who was still out of earshot. "No, I—that is, not about the case, no. I just wondered . . ."

"Yes?" Cecilia said, as gently as she could.

"Is Miss Hughes—walking out with anyone?"

Cecilia almost laughed in surprise. So she *had* been right! The sergeant was sweet on Jane. But was Jane sweet on Collins? It was all much more pleasant to think about than murder. "Not that I know of, Sergeant. I doubt Miss Clarke would want to lose her lady's maid right now." And Cecilia certainly didn't want to lose her friend. Jane and Jack had made life at Danby much less lonely since they arrived. Yet Sergeant

Dunn did look so dear and earnest as he asked. "Perhaps, once things have settled a bit, you might like to call on her? Her half days are usually Wednesdays."

He looked quite relieved. "I just might do that. Thank you, Lady Cecilia."

"Sergeant!" Inspector Hennesy barked. "What are you yammering on about over there? Our work isn't finished, you know." Mr. Brown had gone, and the inspector loomed in the doorway.

"Yes, Inspector. Of course. Right away." The sergeant put his helmet back on and hurried away.

Cecilia turned away, only to come back when the inspector called her name.

"Was it only those letters that made you suspect Mrs. Winter, Lady Cecilia?" he asked.

Cecilia thought of all she and Jane, and Annabel, too, had done in the last few days, all they had heard in London. But she decided it would be far more useful if Inspector Hennesy thought her a silly Society fribble than a busybody—just in case such an unlikely situation ever arose at Danby again. Not that it would, of course. Surely, life was going to go back to tea parties and lawn tennis and dancing with sweaty-palmed cricket chaps again. This year's church bazaar would just pass into legend.

"It was the séance," she said.

He looked baffled. "Séance?"

"Yes. Miss Black is a spirit medium, didn't you know? She held a séance at Primrose Cottage to contact Mrs. Price. It was most enlightening."

Now he scowled. "A séance?"

"Yes. The other side can be most fascinating, Inspector."
She gave him one more light smile and decided to go back to
fetch another cup of tea from Mrs. Caffey.

As Cecilia gulped down the welcome, bracingly strong
and sweet brew, she saw that her mother had gone around to
sit on the terrace with her father, Annabel, Patrick, and her
grandmother. Mr. Brown had joined them as well, with the
ruins of the empty bazaar just beyond. It looked most strange,
the abandoned tents, the overturned tables, and a tea party
on the terrace as if nothing had happened.

"I never knew the countryside could be quite so wildly
fascinating," she heard someone say, and she turned to see
that Lord Eversham was still there. He, too, looked utterly
unruffled, perfectly dressed in his stylish brown suit, and
bright hair shining. His eyes were full of laughter, though
they held a tinge of concern.

She was shocked he hadn't fled with the others, to spread
the word of the curse of Danby Hall. To forget he had ever
danced with or sent flowers to that odd Lady Cecilia Bates.

She shouldn't have been surprised, though. He didn't really seem at all the sort to let a bit of drama discourage him
from an amusing afternoon.

"Don't you have your own country home, Lord Eversham?"
she said. "I hear Eversham Abbey is quite grand indeed."

"Oh yes, it is. Terribly. And cold and empty. Nothing ever
happens there at all. I think at the last church fete my mother
hosted, the most scandalous thing that happened was the
vicar imbibing too much cider and falling into the lake."

Lady Rights a Wrong

Cecilia couldn't help but laugh. She could never picture handsome, sweet Mr. Brown doing such a thing. "Our vicar is—quite different."

Eversham nodded, looking suddenly serious. "Still—are you sure you are quite well now, Lady Cecilia? It must have been a shocking sight to see a man die like that."

Cecilia swallowed hard and then turned to look at Danby, her home, the familiar paintings and carpets, the terrace beyond with her family. She was suddenly very, very glad to be alive to see it all again. "Yes, I am quite well now."

"Good. Though if you feel at all faint, I am quite happy to carry you to that chaise over there."

Cecilia laughed again. He was a silly marquess—but a handsome one. "Like Marianne Dashwood and Colonel Brandon? Perhaps one day . . ." She saw her mother wave. "But you must not encourage my mother. I fear she may be about to ask you to dinner."

"Will someone keel over in the soup?"

She remembered poor Mr. Hayes back in the spring, who had nearly done just that, and she sighed. "I can guarantee nothing, Lord Eversham. Anything might happen."

"In that case, I shall happily accept. I would certainly hate to miss whatever happens next."

❧

Jane walked Lady Cecilia's bicycle across the graveled drive toward the garage, half-afraid the heavy contraption was going to collapse on her and somehow pin her to the ground. She had no idea how Lady Cecilia was brave enough to ride it as she did, but she did seem to enjoy it a lot, despite her ear-lier accident. And it was surely a lovely day to be out and about on the Danby grounds, freed from duties for a while.

Jane turned her face up to the sky and closed her eyes for a moment, relishing the warm sun on her cheeks. Despite the blue, cloudless expanse above, the nip of autumn was at the edges of the breeze, and the leaves were starting to fall from the trees. Soon it would be winter.

She thought of winter back home, the streets muddy, the skies leaden, the fireplace smoking. She didn't miss the idea of that very much at all, though she did miss her family quite a lot.

She peeked back over her shoulder at the house, all tinged gold by the afternoon light, quiet and solid and beautiful. De-spite that little flash of homesickness, she felt such a thrill of excitement to know that Danby was where she was now. And what adventures she had there! She could never have imag-ined them before.

She continued on toward the garage, a little bounce to her step, and she had to admit her happiness that day wasn't *just* about adventure and grand houses. It might be, just a tiny bit, about the man who was in the garage.

Jane pushed the bicycle through the open doors and blinked at the sudden shadow after the bright day. The air was warm and smelled of oil and the fine leather seats of the car, and she could hear mysterious clinkings and clankings coming from the caverns of the space.

"Hello?" she called. "Mr. Collins?"

He appeared from behind a screen, wiping his hands on

a rag. His hair was rumpled, he wore only a plain gray cover-all, and a smear of grease was on his cheek, but it didn't take away from how handsome he was. How her heart pounded to see him.

"Why, hello, Miss Jane, what a fine surprise," he said with a smile. He tossed aside the rag. "What can I do for you today?"

"It's Lady Cecilia's bicycle," Jane said, glad to turn her gaze away from him and to the contraption. Maybe then he couldn't see how flustered she felt. "She thinks there's something wrong with this—thingamie here. She's having a hard time stopping."

Collins knelt down to examine the bicycle, his shoulders flexing in a way that made Jane want to touch them in a most improper fashion. Some proper lady's maid *she* was turning out to be! "Just looks like the chain is loose. I can fix that for her in a trice."

"Thank you. She wants to ride into the village tomorrow for some flower-arranging thing at the church." And maybe Lady Cecilia would see the vicar while she was there. But Jane daren't ask her.

"And what about you? Are you going to take up bicy-cling, too?"

Jane grinned. "I do doubt it. This thing scares me to bits."

Collins laughed. "I agree. Give me a solid automobile any day."

Jane laughed, too, feeling that wonderful ease she had with him return. "You do drive them so well. I'm never afraid when you're behind the wheel."

He stood up and smiled at her rather shyly. "Speaking

of which—I have permission to take out the car myself on Tuesday evening, when the family is dining at home. There's a dance at the Guildhall, a ragtime band all the way from Liverpool."

"Ragtime?" Jane sighed. "How wonderful! I heard a bit of that music when I was in America. I love the bounce of it all."

He traced his toe along the stained concrete floor, not quite meeting her gaze. "I wonder if—well, if it's your evening off, maybe—you'd like to go with me? We could learn some of those new dances together. I warn you, though, I'm a bit of a two-left-footer on the dance floor sometimes."

Jane was astonished, afraid—and wonderfully excited. She pressed her hand to the sudden flutter in her stomach. "Oh. I— I suppose I could find a sturdy enough pair of dancing shoes and trade for a day off with one of the other maids. And Miss Clarke won't mind as long as I'm home in time to help her change after dinner. If you're sure you want me to go . . ."

His smile widened. "Of course I'm sure. I've been wanting to ask you for ages, but I just . . ." He broke off with a rueful laugh, making Jane smile, too. "So, I'll see you Tuesday, then?"

"Yes. Tuesday it is." Jane spun around and hurried out of the garage, afraid she was grinning like a total idiot, but she just didn't quite care. She couldn't wait to tell Lady Cecilia!

Epilogue

❧

O h, Jane, you are an absolute miracle worker!" Cecilia cried happily. She spun around in front of her looking glass, feeling quite as if she floated on a wonderful marshmallow cream cloud.

"Be careful, my lady!" Jane admonished. "We don't want it all to come tumbling apart again."

Cecilia laughed and stood obediently still as Jane adjusted the sleeves of Cecilia's new ball gown and then knelt down to check the hem. The dress had just arrived from London, a confection of white satin with a white tulle tunic overlay embroidered with pearls and sequins in patterns of twisting vines and lilies. It was perfect for the après–shooting party ball Cecilia's mother had planned so carefully. Something had to distract everyone from Danby's latest murderous scandal, and what better way to do that than a lavish dance?

Cecilia patted her hair, an elaborate arrangement of curls

and waves Jane had bound with a satin and crystal-studded bandeau. "You are utterly wasted as a lady's maid, Jane. You should be working in some elegant London couture salon, which one day you would own yourself."

"Oh, I don't know about that." Jane shooed Jack away from the lace trim on the gown's train. "London was certainly exciting to see, and I wouldn't mind visiting again. But I like my work here. And there's a lot to be said for the peace and quiet of a house like Danby, isn't there?"

"Yes, indeed," Cecilia murmured. It had certainly been "quiet" since the Price affair. There had been shooting luncheons, dinner parties, walks, and books. Now even the autumn sport was going to be done, and Christmas to plan for next. She wished she knew what to do after that. After feeling so useful, having work and a purpose, she felt terribly at loose ends.

"Let's do your jewelry, my lady, and you'll be all ready to go," Jane said.

Cecilia sat down at her dressing table and studied her reflection in the silver-framed glass. It was dark beyond her windows now, night falling earlier every day, but she could see the garden lit up by golden fairy lights. Every sign of the bazaar was long gone now. The trees were turning bare and the flower beds were going to their winter sleep. The looming tower stood beyond as an ominous reminder of what had happened.

"Maybe we could go back to London soon," she said, tearing her eyes from the tower. "Aunt Maggie should be back from climbing in the Alps by then, and we could attend some meetings at the Women's Suffrage Union."

Jane sorted through the meager contents of Cecilia's jewel case, studying the earrings and brooches and lockets with narrowed eyes. "Have you heard from Miss Price, then, my lady?"

Cecilia nodded and took out Anne's letter from where it was tucked behind the red-haired china shepherdess, along with the rest of the day's post. "Yes, she sounds just as sensible and unflappable as ever, considering the terrible things that have happened. Miss Black is staying for a time at a clinic at Lake Geneva but is still writing pamphlets for the Union and is expected to be able to resume her work in the springtime."

"Oh, I do hope so, my lady." Jane fastened a double strand of pearls at Cecilia's neck. "And what about poor Mrs. Winter?"

Cecilia glanced over Anne's neatly printed words again. It was rather astonishing how close she felt she had become to those people in such a short, yet quite intense, moment of time. They felt like friends now.

"Mary is living with Anne in her London flat at the moment, while all the complications of Mr. Winter's estate are settled, and surprisingly, she is helping Anne organize the Union's files as Anne and Mrs. Palmer decide how to structure everything now," Cecilia said. She wondered how the two almost-reconciled sisters got on day-to-day. "Poor Mary indeed, I am sure she is rather penniless and lost right now. Maybe she will find suffrage is useful to her after all."

"At least she isn't married to a monster anymore," Jane said with a shiver. "We can all make fresh starts, if we want to."

Cecilia thought of Jane's life in America, which sounded so different from Danby, and her own dull past. But it was

1912 now. Things were changing. "Indeed we can, Jane. And with her sister's help, I'm sure Mary will be fine."

"What about their father, my lady? Would he help? He seems rich enough. That car of his! Mr. Collins says it's quite *au courant*."

Cecilia had to smile at the twinkle in Jane's eyes when she mentioned Collins. Collins *was* handsome, and well-spoken, and if Jane did want to marry him, she could live with him in the flat above the garage and never leave Danby. Selfishly, the thought made Cecilia quite happy, though she did rather pity Sergeant Dunn.

"I am sure Mr. Price *is* quite comfortable," she said. Jane held out two pairs of earrings, one of pearl drops and one of diamond studs, and Cecilia chose the diamonds. "But Anne's postscript here says he means to marry soon, and the new Mrs. Price wants a fresh house in Cheyne Walk."

"Cheyne Walk? Sounds artistic. Is it that young lady we heard about in London, then?" Jane said, referring to the gossip about Mr. Price's "special friend," even before his wife's demise. Mrs. Price's friend, however, was probably always going to be a secret.

"Indeed so. I'm sure they'll be quite happy, aren't you, Jane?" Cecilia tucked Anne's letter away.

"As happy as people like that *can* be, I suppose." Jane straightened the bandeau in Cecilia's hair. "But maybe they won't be the only ones?"

Cecilia wasn't sure she liked the laughing look in Jane's eyes. "Whatever do you mean?"

Jane gestured to the other letter on the dressing table,

one on thick, creamy paper with an embossed blue-and-gold crest. "I see you got even more in the post today, my lady."

Cecilia felt her cheeks turn warm and fussed with the silver-capped scent bottle to cover up her silly blushes. If only she didn't have that ridiculously pale, freckled Bates complexion that showed every emotion! "I did get a note from Lord Eversham, yes. Just a message to say what a terribly interesting time he had here. He wishes all church bazaars could be so eventful."

Jane laughed. "Not me, my lady! If they have it next year, I hope the most exciting thing to happen will be that lemon drizzle cake coming in second place for the first time."

"Do you think you'll be here next year, then, Jane? I do hope so!" The room was quiet for a moment as Jane looked for Cecilia's gloves and Jack groomed his paws by the fire. All so peaceful. So exactly as it should be.

"I like it here, my lady," Jane said. "I do miss my family, but I love Danby, and all your strange English ways. I think I'll stay as long as you and Miss Clarke need me."

That was one of the rubs, though, wasn't it? Cecilia wondered how long Annabel *would* stay. After London, Cecilia was quite starting to like her. However proper and uppity she may be, she was also sharp and funny and mischievous. Cecilia enjoyed the morning rides they had gotten into the habit of taking together. But Annabel was beautiful, intelligent, lively, and above all rich. What would she see in dear, sweet, vague Patrick and falling-down Danby?

"What about you, my lady?" Jane handed Cecilia her fan.

"Me, Jane?"

"Won't you want to marry and have your own house-hold?" Jane nodded toward that crested stationery. "I bet a marquess must have a nice house indeed."

"I am quite sure he does." Cecilia thought of what she had heard of Eversham Abbey, a house even older than Danby and twice as large. And there was Lord Eversham himself, handsome and witty. Life as a marchioness would mean a leading place in Society. But there were other things out in the world, too. Travel, like Aunt Maggie, and college, like Maud Rainsley. Running the church as a vicar's wife, maybe, close to Danby. So many things.

"To tell you the truth, Jane, I have absolutely no idea what I'll do now. Except go downstairs before my mother comes looking for me!"

Jane helped button up the myriad tiny pearl buttons on the kid gloves, made sure the hem of the gown was straight, and stepped back to study her handiwork with narrowed eyes.

"Am I presentable, then, Jane?" Cecilia asked.

"Very nice indeed, my lady, if I do say so myself." Jane smiled brightly. "Say, if you were a marchioness, we could do this every night!"

Cecilia groaned. "Heaven forfend! It would be too ex-hausting." She glanced at Jack, who had jumped up onto his favorite cushion on the bed. "What do you think, Sir Jack?"

He squeezed his green eyes in agreement. Or maybe he was just looking forward to Mrs. Frazer's lobster patties, one of which he would be sure to steal later.

Cecilia and Jane made their way along the old Elizabe-than gallery, darkened now with the tapestry draperies closed, and down the stairs, where the sounds of the party were already floating upward. Jane left her at the landing, along with all the other servants who could escape from Redvers's stern eye, to watch the arrivals. Jane sat down on the top step between Collins and Rose and waved Cecilia on.

The White Drawing Room had been transformed into a ballroom for the evening, and for a moment Cecilia stood transfixed in the doorway. It had been quite some time since Danby had put on such a glorious show. The red Venetian velvet chairs and settees had been pushed back to the walls to make room for a dance floor. Mr. Smithfield's florist had quite outdone themselves with garlands and bowers of crimson and dark-gold roses, set off by deep-green leaves and vines and tied with crimson satin bows. Autumn-leafed trees in silver pots towered in each corner, giving the feeling of an enchanted fall forest. The air was rich with the scent of the roses and the mingled perfumes of the guests. Jasmine, lilies, violets, and Cecilia's own lilac scent.

She certainly never again wanted to smell anything like Monty Winter's greenish cologne, which had clung to his threatening letters.

She shivered and reminded herself that tonight was for having fun. For forgetting. The orchestra that sat on a dais at the far end of the room, half-hidden by potted palms, played a lively polka. Couples already spun around the floor, a whirl of bright silks and satins and lush velvets, set off by the black of the men's evening suits, the glitter of jewels, and wafting of feathers. It was all so beautiful, so joyful, so seemingly permanent, as if the loveliness of Danby would go on forever.

Cecilia now knew all too well it couldn't. It was as fleeting as a butterfly fluttering higher and higher until it vanished into the sky. But she would certainly enjoy it while she could.

"Champagne, my lady?" Redvers appeared beside her with a silver tray of cut-crystal coupes, filled to the gilded brim with bubbling golden liquid. James and Paul were also moving through the crowd, offering champagne and claret cup to the guests, but she didn't see Jesse. She tried to tell herself that small, sinking feeling was certainly *not* disappointment.

"Oh, thank you, Redvers. How delicious." Cecilia took a sip and laughed as the bubbles tickled her nose. Redvers smiled indulgently. He had always spoiled her, even when she was a small child, slipping her biscuits and hot chocolate for her sweet tooth. Now champagne.

She glimpsed her parents standing near the grand carved marble fireplace, chatting with the Byswaters as her mother ran a careful eye over her party. Cecilia's grandmother sat in an armchair nearby, grand as always in her Edwardian gray satins and pearls, a tiara shimmering in her old-style chignon of hair. To Cecilia's surprise, the dowager was talking to— Lord Elphin! His suit was decidedly rusty looking, as if evening wear had not seen the light of day from his wardrobe in ages, but he nodded and smiled affably enough as he drank some of the claret cup.

"It has been far too long since Danby looked quite so grand, Redvers," she said.

"Much too long, my lady." Redvers sounded strangely wistful as he, too, watched the dancers whirling past. Was he bored, she wondered, pining for the house's glory days when her parents were young?

He smiled at her and drifted away, disappearing into the crowd who eagerly reached for his tray. Cecilia wandered around the edge of the room, greeting neighbors, laughing, talking, sharing the local gossip. Who was engaged, who had gone abroad, who was redecorating their house—nothing about what had happened at the bazaar. It was all quite lovely, quite ordinary, yet somehow she, like Redvers, felt a touch of some cold wistfulness deep down inside.

"Lady Cecilia," she heard Mr. Brown say, and she smiled at him when she saw he was examining the cases of jeweled snuffboxes her grandfather had collected. No doubt he was hiding at the edge of the room from all his eager female parishioners. Not that she could blame them—he did look quite splendid in his evening dress, his brown hair gleaming in the lights that wound their way through the bowers of roses. "How beautiful you look tonight."

"Thank you, Mr. Brown. You do look quite well yourself."

He laughed and ruefully smoothed his hair. "It's not every day a vicar gets to drag out his best city clothes, you know." Then his expression grew serious as he watched her. "I do hope you have recovered from—well, from everything that has happened. It's all been most shocking."

"I have recovered—I think. I am glad justice was served. But I'm sorry your lovely bazaar was ruined. The St. Swithin's roof . . ."

He laughed gently. "You mustn't worry about that, Lady Cecilia. Drama does seem to be a boon for charity. We now have more than enough for the repairs. In fact, I'm hoping to have a small dinner at the vicarage to celebrate. My own cook is nothing like your splendid Mrs. Frazer, of course, but I think we can carry something off creditably. It would be splendid if you and your family could attend. Nothing as large as this . . ."

Cecilia studied the dancers again. The drawing room seemed even more crowded now, warmer, more filled with the kaleidoscopic whirl of color. "Nothing ever really is *this* grand, Mr. Brown."

The orchestra finished the polka with a flourish, and she heard the opening strains of an old-fashioned waltz.

"May I have the honor of this dance, Lady Cecilia?" Mr. Brown asked.

Cecilia smiled and nodded as she reached for his hand. His clasp was light, gentle, but his fingers felt warm and safe through their gloves. He whirled her into the dance, quite graceful for a vicar, leading her into a series of twirls and swoops that made her laugh. Her silken skirts swayed, and for a moment she felt just as she had told Jane—as if she floated on a marshmallow cloud, held up by Mr. Brown.

As the music swirled to an end, her head was quite spinning, giddy with what a surprisingly good dancer he was, how far from the world she had felt for just a moment. She curtsied to him, and he bowed, his velvety dark eyes smiling down at her.

She felt herself blushing and was glad of the distraction from Mr. Brown's eyes when her father stepped onto the dais.

"Our dear friends," Lord Avebury said, beaming out over the crowd. "How very kind of you to join us on this special evening. For not only has our neighbor Lord Byswater bagged dozens of pheasants on our shoot, lucky fellow . . ." A cheer went up, and Lord Byswater gave an exaggerated bow as Lord Avebury laughed. "But we also have our own very special family news. I am most pleased to announce the betrothal of my son, Lord Bellham, to Miss Annabel Clarke. The wedding will be at Christmastime."

Cecilia felt a pleasant shock of warmth at the sudden news. Annabel would be her sister-in-law! She and Jane would not leave, and Danby would be saved! It would have Annabel's American money, plus her energy and ambition.

Patrick and Annabel joined Lord and Lady Avebury on the dais, holding hands. Annabel looked as fashionable and elegant as always, in one of her new London gowns in bronze chiffon and burgundy velvet, and a tiara of rubies in her golden hair. Patrick appeared as careless as ever with his collar crooked and his hair tousled. No one would ever have imagined, looking at them, that they belonged together. But the pleasure in their eyes as they looked at each other, the tender way they squeezed each other's hand, was unmistakable.

Cecilia felt Mr. Brown studying her, and that blasted blush burned hotter in her cheeks. Bates complexion indeed! She clapped harder to cover her flustered confusion.

"So please, everyone, raise your glasses to the happy couple," Lord Avebury said. "And to Danby Hall. May we see many happy years to come."

"To Danby!" everyone cried, and the orchestra played a fanfare as Patrick kissed Annabel's cheek. It was as if all the good things would go on and on now, forever.

Ready to find
your next great read?

Let us help.

Visit prh.com/nextread

Penguin
Random
House